A COLD BLUE CALL

A.J. DOWNEY

BOOK SIX

COPYRIGHT

ISBN: 978-1-950222-15-5

Editing by Barbara J. Bailey

Book design by Maggie Kern

Cover art and Indigo Knights logo by Dar Albert at Wicked Smart Designs

Model Salvador Herrera

Photographer - JW Photography & Covers

DEDICATION

To Derek Cromwell, one of the unsung heroes before he folded up his cape. Don't worry, world. He still unfolds it every once in a while for various causes and old times' sake, and lucky us, it sounds like he might be fully coming out of superhero retirement soon.

PROLOGUE

*A*ngel…

I stared at the Springfield XDS on my galley table. I had it for home protection, even though my home was actually a boat right now. I liked it, although with my big hands, I needed the extended magazine with the grip extender for a comfortable fit. Golden thought I should have just gone with something that fit my hand naturally, but I liked the feel of this one when I fired.

I was thinking about putting it to my head and firing it for the last time. I had it sitting on the table in front of me, mostly empty, just the one round it would take to end me in the chamber, the rest of the magazine's contents lined up like soldiers on the lacquered wood, by the bottle of Johnny Walker and the glass of whiskey that I'd just poured, my second of the night.

I kept staring at the gun, and thinking about my brother, my sister, and her kid. How Maria would be angry, and how Golden, he would hurt, but he'd hold her and Manolo together okay. When he fell apart, the club would be there to put him back together. My twin was strong. Way stronger than me. He'd eventually be okay. I had to believe that.

I *did* believe that.

He was the better of the two of us, always had been. He was braver, stronger; more resilient. Me? I wasn't any of those things. I was just going through the motions, saving as many as I could, but man, when I needed someone there to save me? There wasn't nothing for it. I was alone and I didn't have anybody I was comfortable reaching out to. Not my brother, not my club, no one. They all had their own things going and handled their shit so well, while me? I just seemed to fuck everything up. Except that when I fucked up, people died.

I couldn't do this shit anymore. I couldn't save my sister from her douchebag baby-daddy, I couldn't help my nephew, and my brother had just gone back out on the street after being shot, for fuck's sake. I felt paralyzed. By guilt, by fear, by remorse; hopelessness ran through my veins, and not even God was watching anymore. I was alone. Bereft.

I just couldn't do this anymore.

I started to reach for the Springfield, and found my hand deviating for the whiskey, instead. I downed what was in the glass and poured another, staring at the amber liquid subtly rising and falling against the edge of the glass as my live-aboard gently rocked in the bay.

Was it going to hurt? Would it be quick or would I linger? I was tired of hurting, I didn't want to hurt more. Please God, just give me a sign, and get me through just one more night...

There was a faint shout outside my boat, thumping and thudding, and a woman swearing, her voice edged in pain. I got up as if pulled by strings, and went up and out on deck, looking over toward the dock and saw her, sprawled across the creosote-soaked wood.

She sat up, hissing between her teeth, one hand wrapped around her delicate wrist, inspecting the palm of her hand in the dark.

She groaned and looked around her at her spilled groceries and I called out softly.

"Are you all right?"

"Yeah," she called back automatically, and then took another look at her hand. Her shoulders dropped and she hung her head, a little defeated. "No."

"I'm coming to help you," I said. I moved across the deck and went to the dock. It was low tide, so I gripped one of the mooring lines and braced a boot against the edge of the dock, hauling myself up onto it.

"I think I'll be okay, I don't know what happened, I think my heel caught –"

She stopped when I gently grasped her hand and turned it to the light from one of the poles. A wicked sliver cut across the heel of her palm, almost the entire width of her hand. I hissed between my teeth at the sight; that was nasty and had to hurt.

"What's your name?" I asked gently, all business, going right into paramedic mode.

"Claire," she said.

"Hi, Claire. I'm Angel, and it's your lucky night. I'm an Indigo City medic and we're going to get you taken care of."

She laughed faintly and said, "I appreciate that, Angel, but, would you mind grabbing my oranges before they end up rolling into the drink?"

I said, "Sure. Hang tight, I'll get your things. Just don't try to move yet."

"Oh, I'm sure everything else is fine; ankle hurts a little, but it doesn't feel broken."

"Just don't move for me, okay?"

"Aren't you sweet?" she asked and I could hear the smile edging her voice.

I looked at her finally, and, Wow! She was breathtaking. Large dark eyes were set in a slender face with high cheekbones, her skin still sun-kissed despite the winter's chill around us, a smattering of freckles across her nose and cheeks. Her long, dark hair was in a high ponytail, and a fringe of bangs fell across her forehead, longer on the sides, sending sweeping tendrils of all that deep brunette satin to frame her face, like the work of art that it was.

"Just doing my job," I stammered, and her smile grew, showing straight white teeth.

"Pretty sure you're off the clock," she murmured.

I felt an answering smile cross my lips, and it almost felt foreign on my face, it'd been so long since I'd done it genuinely, without it being superficial.

"I'm a medic, I'm never off the clock."

She laughed and the sound was good.

She raised her perfect sweep of eyebrows and said, "My oranges?"

"Right!" I jumped slightly, startled back into action and realizing I'd been staring like some gob-smacked idiot. I gathered up her fruit into the canvas grocery sack and lowered it over the edge of my boat, onto the bench fixed to the port side.

I went back to Claire and held down my hands, and said, "Easy now, don't put any weight onto the ankle you've hurt until I can get a look at it."

"Um, okay." She took my hands and I pulled her up easily onto her one good foot. She let out a little surprised yip and said, "Wow! Okay, you're pretty strong."

I gave a nod and said, "Yup, and I'm going to pick you up."

"What? Oh!"

Too late. I'd already lifted her easily, one arm behind her back, the other beneath her knees, and I swear her thick, stylish wool coat and the sweater dress she wore beneath it weighed almost as much as her. I stepped off the dock and down into my boat while she clung to me, her arms around my neck. I murmured, "Okay, tough part is over, I'm going to put you down. Remember, no weight on that ankle until I can get a look at it."

"Okay," she said, breathy, and I carefully set her down. She hopped on one foot, using me to find her balance for a moment and let go once she had it.

"Oh, shit, my purse," she said.

"I'll get it, go on down below deck and sit. I'll be right down to look at that ankle and take care of that hand."

"Um, okay. Thank you."

"No problem, it's what I do."

I went back up on the dock and bent, snatching up her purse from the wood and dusting a few stray slivers off of it. I leapt back down onto my boat, and went for the door and the few steps leading below deck.

I found her stopped in the galley, staring wide-eyed at the table.

"Shit," I grunted.

She turned, slightly open-mouthed, and transferred the stare to me. "Did I interrupt something?"

"It's nothing," I stated. "I was just cleaning it."

"Uh-huh," she said flatly, like she didn't believe me.

I decided against trying another lie as she picked up the Springfield, removing the magazine and having a look. She set that down and pulled back the slide, ejecting the bullet in the chamber. She rolled her lips together, her eyes closing, the lashes fluttering against her cheeks for a moment before she opened those bottomless dark eyes and stared into mine.

"Looks like this was a happy accident, then," she said softly, and palmed the round, shoving it into her coat's pocket. She put the magazine back and hit the switch on the side, the slide popped forward, and she handed me my weapon.

I dumped it in the empty stainless steel sink of my galley with a clatter and moved further into my boat.

"Please, sit," I said, swallowing nervously. "I'm going to grab my first aid kit."

"Okay," she said gently.

I moved past her in the narrow space and went back, past the stair, to the stern of my boat and the berth. I opened up the cabinet door beneath my bed and pulled out the soft-sided first aid kit. It was the size of a small suitcase; I had everything for any kind of emergency in here. I think every good medic's first aid kit was essentially the same kit we carried out in the field, fully-stocked and ready to rock.

I expected her to be gone, but when I came back out, she was in my recliner in front of the TV, spun out to where I would have the most room to work. I knelt at her feet and opened up my kit. I was still in uniform from the shift I'd just worked, which I guess had helped sell the believability that I was, in fact, a medic. Why else would she just take my word for it?

"You okay?" she asked softly, and I couldn't look at her. I nodded and unzipped compartments and sat back on my haunches with a sigh.

"I'm supposed to be taking care of *you*," I reminded her and she smiled a charmed, if sad, little half-smile.

"Can't take care of anybody if you don't take care of yourself, first," she said and her voice was gentle with just an edge of seduction that I don't think was intentional. I think that was just her voice. I nodded and switched subjects. She'd already taken off her coat. It sat, with her purse on top, on the bench back by the table my bullets were still lined up on. My glass was empty and I had to smile at that. I mean, wasn't that why I'd been drinking it? For the liquid courage? Not that she had anything to fear from me at all. I was genuinely just looking to help her.

"Not trying to get fresh with you," I murmured, slipping my hands up the long skirt of her knit dress and finding the top of her heeled boot, up over her knee.

"I think it would be fine if you were," she said dryly and I nearly swallowed my own tongue. I felt my face heat and didn't respond to the overt flirtation, instead trying to remain all business.

I trailed my fingertips across the smooth leather and found a zipper at the inside of her ankle, let it down and gripped her heel gently; the high heel of her boot was loose and flopping.

"Think I found why you fell in the first place," I murmured. "Boots might be toast. Shame too, they're nice."

"Dammit, they're my favorite pair," she pouted.

"Brace yourself, this might hurt a little bit." I eased the boot off her foot and she sucked in a sharp breath, tensing as I carefully brought it down and all the way off.

"Ooo yeah, that's a nasty sprain. You're already swelling. Hang tight." I rooted through my bag and found one of the chemical ice packs, popping the inner bladder and shaking it up; it instantly grew cold. I found a roll of Ace bandage and gently wrapped it onto the affected area temporarily so I could deal with her hand, which she was still cradling to her breast.

"Okay, onto the main event, let's see it." I held out my hand and waved at her to give up hers.

"This is probably going to suck, digging that bitch out, isn't it?" she asked.

"It's not going to be fun, but it's not going to be too bad. I don't think you're going to feel it, the way I think I'm going to have to do it; it's the disinfecting that's going to sting a little. But, we'll see what I've got in here to minimize that."

"Okay, just get it out quickly," she said, through gritted teeth and I chuckled.

"More whiskey?" I asked.

"Yes, if you please."

I laughed outright then, and stood up. "All right."

I poured her a little more and handed her the glass. She took it with her uninjured hand and sipped, while eyeing me with some trepidation. I smiled and turned my back to her, pulling her forward against it and resting her hand, palm up, on my knee.

"Don't move, and no peeking," I told her.

"Are you serious?" she asked, laughing a little.

"I am. Just relax, don't look, and let me do my job. It'll be over before you know it."

"Okay, cool," she said, her voice buzzing with nervousness, and I heard her take another sip.

I pulled out a scalpel and uncapped it. The sliver was under a few layers of skin but I didn't think she would bleed much if I just parted them and lifted it out. If I went after it with a needle, we'd be here all night and I would have to break it up and pull it out in chunks. It would be better to get it out in one piece, disinfect, and bandage it up. No fuss, quick and easy. I didn't want or need the scalpel freaking her out, though.

"Okay, here we go, ready?"

"No!" she blurted after exhaling a breath but it was too late, I was already drawing a sharp, clean line down the middle, the skin parting easily, the sliver emerging almost as if her body rejected its presence, offended that it'd even tried to take up residence there.

"Doing all right?" I asked, when I didn't hear anything. I set the scalpel, still out of sight, on my kit and picked out a pair of tweezers from their pocket, flicking off the plastic keeping them together with my thumbnail.

"No!" Her voice was tight and clipped.

I could hear the smile in my voice as I told her calmly and evenly, "You're doing great, Claire. Just a couple more things and we'll be all done."

"Mm," she said noncommittally, her voice strained, her breath held tight. I set the sliver aside on a piece of gauze and pressed another piece to the palm of her hand while I pulled a bottle of hydrogen peroxide from its spot. I pulled the cap off with thumb and forefinger and moved the gauze away. It was dotted with crimson and I frowned; it was bleeding a little more than I expected, but still not too bad.

"Maybe a slight sting." I sprayed the disinfectant solution onto the cut and it frothed and foamed with a vengeance. She jumped and let out an explosive breath that tickled across the back of my neck before her forehead dropped below it, to press just between my shoulder blades. I tingled all over at the contact.

"That's not as bad as I thought it would be," she confessed.

I dabbed at the cut and said, "Yeah, this is pretty mild stuff."

"Thanks for that," she murmured, muffled, and I smiled.

"You're a tough girl, Claire."

"Ha!" she mocked and I smiled some more.

She eased more against my back and I tried not to freeze and revel in the contact. I missed human touch something fierce. I ached for it, but I just couldn't bring myself to go my twin's route and find it in a string of meaningless hookups. That just wasn't for me.

I doctored Claire's hand with antibiotic ointment and bandaged it like the pro I was, splitting the bandage and tying it securely before relinquishing her hand. She lingered against my back and as much as I wanted to stay like that, I needed to have a look and bandage her ankle.

I sighed, partially from frustration and partially from longing, and murmured, "Claire, you can sit up now."

"Sorry!" she blurted, and sat up sharply.

"'S'okay. It was nice while it lasted," I gave her, and I turned back around to face her. I checked my watch and said, "Leave the ice on a few minutes more."

"Wow, that thing is huge," she said, staring at the bloody piece of dock I'd pulled from beneath her lovely skin.

"Yeah, it's out though." I stood up and cleaned up my wrappers and detritus. I disposed of the capped scalpel in the sharps' container I kept under the sink, the only thing in it, and put everything in the trash where it belonged, or back in the kit, leaving out only what I would need to wrap her ankle securely.

"I'm going to put this back, be right back, okay?"

"Okay," she said softly.

I returned to her sitting quietly, empty glass on the little table by the chair, staring at the crisp, white bandaging around her hand, face screwed up into an expression that said she was deep in thought.

I sat at her feet and she stared into my eyes, searching, for a long time. I know it sounds cliché as hell, but I felt a connection with her. Something inside me touched something inside her, like for like, moving against each other like two cats, greeting one another.

She asked me, her voice quiet in the small, intimate space of my live-aboard, "Angel, what did I interrupt?"

"Nothing," I lied, ashamed, and she gave me a look that said, *don't lie to me, please. I'm not a fool.* I swallowed hard and she waited me out.

"I work a tough job. It was a bad night, more deaths than saves, I don't want to talk about it."

The fingertips of her good hand grazed my cheek and I looked up sharply.

"Don't want to talk about it, or feel like you've got no one to talk to?" she asked.

Hit the nail right on the head.

"Both," I hazarded and she nodded carefully.

"I understand."

"You do?"

"Yeah," she said and something on her face, in her eyes; I believed her. I grunted and went to pay attention to her ankle, but she stopped me with a hand on my shoulder. I looked up.

"I'm here, I'm listening, and I won't judge," she said.

"Just… I've just been lonely, I guess," picking that off the monumental pile of shit that was wrong with me.

"I can understand that, too," she said and again, I believed her.

I went back to that ankle, wrapping it carefully to make sure she had the support she needed while at the same time I wasn't cutting off circulation or anything. I affixed the two butterfly clips, digging their little teeth into the tan bandage and pulling it taut before hooking it into the other side. I let her foot go, my fingers leaving the soft, warm covering of the Ace bandage over her silky skin, and jumped slightly when her fingertips touched the side of my face and her lips were suddenly on mine.

I froze for a heartbeat, unsure what to do, but my body, craving this sort of contact as much as my heart did, took right over. Before I knew it, I was kissing her back, drinking in what she had to offer, the taste of my whiskey sweeter somehow coming from her soft mouth, as her tongue plunged past my lips and swept against mine, exploring, asking silently, for what I didn't know, but it didn't matter. My soul called out to hers and for some reason, I could swear I heard an echoing, yet silent, cry from her, and it was like I just knew what to do.

I took the lifeline she was throwing me, her hands to either side of my face, holding me to her, her body on the edge of the seat in a bid to get closer. I felt my hands caress over the soft knit material of her sweater dress, the turtleneck and her decorative scarf covering her neck to her chin. I didn't like that. I wanted to play my lips along the skin there. I wanted to hear her gasp as I found that sweet spot every woman had, and I wanted to send shivers and chills through her body like she was suddenly sending through mine.

I was desperate, starving for some skin-on-skin contact with her and I started by unwinding the scarf, pulling my mouth from hers briefly to lift it over her head. She let me take it, her hands going to the wide, black decorative belt around her trim waist and undoing it, letting it fall into the recliner.

I pulled the other boot from her uninjured leg awkwardly as we couldn't seem to stop our mouths from feasting on one another. She whimpered softly when I pulled her by her thighs practically into my lap and she felt the hard length of my cock through my EMT pants, pressing against the fabric of her panties.

"Hold onto me," I whispered harshly and her arms went around my neck, her legs locking behind my back as I stood in one fluid motion and turned, carrying her back to my berth and the queen-sized bed I had back there.

It was a mess, unmade, a triangle of blankets pulled back from where I'd carelessly thrown them that way getting out of bed that morning. I sat her on the end of the bed and continued to kiss her while I awkwardly raised one leg and then the other, blindly letting down the zippers on the inside of my own boot's ankles. She was gathering the skirt of her dress in her hands as I toed off my boots and pulled my shirt over my head. I was suddenly possessed, needing her body against mine in the worst way.

She lifted her dress over her head at the same time I got started on my pants and I just had to stop and stare for a minute. She was fit, toned, and wore a black lace matching bra and panty set that made her look like some Victoria's Secret runway angel. She tossed the grey dress on my floor, and when she reached up and let down her hair I think I forgot how to breathe for a minute.

She hauled herself back onto my bed with her hands and asked, "What's wrong?"

"You're beautiful," I said and shoved my pants off, dragging my feet along the carpet to shuck off my socks, which peeled off perfectly with the friction like they did every time. I got up onto my bed and lay beside her, rolling so one arm was over her and half my body was paired with hers, putting as much skin as possible against hers.

She was warm and so soft, her body rocking against mine, putting her closer, her arms going around me and cradling me gently while my mouth found first her shoulder and climbed its way along her freckled skin to the slope of her neck. She writhed a little when I found that spot, her breath coming in impassioned pants as my hands smoothed their way over her body from hip to breast, cupping and squeezing through the rough lace of her bra.

She let her own hands explore my shoulders and chest in a silken caress before she boldly reached into the waistband of my boxer-briefs and wrapped gentle but firm fingers around my straining cock.

A jolt of electric pleasure arched through my body, forking out from that intimate touch and crackling along every nerve from it, out through my limbs. I unhooked the front of her bra and dragged the straps off her arms, which forced her to let go of me for just a moment.

"Come up here, I want to blow you," she said and I blinked in surprise.

She dug her nails into my ass through the fabric of my boxer-briefs and

I moved up, letting her drag the offending garment down to my mid-thigh. As soon as my cock sprang free, her mouth went over it, hot, wet, and velvety-soft, pushing down over it until the head nudged the back of her throat. I expected her to back off, but she didn't, her throat relaxing around me and she took me in just that little bit more.

"Dios mío," I uttered, breathlessly.

I threw my head back and held still, eyes closed, and just gave myself over to the sensation of her mouth on me. She bobbed her head gently, making love to me with her mouth, worshiping my cock with her lips and tongue and I couldn't get enough of it.

I pressed my hands to my lower back, my fingers digging slightly into my skin, and fought the urge to thrust; my breath filled my chest, falling from my lips in a craze of passion as I let myself go and just gave myself over to the feel of this sensual stranger and the things she did to me. I dropped my chin to my chest and opened my eyes, meeting the heat sliding behind her gaze as she stared up at me, the sight of my dick disappearing between her lips almost too much.

"I don't want to come," I rushed out. "Not yet."

She drew back off of me, freeing my cock from her mouth with a little pop. I reached for her, sliding a hand down her body, dipping it into her panties, teasing at her pussy lips with my middle finger as she rolled like a cat, arching her back, thrusting her hips against my hand, grinding herself against it, hot and wet, slick to the touch, begging for a touch from me that went much deeper than just my fingers.

"I want you inside of me," she murmured in a sultry bedroom voice that had my cock twitching.

I made quick work of pulling my boxer-briefs off and reached into a cubby in the headboard for one of the dust-coated condoms there. I tore the package open and rolled it on while she followed every one of my moves, her gaze like heated mercury, liquid and smooth.

I hooked my fingers in her panties and she lifted her hips off the bed, letting me skate them down over her long, toned legs and off. I dropped them, my eyes transfixed by the sight of her spread legs, her fingers working against her swollen pussy lips, glistening with her arousal. I got between her thighs and she reached for me, dragging my mouth to hers, working her pussy against me, sliding it along my shaft tantalizingly in a display of raw, organic desire the likes I'd never seen before.

"Please, Angel," she whispered, her voice heated, and I slid inside of her. The union of our two bodies was like being touched soul-deep. She gave a little cry and pressed herself down over the top of me, her body shaking and trembling with the first fine start of orgasm.

I let her calm, let her settle, and then began to move, slow, sensual, deep thrusting. So careful that the only sound in the small space of my berth was our heavy, liquid breathing, washing out to meet the lapping water on the other side of the hull. Her arms went around my neck and she arched, causing me to look down our conjoined bodies and groan. The sight of me disappearing into the depths of her pussy was so erotic, so hot, I wanted to commit the sight to memory forever more.

"Angel..." My name was like a whispered prayer falling from her lips as her body began to tremble finely against mine. Our synapses on overload, the pleasure between us rose, wrapping around us, swallowing us whole, drowning us, until with a few tightly-controlled final thrusts we both broke through the other side and it was like I could suddenly breathe again.

I collapse over her and she cradled me to her body, gasping against my shoulder, shuddering beneath me, her tight pussy milking me with aftershocks as I settled over the top of her, carefully holding my weight on my arms and knees so I wouldn't crush her.

Her mouth found mine and we kissed for what felt like forever, long into the night.

When I woke the next morning, she was gone. I found my gun in pieces on the table, the single bullet she'd pocketed gone, a note in delicate script left on a notepad I usually kept by the galley's fridge.

You saved one last night. You saved yourself. Now you can go out and save more. It's what you do, it's the kind of man you are. Hopefully, I'll see you around, Angel. Hopefully, our paths will cross again.

-Claire.

Shit. No number. No last name.

No way to track her down.

1

Three Years Later

*A*ngel…

"Dispatch 641."

"Jesus Christ, Tina!" Johnson cried, picking up the radio from its cradle as the call popped on our screen. Tina had the bad habit of calling on the radio before she'd even sent the call to our rig through the tablet.

"641, go ahead Dispatch."

"Alpha 641 you have priority one traffic for a suspected overdose, thirty-one-year-old female, unresponsive, unknown downtime. PD en route."

"Copy. 641 en route."

He hung up the mic with a clatter and glanced at the screen for the address. I'd already tapped the button to accept the call before he was even off the radio, which was redundant nowadays. Tina had just been at it so long, she liked to do it old-school.

"Sounds bad, punch it," I told him, and he flipped switches for lights and sirens, our rig's engine growling like a beast as he dropped the accelerator. He laid on the horn and road-raged some at the fuckwits in our way but I let him go. I missed Ramsay; she'd been my partner for two years before deciding to get out of Indigo City to sunnier climates. I'd been paired with floaters ever since, while they decided who to put full-time in her place with me.

I had a feeling that the top brass was going to put me with Johnson full-time, which wouldn't be the worst thing in the world, but it wouldn't exactly be the best, either. He had an explosive temper and didn't always do well under pressure. He was good for a basic rig but not for an advanced medicine truck like this one.

"Are you fuckin' kidding me? Come on!" he shouted at the windshield. An ICPD rig had pulled up to the curb in front of us at the building we'd been dispatched to, but it hadn't pulled up far enough or fast enough for Johnson's liking. I shook my head and tried to cover my ass with a laugh even though the dude was making me seriously uncomfortable. I gritted my teeth and bailed out of the passenger side of the rig before he'd even finished slamming it in park. He met me by the back doors to get the gurney.

"You cool?" I asked and he scowled at me, his head jerking back like I'd spit in his face or something.

"Yeah, man, just another day at the office."

I gave a curt nod and we wheeled the gurney into the lobby of the building and hit the elevator button for the fifth floor. The cops joined us a second later.

"Hey," one of them said, and gave a nod.

"'Sup guys?" Johnson asked.

"Not much, what do you think it is? Junkie or suicide?" the second cop asked.

"Doesn't matter," I said. "A patient is a patient, no matter what their story. We're here to save them." I swallowed hard and thought back to my own battle with my demons; how close I'd come, until a real angel had been sent out of nowhere to save me.

Johnson snorted.

"They wanna die so fuckin' bad, I say let 'em go. We got real patients to deal with. Ones that wanna live."

That put the nail in his coffin where I was concerned. I fought not to roll my eyes and the cops exchanged a sharp look between each other. The taller of the two of them asked, "Isn't that kind of an unprofessional point of view for a paramedic to have?"

He didn't get an answer. The elevator pinged, the doors slid open, and we rolled out onto the floor and up to the apartment door we'd been called to. A man was standing in the open doorway looking frantic, looking shook, his cell pressed to his ear as he said, "Oh, thank God! They're here. Yes, thank you." He hung up and said to us, "Please help. It's my sister, she's back here."

We left the gurney in the hall, one of the uniforms nodding and standing with it, the other taking the brother aside.

"What's her name?" I called out to him.

"Claire. Claire Montgomery."

Twilight Zone. I thought to myself. *Creepy coincidence.*

I rounded into the bedroom he indicated and she was laying on the floor. Claire.

My Claire.

"Son of a bitch," Johnson muttered, and I agreed, just for completely different reasons. I knelt down by her side and checked her pulse and for breathing. Both were barely there.

"Do you know what she took?" I shouted.

"No! I wasn't home. I came home and found her like this, I couldn't wake her up!"

I shone a light in her dark eyes and couldn't find a damn pupil, but had to guess they were pinpoints.

"Opiate?" Johnson asked.

"Think so, can't be sure."

He hooked her up to the monitor, and her heartbeat was barely hanging on by a thread. I cursed and put an oxygen mask over her mouth and nose, bagging her while Johnson got the Narcan going. If it wasn't opioids it wouldn't do anything but better safe than sorry.

"Claire!" I called loudly, and rubbed my knuckles across her sternum through her thin tee. "Claire, come on, baby! Wake up. Talk to me!"

"Here, move." Johnson administered the Narcan and I went back to bagging. I swear to God, those were the longest, roughest few heartbeats of my life before her dark eyes flew open and she sucked in a hard breath, crying out.

"It's okay, Claire. I got you, just hang on, breathe. Breathe for me."

"Angel?" she asked tremulously, and I smiled.

"Yeah. Yeah, I got you."

"You know her?" Johnson asked.

"Yeah. Grab the gear," I ordered, and I scooped Claire up without a second thought and carried her out past the cops and her brother.

"Claire!" her brother cried, and she hid her face against my chest. I set her on the gurney, my muscles just beginning to strain. She was so light, fragile, like a bird. I set her down and she was still out of it.

Jesus, how much did she take?

Tears gathered in a constellation on her lashes and she whispered, "Why did it have to be you?"

She reached up and clutched her necklace.

I said, "Just hang on. We're gonna get you taken care of."

She closed her eyes and lay back and I said, "Let's move. I'm not sure the one dose is going to hold her."

I pulled the last strap tight across her legs, securing her to the gurney, and took her hand as we wheeled her to the elevator.

"Where are you taking her?" the officer who had waited with our stretcher asked.

"Trinity Gen."

"Cool, we'll bring the brother."

"Thanks," I grunted and checked her. She was sliding again already.

"Johnson, haul ass, we gotta get her another dose."

"Can only go as fast as the elevator, man."

"Claire, come on. Talk to me. Look at me."

Her head lolled on her neck and she dragged her eyes open. She let go of her necklace and reached up to touch the side of my face. I captured the hand and brought it back down.

"I wished for you," she murmured, and then she was out again. The Narcan was working; she was breathing, but she wasn't out of the woods yet. Sometimes it took more than one dose. It was a miracle drug, for sure, but it had some limits.

We rattled onto the elevator and I stared at her necklace, a bullet, wire wrapped around its base and hanging from the black cord. My heart ached. Apparently, she had never forgot about me, but why didn't she come find me?

We rode down in silence, I kept checking her vitals and she lay, her eyes closed, head faintly rolling back and forth. She was coming back, but she wasn't quite *here,* and as soon as I passed her off through the doors at Trinity Gen, I was going to lose her all over again.

Not this time. You have a last name and you have connections.

I swallowed hard and loaded her into the back of our rig, climbing up behind her. Johnson, to his credit, didn't say a word about it. Just closed us in and hopped in the driver's seat, radioing ahead to the hospital while I went to work on Claire.

She would be okay. We had got to her in time. Still, it felt like the stakes were incredibly high for me. I sat in the back of the rig, calling out the info the hospital needed for Johnson to relay, while I started an IV and dosed her with another shot of Narcan to counteract whatever she'd taken.

I leaned in close and said, "Claire, *mi alma,* I need you to tell me what you took and how you took it."

"Pills," she mumbled, and I called it out to Johnson.

"Where'd you get them, hm?" I asked but there was no answer. She just lay there, eyes closed, but her breathing and heart-rate were good, oxygen saturation a little lower than I would like, but rising. I thought we'd got to her in time to stave off any permanent damage, which I was grateful for.

I whispered to her in Spanish, encouraging things. Johnson didn't know the language, and I didn't think Claire did either, but where she was, between life and death, she didn't need to know the words, she just needed to feel safe, which I could provide if only for a fleeting moment. We pulled into the ambulance entrance outside Trinity Gen's emergency room doors and I was about to lose her again.

Only for the moment. I reminded myself.

Before Johnson came around to the back, I lifted my bullet from around her head and stuffed it quickly into my pocket. I would give it back. It just wasn't something I think they'd let her keep and I didn't want her to lose it forever, because I would see her again. I had to. Fate wouldn't have put each other in our respective paths during these moments in our lives if we weren't meant to be.

I'd prayed and God had given me her when I needed her the most. I didn't know if she prayed. I didn't know if she was a believer, but I couldn't chalk it up to coincidence that I had been the one to respond to this call. Out of every rig in Indigo City and the surrounding area, it was mine to come to her rescue.

"Angel, don't go!" she cried, grabbing onto my hand where it gripped the rail of the gurney, as we passed her into the emergency room team's care.

"Don't worry, just get well, I'll see you again soon," I promised her and Georgia, one of the emergency room nurses, gave me a funny look. I gave her back a meaningful one and she nodded.

Anything to keep the patient calm, right?

I stood in the brightly-lit hub of Trinity Gen's emergency room, and I had already started plotting and scheming as to how we would meet again. I was about to break some hardcore ethical rules.

"Okay, bitch. You *know* I can't do that." Pasquale glared at me from across the two-person booth at the *10-13*.

I held out my hands, helpless and said, "I'm begging you, you're the best 'in' I have at Trinity Gen. I just need you to pass her a note. I'm begging you, Pasquale. I just need to get her my number. She can do the rest. *Please.*"

"Oh, no. Not until you tell me *why*."

I gritted my teeth and he sat taller, crossing his arms over his narrow chest and raising an eyebrow. He had on a blonde wig and was rocking a retro-fifties look, complete with breasts this time. He was drag-queen-fabulous and wasn't about to give me an inch. I let out a breath that turned into a sound of defeat.

"Okay, but you have to swear not to tell Golden."

He perked up at that and asked with genuine interest, "Since when have you started keeping secrets from your twin, Sugar?"

"Since if he found out about this, it'd probably destroy how he looks at me and what he thinks of me forever."

Pasquale's posture eased as he searched my face and finally his arms came down. He hung up his usual biting sarcasm and said, "Okay, talk. I'm sworn to secrecy."

I gave a reluctant nod, and told him how Claire and I met. He stared at me, dumbfounded, and said, "Baby, that ain't nothing to be ashamed about. We all go through hard times, believe me."

"I know, but…" I trailed off and looked out into the restaurant, and sighed. I shook my head and refocused on Pasquale's heavily-made up face. The only thing thicker than his make-up was his expression of concerned empathy.

"It was three years ago, and I haven't stopped thinking about her since. I don't think a single day has gone by. I don't want to lose her again and not try."

He huffed out a breath and stared at me, the internal debate raging in his eyes and written in the unhappy lines of his face. This had the potential to be a huge HIPAA violation and it could cost him dearly. I wasn't asking for a small thing here.

"Gimme what you got," he demanded, snapping his fingers at me and holding out his hand, waving his fingers at me to hand it over impatiently.

I handed him a 6x9 manila envelope with a note and her necklace in it, and a piece of paper with her admit date and first and last name. He looked over the paper and squeezed the envelope with his long, perfectly-manicured nails.

"What's in here?"

I told him.

"Motherfucker, and if she hangs herself with it?" he demanded.

"She won't," I said with dead certainty.

"She is in there for a suicide attempt."

"She won't, Pasquale."

He sighed and dropped his shoulders.

"A deal. I'll show her the necklace, then I'll bring it back to you. She can get it from you herself when she gets out of there."

"I wish you could get me onto the ward to see her," I said grimly.

"Baby, ain't even *family* allowed to see her. She is on a seventy-two-hour hold. Probably longer if she don't open up and share her problems. She almost succeeded in offing herself, yeah?"

I nodded and said, "Got there in the nick of time."

"Honey, I don't doubt that. You are as your name implies. Look, I said I would do this thing for you and I will. I've done rotations on that ward and I can get in. I'll bring whatever message I can out, but then you are on your own, and I don't ever want to hear this spoken about *ever*."

"You keep my secret, I'll keep yours," I said honestly.

"Oh, you can count on that, baby. You narc me out I'm gonna fuckin' kill you."

He picked up his pink martini and downed it in one swallow and gave me a contemptuous look. "I cannot believe what I do for y'all, sometimes. It is unreal."

"And appreciated," I said leaning back in my seat. "You have no idea how much."

He shook his head and said, "You fuck me, I better at least get the courtesy of a reach-around." I nearly choked on my beer and he gave me a flat look and raised a slender hand calling, "Waitress, can we get some napkins please, honey?"

2

───────────

*C*laire…

I was sitting, curled on the bed in the single-occupancy room. I'd graduated today to real clothes. They'd given me a set of blue hospital scrubs and a one-size-fits-all grey sweatshirt with the hospital logo emblazoned on it. The sweatshirt was something like four sizes too big for me, but I liked it well enough. I put it on and pretended that it was Angel's, which was ridiculous, I know. A fit of drug-induced wishful thinking. There was no way he was the medic that had brought me here.

I was emotionally exhausted and still felt like shit from my suicide attempt. I'd talked to the social worker, and the doctor on this floor, and they'd taken me back to my room. I hadn't been locked in, but it still felt like a jail. The door was big, and grey-painted steel, set with those windows with the chicken wire in them in two panels, one high and one low. I could see the nurse's station through it, the nurses in a bubble of more glass and chicken wire. The med carts were secured there.

I was embarrassed more than anything, now, and I just wanted to go

27

home. Well, back to my brother's. Home wasn't exactly something I had.

The night I'd met Angel, over three years ago now, I had been offered a deal with the prestigious Night Circus. I had been a champion gymnast all through high school and college and had skipped out on a final run at the Olympics in order to join the Night Circus as one of their aerial *tissu* performers.

It was the opportunity of a lifetime, traveling all over the world, and as much as my soul had connected with Angel that night, I didn't want to give up on my dream. I should have stayed. That dream had become a nightmare.

I looked up sharply from where I sat, curled at the head of my bed, when the door to my room opened. An orderly, no, a male nurse came in and closed the door behind himself and stood with his back to the windows.

"Christ on a cracker, I cannot *believe* I am doing this," he said as he slipped a manila envelope out of his scrub pocket. "Hurry up, now, and give me back that necklace. I can't leave it here with you."

I frowned and took the envelope, tearing it open and upending it. My bullet necklace fell into my hand and my eyes widened. I hadn't thought I would ever see it again. I looked up sharply.

"Who are you?"

"A friend of a friend, sweetheart, and I have got to *go*." He held out his hand like 'Gimme', his nails acrylic and with a nice burgundy sparkle polish on them. I bit my bottom lip, trying to decide. I handed the necklace back, and he said, "Don't get caught with that," stabbing one of those manicured nails at the envelope in my hands. "Hide it until I'm the only one at the desk."

I nodded and he went back out, shoving my necklace into his pocket. I tucked the envelope behind my back, under the pillow. I had spotted a sheet of paper in it and I was dying to know what it said.

The nurses worked on a rotating schedule serving up medication to their patients while one always remained at the central desk. It was run efficiently, like a prison, and thoroughly creeped me out, being here. I couldn't complain, though. I had legitimately given up and tried to take my own life. I belonged here, but at the same time I felt like I didn't. Now it was just follow the plan set forth by the good doctors in white coats and get out.

The bald man with the nails looked up from his post, down his nose at me, and gave me an imperious nod. I pulled the envelope out from under my pillow and the single sheet of paper out of the envelope.

Mi Alma – Claire –

Please. Call me when you're better. I've thought about you every day since that night and never gave up hope our paths would cross again. I've saved countless since that night, but you're the only one that's mattered.

–Angel

It had his phone number under his name and I swallowed hard and quickly hid the envelope and message. I met the nurse's eyes through the wire cage in the thick glass of my hospital room door and gave a single nod. He cracked his first genuine smile, and gave a single nod back.

It *had* been Angel to save me.

I reeled slightly from the information and yearned to talk to him again. The only problem was, I was trapped in here while he was out there. I had to put my time here to good use, and so I just sat there to think.

3

______

*A*ngel…

My phone rang and I set the beer I had in my hand down on the railing of my porch. I answered it without really looking, my eyes locked on the boat traffic passing on the Chesapeake as my houseboat bobbed at the end of its dock. I'd moved in at the beginning of the summer.

"Hello?"

"Hi, um, it's me."

My heart stopped.

"Claire?"

"Yeah. I memorized your number, asked to call my brother… I hope you don't mind me calling like this."

"No! No, *mi alma*, I don't mind. Why would I mind?"

She sniffed, and her voice came hesitant and broken over the line as she whispered, "I'm so sorry…"

"Claire, don't be. I'm the last person who can judge on that score."

"Thank you," she murmured, and I knew it wasn't about the 'no judgement'.

"Baby, if it weren't for you, I wouldn't have been there. Thank *you*. You have no idea how many lives you saved that night. Shit, hundreds. Hundreds, all alive because of you."

"Really?"

"Really."

"God, everything got so fucked up, and just hopeless and there wasn't anyone, you know?"

I wanted to tell her, 'Yes, there was. I was there, I was *always* there…' but it wouldn't help anything. It wouldn't serve any purpose except to pile on the guilt and make her feel worse about herself.

"Can you tell me what happened?" I asked.

"Um, yeah, just, not now, not while I'm here. I'm trying to get out. Doing everything they say…"

"How long does it look like they're going to keep you?" I asked.

"I don't know. A few more days, maybe? I'm not sure where I'm going to go. I don't have a home and my brother… God, he's so angry with me."

"One thing at a time, *mi alma*. Work on you, work on getting better. You can't take care of anyone else unless you take care of yourself first," I reminded her.

"Okay." There was a long pause while she considered what I said and finally she said, "Angel?"

"Yeah?"

"I'm glad it was you."

"I thank God it was me," I whispered and she gave a slightly-broken laugh. I didn't think her faith was intact, but that was okay. She didn't need to believe in God. He believed in her and had done his miracle-working already. It was my turn, and I only hoped I could live up to the task He'd put before me.

He never gives you that which you cannot handle. It may not be easy, but you can do it. I reminded myself.

"I have to go, another patient wants to use the phone."

I tried not to feel bitter about that; she'd only just called.

"Okay, call me again when you have a release date, and Claire?"

"Yeah?"

"Take care of yourself, and I'll see you again."

"Promise?" she asked, and she sounded so fragile.

"I promise."

"Okay, bye."

"Bye for now," I said, and it killed me.

I hung up and heaved out a huge sigh of both relief and trepidation at what lay ahead. I leaned heavily on my porch rail and stared out over the water and prayed.

I prayed fervently, as hard as I'd ever prayed before in my life.

4

laire…

"I don't even know who you are, anymore, Claire."

"I'm sorry," I said, and felt that black hole of hopelessness open up underneath me. Carter had never understood me. Of the two of us, he had always been the rock while I'd always been the free spirit. It'd put us at odds before, but now, I was afraid my rash decision had absolutely broken us.

He shook his head and heaved a giant sigh weighted with emotion. I felt despondent. I could see the silent rage in my brother's eyes and it wasn't good. The therapist gently interjected.

"Claire, what would you like to tell your brother?"

"I don't know what I *can* tell him other than what I've already said. I'm sorry, and it won't happen again." I crossed my arms over my chest as much to shut everyone out as to hold myself in. I felt gutted, like everything was spilling out onto the spotless linoleum floor. Carter just kept shaking his head.

"Carter, you seem angry." The therapist gently prodded and my brother seethed.

"You're damn right, I'm angry. What if Gracie had found you? What if it'd been your niece or my wife, Claire? Jesus, you have to stop making these selfish decisions!"

"Like what? What else, Carter?" I demanded, scowling. Okay, I'd fucked up this time, but I was genuinely confused now. What was he trying to say?

"Like leaving in the first place. You didn't even ask. You literally showed up, said you quit the Olympic team and were joining the circus. The goddamn *circus*, Claire!" He threw up his hands and dropped them to his khaki-covered lap with a meaty '*Thwack!*'

"I'm sorry, I didn't realize I needed your permission, Carter!"

"You can't make a living at art, not a reliable one, at least. You need to get your head out of the clouds and –"

"I make over a hundred thousand dollars a year! Is that not enough for you?"

"And you live out of a fucking suitcase! You crash at my place any time you come through town and you tried to kill yourself, Claire!"

"Okay, I'm going to stop you," the therapist finally interceded. "There's a lot to unpack here…"

I stopped listening, my brother and I staring each other down. I'd never seen him like this, so angry with me. I mean, I'd pissed him off before, sure, but never had I seen him so enraged. It was scary, and I suddenly felt like I was on shaky ground. Panic began to take hold. *Had I fucked this up past fixing?* A sudden dark welling of emotion surged angrily to the surface. Angry at myself for not finishing the job, I closed my eyes and clung to Angel's face, my niece Gracie's, my brother's, the other performers who, despite how hard life was at the Night Circus, had become my family.

Did they even know I was in here? Had I just disappeared? God, did I even still have a job?

I didn't know. I also didn't know why I suddenly thought of those things now… I mean, we were basically on a week's leave, but the end of that leave was coming up fast.

"Are you even listening right now? God, Claire!"

I opened my eyes. My brother was sitting there in his business casual attire, his arms crossed, a look of utter disgust on his face, and I broke cleanly in two.

You did this, you total waste of space. You fail at everything.

"I'm listening," I lied, and hoped that it sounded believable enough. My brother shook his head.

"I'll bring your things, but when you get out of here, you have to figure things out on your own this time."

"Carter, I don't know that's the best thing for Claire, right now. She needs your support dur– "

He cut her off.

"No, she *had* my support. Right now, my family, my wife, my daughter, *they* need me. Claire, you chose to throw your life away. I can't help you anymore. I'm not going to risk a second time around. Gracie doesn't deserve it. Mallory doesn't deserve it, and I don't want to walk in and find you dead next time."

"There won't *be* a next time!" I tried, but he shook his head.

"I'll bring your stuff tomorrow," he said, getting up.

"Carter…" the therapist beseeched him and I shook my head. I couldn't look at him but then again, he couldn't look at me, either.

"I love you," he said.

"If you love me, you wouldn't walk out on me," I said softly.

"You walked out first," he shot at me and he leaned down to hug me. I jerked back and he dropped his chin to his chest.

"Fine."

He walked out. The therapist was even caught off-guard, staring after him, her mouth agape. I shot her an apologetic look and said, "Guess you know why I ran off and joined the circus."

She shook her head in disbelief and I felt sorry for her. I felt sorry for myself, too, but I think I was so used to this kind of treatment from my family that it wasn't quite so keen after all this time.

"Let's talk about that," she said gently, and I took a deep breath and nodded.

There was a lot to talk about. Carter was a year older than me. My father walked out on our mom when I was four. I barely remembered him. My mom relied on Carter for a lot of things where I was concerned. She worked long hours, day in and day out, and still collected welfare for our entire childhoods. I mean, there was only so much she could do with a high school diploma and no prior work experience. She ended up a clerk at a grocery store and worked her way to management, but it wasn't easy and the pay was very little.

Still, she managed to keep me in both dance and gymnastics. I didn't find out until after she died that it was by selling her jewelry, little by little, when the need called for it. Carter had gone to college on a basketball scholarship. He had been *this* close to going pro, before he'd blown out one of his knees.

We were both athletically inclined and gifted in our own right, his injury hadn't affected his scholarship money and he'd worked hard to fill the gaps with grant money, earning his degree. He had gone into teaching, but he felt cheated. Had felt robbed of his opportunity to go professional and he hated the fact that I'd given up the chance at another shot at Olympic gold for gymnastics to join the Night Circus.

Had thought I was wasting my talent, but I loved my art so much and the world of professional sports had always been his dream, not mine.

I felt exhausted by the time we finished talking and the therapist looked genuinely sympathetic. She seemed disappointed that I couldn't think of anyone to call. She didn't feel comfortable releasing me without a contact person in the outside world that could help me get over the hump. I felt like a prisoner and just wanted out, but until I could come up with someone, the chances of her extending my stay looked like a real possibility.

I went back to my room and picked up the book on my end table. I opened it, not that I was reading it, but to the note that Angel had had smuggled in to me. I read it and reread it, taking comfort in it, and on my last wing and a prayer went back out onto the ward and to the therapist's office door.

I knocked gently on the doorjamb and she looked up from behind her computer screen, her glasses perched on the end of her nose.

"Yes, Claire?"

I chewed my bottom lip hesitantly and said, "Actually, there's one person I could try to call…"

"Oh?"

"Yeah. Could I try please?"

5

*A*ngel…

I couldn't believe the things she told me. Her own brother… fuck me. I got it, to some extent, but at the same time, I didn't. I couldn't. Still, at the same time, it was as if God had a plan for me and for her, and was throwing us back together again. I couldn't say I felt bad about that in the slightest, even though I had the vague, nagging worry that this could be a bad idea and do more harm than good.

I mean, what if we just weren't compatible? What if I hadn't saved her, but just delayed the inevitable? *What if I fucked this up?*

I swallowed hard and got out of the back of the taxi at the curb in front of the main entrance to the hospital. I'd called off sick so I could be here, and I wanted to get Claire and get her home. I didn't want one of the city's finest all up in my business. It's why I'd chosen the plain black bomber jacket over my more-recognizable leather jacket and cut.

That, and I didn't know how Claire felt about MC's, even legit above-board clubs. They had a rough rep when it came to the average citizen. They saw the leather and patches and automatically went to some of the worst of the worst, like the Sacred Hearts.

38

There wasn't anything 'Sacred' or full of heart about those assholes.

Their original charter had thought it would be a good idea to use the Catholic faith to generate their name, in order to skate under the radar for the first couple of years they were in business. It'd worked to some extent, and by the time any cops had decided to look at them, it'd been too late. They'd already had a strong foothold in criminal enterprise. Their penchant for being slippery hadn't ended there, though. Aside from a member or chapter here or there getting busted the rest of the club managed to squeak out from under any charges. In fact, they were slicker than fucking owl shit when it came to avoiding RICO.

Then, some years back, *something* went down and they'd sort of flamed out and gone quiet. No one in law enforcement believed it was going to stay that way, but I think all of them hoped for it. My brother and the rest of the guys were sure they had been responsible for a fair bit of the drug trade coming up through south of the border, just damned if it could be proven. Of course, the Marianas cartel had all but dried up overnight, precipitating the last several years of calm out of them. Theory was, there may have been some sort of trouble in paradise and that the Sacred Hearts had took the Marianas cartel the fuck out.

If that were the case, they weren't dudes you wanted to fuck with. Like *at all*. A year or two back, our president had a run in with one of them at the *10-13*. Some guy coming up through his basement with some chick. He'd let them go, and I didn't blame him. Sometimes, out here on the street, you had to pick your battles. Even as a cop. As a retired cop? Even more so.

The taxi driver popped his horn and I turned around, scowling and waved him down. When I turned back to the hospital doors, she was there, like magic, two suitcases, one full-sized and one carry-on, a gym bag slung across her chest, along with her purse.

I shook my head in disbelief. Her brother had seriously just up and abandoned her in her time of need. Brought her things, dropped them off, and that was it. It was unconscionable, but then again, I didn't know everything. I was going to find out, though. I needed to know everything there was about her.

"You look good," I said breaking the spell of silence. She smiled and it was almost shy. She fell back a slight step, and then the girl I knew, the girl from three years ago in my tired little live-aboard stepped forward, dragging her suitcases with her and abandoned the handles to wind her arms around me. She buried her face in the front of my chest and breathed deeply, cuddling into me like she was coming home.

I put my arms around her and held her tight, kissing the top of her head and it felt so natural to have her back in my arms, like no time at all had passed. We might as well be back on that boat on a cold winter's morning, not on the sidewalk in front of Trinity Gen in the moderate temperature of the sunny afternoon of three years and some change later.

"I missed you," she murmured and I smiled, I couldn't help it. I'd missed her, too.

The cabbie, impatient as fuck, beeped his horn. Claire jumped and I turned back to him, annoyed and scowling.

"Pop the trunk!" I called out and he obliged. I opened the car door for Claire and she got in, sliding across the seat to make room for me. I loaded her bags in the trunk and got into the back of the cab, telling the obnoxious cabbie, "Take us back to where you picked me up."

Claire threaded her fingers between mine before he could even switch on his signal indicating he wanted back into the flow of traffic. I put my arm around her and she rested her head on my shoulder.

"We'll get you home, you can have a hot shower, and I'll cook us dinner. How does that sound?"

"Sounds wonderful."

"Sleeping arrangements are a bit tight. If you wanted your own room, I can crash on the floor or –"

"Don't be stupid," she murmured and raised her head to capture my lips with hers.

That kiss was as sweet as the first we had ever shared. Deep and full of meaning, though with a lot less tongue, for modesty's sake. The cabbie was staring at us a little too hard in his rearview mirror and I said, "Hey, eyes forward, buddy. I'm not paying you to land either of us back at the hospital."

He grumbled and griped in whatever his native language was. Some sort of eastern European. Maybe Polish, or Czechoslovakian. I wasn't familiar with them. Claire's eyes flashed and she responded in broken whatever-it-was and the driver kept his eyes on the road after that, a deep blush painting the back of his neck red. I laughed. I couldn't help it.

"What did you say?" I asked when we were safely deposited at the marina my houseboat was moored at. Her bags were out of the car and the driver had been paid and was on his way.

"Asked him if he kissed his mother with that mouth," she replied.

"What language was that?"

"Russian."

"You speak Russian?"

"A little. We spent a few months there performing and recruiting performers before making our way back through the rest of Europe and a circuit through the States."

I took her big suitcase and shouldered her gym bag. She kept her purse and her little carry-on and followed me.

"You moved," she said, carefully, and I nodded.

"Around the end of last summer. It's still pretty new. I've always wanted one of these houseboats, and when I finally finished working on my live-aboard, restoring it? I sold it. I'd saved the down payment for one of these and selling the boat I had when we first met pushed me the rest of the way. I just need to pay for moorage and upkeep."

"Wow."

"Yeah. I, um, well, I hope you like it," I said, suddenly nervous. I collapsed the handle on her suitcase and stepped off the dock onto what was essentially my back porch. It was closer than what served as the front door. The narrow French doors back here opened up onto my galley kitchen and four-person dining room. It was a little quirky in layout, because the bathroom was also down here. To the right, just as you entered through the back door, was a doorway that led into the bathroom, which had open spaces to two sides, one leading into the kitchen along the long side of the whirlpool tub, and one at the end of the tub leading into the living room, taking advantage of the view off the bow of the boat.

That view was *everything*, though. It went straight out the three-panel bay window over the few sailboats docked in the marina and out over the Chesapeake. It was a million-dollar view that I was paying around a thousand bucks a month moorage fees for. It was worth every penny, too.

The blinds in the bathroom out to those two open spaces were up, for right now. One of my favorite things to do after a long shift was to draw a hot bath and lean back with a beer and just stare out over the water through my windows. I had the sudden urge to strip down, draw a bath, and hold Claire and show her how meditative and peaceful that could be. She came in behind me as I set her things down on the twin bench seat across from my wood stove. The bench seat was made up with a set of Spiderman bedding right now. It doubled as Manolo's bed when he was here.

Claire hadn't seen it yet, she was fixated, with a longing look on the tub. I smiled and said, "Yeah, there's no showering in the traditional sense of the word here. It was either the tub or a shower. Couldn't do both. When it came to the building phase, I went with the tub but had a removable faucet put in. You want a shower, you kind of have to kneel there and use the faucet. Not ideal, but once you lay back in that thing with a glass of wine at night with the jets going, you'll see it was worth the sacrifice."

"Oh, no, with a view like that it's totally worth the sacrifice. I want to get naked so bad right now."

I laughed and said, "Don't let me stop you, *mi alma*. I am going to get some dinner going. You're probably starving. Any special dietary needs or requests?"

She let me take her carry-on and her purse and followed me through the kitchen asking, "What, like allergies?"

"Yeah, or, you know, vegetarian, gluten-free, any of that."

She shook her head, some of her bangs getting into her eyes. She brushed them away and said, "No, I don't *like* red meat all that much, but I'll eat it occasionally."

"Okay, good to know."

"You, um, have a son?" she asked softly, looking at the Spiderman bedding her stuff was on.

I shook my head. "Nephew. My sister's son. She's, um, in prison serving a sentence for drug trafficking. Manolo lives with my brother, Rodrigo and his girlfriend Lys. I have him every Saturday night to Sunday morning so I can take him to Mass with me."

"Catholic?" she asked and I nodded.

"You?" I asked.

"Spiritual but not religious. Still, there's a certain melancholy beauty to the Catholic services."

"You maybe want to go with us?" I asked.

"Sure," she nodded. "I won't partake in the sacrament, though. I mean, don't you or shouldn't you go to confession first?"

I smiled. "That's right. For not being Catholic, you sure know a lot about it."

"The Italians in the circus are pretty devout. They find a church and go to Mass as often as they can, even while we're out on the road. They're kind of inspirational in their devotion to it."

She stepped closer to me and I opened my arms to her. She sank against my chest gratefully and I held her, falling silent as things suddenly became serious and intimate, the air heavy with a crackling tension, some of it sexual, some of it something undefinable. I waited her out and she finally asked softly.

"Show me the rest?"

"Sure," I whispered and she looked up at me. I couldn't help myself. I closed the distance between our mouths, carefully kissing her with a feather-light touch that accepted rejection if that's what she wanted or needed. She didn't. Instead, her hands found my jawline and the side of my neck, and held me to her as she deepened that kiss into something bottomless, with the depth of emotion in it.

She moaned against my mouth and wilted against me and I held her tightly, swearing to myself that I couldn't and wouldn't ever let her go again. I didn't even know her, I couldn't explain it to you, but she was my match. She was my soul, which is precisely what I called her. '*Mi alma.*' 'My soul'.

"Why does it feel like this with you and no one else?" she breathed and I smiled slightly and shook my head, smoothing some of her silk dark hair out of her eyes.

"I don't know. It's the same for me, though."

"Good to know," she whispered, and laid her ear over my heart.

We stood like that, gently twisting, rocking in each other's embrace for a little while, before I reluctantly asked, "You still want to see the rest?"

"Mm-hm."

I led her up the open staircase and she eyed the fan-work of beams above our heads. It was open, the second floor, loft-like with a high ceiling above the living room area. The stairs led directly to the bedroom with a king-sized bed and little else. I had bookshelves built into the low, waist-high wall with its open-air view over the living room below. The wide open space made the little houseboat seem bigger which was nice, and allowed the heat from the little stove to get up here in the winter.

At the foot of the bed, across an expanse of carpet allowing a walkway, was a television mounted to the wall between the windows, and a little entertainment stand below it to allow for the cable box and such. I didn't much like the idea of having a TV downstairs in my little living room. I liked to lounge and watch TV; downstairs was really only enough room for the bench seat Manolo crashed on, the two wing-back chairs I had facing the four-person dining table, and the little oval coffee table I had to hold whatever book I was reading and to prop my feet on.

This houseboat, while huge and spacious as compared to the little live-aboard I had come from, was still the epitome of tiny-house living by the rest of America's standards. I just didn't need that much space for myself. I certainly didn't need as much house as my brother had bought with his brownstone. *Dios mio*, that place was way more than he and Lys needed, even with Manolo.

I couldn't complain too much, though. When storms bordering on hurricane rolled through, it just wasn't safe staying aboard my boat. I took up residence in their guest room with the Harley safe in their garage when that shit went down.

I told Claire all of this while she stood, somber and amazed; taking everything in. She drifted past the bed to the open expanse of bedroom floor before the set of doors leading into the sunroom overlooking the back deck. I had a small, wrought iron table and matching chairs up here to take my coffee. Plants on stands and hanging from baskets providing greenery, thriving through the many windows. She passed the armoire that served as my closet and the large dresser that really had nothing in it, and went into the sun room.

"I could do my yoga in here," she said.

"Plenty of room," I agreed. "The dresser doesn't have a lot in it. I think I have two drawers used and that's mostly for my socks and underwear. The rest of my stuff, including uniforms, are in the armoire. I can rearrange to get you some more hanging space, though."

"What do you do for laundry facilities?"

I gave a laugh. "This way."

I led her back downstairs and out the side door at the end of the kitchen, to the back wrap of the deck on the side of the boat facing away from the dock. I used my keys to unlock the shed out there to reveal the washer and dryer stacked one on top of the other.

"Not ideal when the rain sweeps in from the side back here, but the deck provides enough overhang that it's not too bad."

"Angel," she said abruptly, and I turned to her; her dark eyes were luminous despite their color and I couldn't help but smile.

"What is it, *mi alma*?"

"I love your house," she said. "It's like a fairy-tale home."

I grinned broadly and said, "Thank you. I'm glad to have you here sharing it with me."

She bowed her head and said, without looking at me, her voice trembling, "I don't think I will ever be able to thank you enough for what you did for me."

I chuckled and pulled her gently into my arms. She felt so good there.

Right, like no one else was ever meant to be in them but her. She cuddled close and I told her the truth, at least the way I saw it.

"You're a strong woman, *mi alma*. You saved yourself that night. You just didn't know it yet."

She laughed a little and shook her head, heaving a deep breath and letting it out slowly, getting some control over her emotions.

"I'm starving," she said finally, after she'd soaked up enough calm, enough peace from the surrounding waters.

"Let's get you into a nice bath while I work in the kitchen. You drink?" I asked.

"Yeah, but um, I probably shouldn't. I just started these new medications…"

"Ah, virgin it is," I said and closed up the shed around the laundry. She tucked herself back under my arm as we went back into the house and it felt like, for the first time, I was really coming home.

6

*C*laire...

I knelt in the tub, my back to the kitchen, and washed my hair first. I was a little self-conscious at first and I couldn't tell you why. I mean, I'd already had sex with Angel, even if it had been three years ago. He'd already seen everything there was to see. I'd even performed nude for the circus before when we'd tried something erotic and adult-themed. I guess there was just something different about the act of bathing, something more intimate. Or maybe I was just projecting because of the fragility of my emotional state.

When my hair was as clean as it was going to be, I switched the faucet to the tub setting and pulled up to stopper the bottom so that it would fill. There was an ample ledge surrounding the bathtub all the way around and Angel had lit candles for me as dusk fell outside the houseboat's windows.

I arranged my soaps and shampoos in a corner with the intention of taking them back to my suitcase, which Angel had taken upstairs already. I stared at that little pile and ached faintly in the center of my chest with how much I wished they could live there permanently. It had been a long time since I had been in a place mentally and emotionally where I just didn't know what to do or where to go from here.

Of course, the Night Circus took up residence wherever it did for three months at a time with a week or two off at the beginning of each new location for us to explore, adapt, and settle. I guess I had fouled that up. I was pretty sure I had either missed our first rehearsal or that it was in the next day or two. I leaned back in the tub with a sigh after brushing my hair and clipping it up at the back and Angel glanced over his shoulder. The movement caught the corner of my eye and I met his warm, liquid brown eyes through the strange window cut beside the tub. He came around the kitchen counter and across the little walkway leading to the living room and leaned on the wooden sill.

"Talk to me," he murmured. "What is it?"

"I don't know if I missed my first rehearsal since coming here or not," I said.

"What was the date?" he asked.

"The twenty-first."

"That's tomorrow."

I breathed a sigh of mixed relief and dismay and covered my face with my hands, pressing my fingertips into my eyes.

He sniffed and I lowered my hands back into the water and looked up at him. He smiled down at me and I could tell that he somehow knew, that why I'd tried what I did had to do with the Circus, but it didn't, really. It had to do with the director more than anything.

I still wasn't ready to talk about it yet. I loved the Night Circus, I loved my family of performers and I loved performing. No, I lived for performing, and the mere thought that I might have fucked that up had been filling me with a tense anxiety and dread. Especially after Carter…

"I've made a mess out of everything," I said softly, and Angel shook his head.

"Not here," he said. "Not with me."

I smiled faintly; it was something to cling to. I couldn't deny that.

"How long does rehearsal take, and what time do you have to be there?" he asked.

"It takes as long as it takes for Milo to be happy with it, and it's the Night Circus, so usually we start in the afternoon."

"I have a shift tomorrow," he said, hesitantly.

"It's fine. I can have a car pick me up and take me, and bring me back here."

"It's a sixteen hour shift for me tomorrow. I'm pulling a double."

"When to when?"

"Gotta be at the house at eight in the morning..."

"House?" I asked before he could finish.

"Firehouse. Indigo City runs on kind of a hybrid system. If it's quiet and there aren't a bunch of calls, we hang around the firehouse with the hose boys until we get something. It conserves fuel." I laughed at 'hose boys' and he smiled. "I love that laugh," he said and I couldn't help but smile, too.

"What time will you be home, then?" I asked and the word 'home' felt foreign but nice on my tongue.

"Probably around midnight."

"Make you a deal," I said softly.

"What's that?" he asked.

"First one home makes dinner."

"That's fair enough."

He leaned way over and I met him part-way. We kissed and he kept his hands to himself, even though I ached for him to touch me. I felt like I was dying to feel something pleasant, and the feel of being wrapped in Angel's arms was really high up there when it came to pleasant things to feel.

"Smells good," I whispered.

"Enchiladas, just like mama used to make." He grinned.

"How long?"

"You have a while yet. Relax."

He went around back into the kitchen and made me something cool to drink. I raised an eyebrow, questioning what it was silently, and he handed it over saying, "Just some ginger ale with a squeeze of fresh lime."

"You're spoiling me."

"You've had a hard week."

I couldn't argue with him there.

I finished my bath and dressed in something comfortable before returning to the table downstairs.

Dinner was amazing, the food so good. We talked quietly and I learned more about him and his family. He had left high school and gone to further his education to immediately become a medic. His brother, on the other hand, had joined the military and had served a few tours. He'd come home, had become a police officer, and then had gotten shot in the leg in the line of duty while serving a warrant on a house somewhere in the city.

He had a younger sister, who by all accounts was sort of a spoiled brat. They'd been raised by his mother and his paternal grandmother after his father died when he was seven. It was fascinating hearing where he had come from and there were a few parallels between his upbringing and mine.

I told him about myself and Carter. My absentee father, how I was raised by a single mother. How dance and athletics had become a sort of babysitter for my brother and I, while my mom worked every job she could to keep us in them and a roof over our heads.

"And you ran away and joined the circus?" he asked, a twinkle in his eye as he gently teased me.

"Yep." I smiled and helped him wash the dishes.

"What was that like?"

"A dream come true," I said softly. "I've been all over the world. England, France, Spain, Romania, Russia, China, India. I really hated it, though, when we spent the three months in the United Arab Emirates." I shuddered.

"Why is that?"

"I'm a woman," I answered succinctly. "While it was beautiful and exotic, it was also dangerous. I didn't feel comfortable going out. If I'd been raped, and reported it? I could and would have been jailed for having sex outside of marriage. I had to be hyper-vigilant at all times. It ruined the whole experience."

"I can imagine," he said, and loaded the last plate into the dishwasher.

I leaned back against the counter in my deep blue silk robe and looked at him. He smiled and shut the dishwasher and started it up.

"I still can't quite believe you're here," he murmured and I almost missed it with the dishwasher starting.

"I almost can't believe it myself," I said, taking his hand in both of mine. I led him toward the stairs and he followed.

"Whatever shall we do?" he asked, with a wink.

"Mm, I was sort of hoping you would show me the finer points of that bed of yours."

He switched out the lights down here on the way past the switch plate and took my hands in his. We went up to the second floor with its barn-like ceiling and he took over, leading me from the stairs to the bed.

"Ah!" He stopped me before I could sit down.

"What?" I asked softly, and without warning, he was by my side and had me up in his arms. I shrieked in surprise and laughed, but the serious look in his eyes stopped me. He slowly and carefully lowered me to the bed and I swallowed hard.

"Couldn't carry you over the threshold; I guess this is the next best thing," he murmured, voice husky with emotion and desire.

"Why does it feel like we've known each other forever?" I whispered.

"I don't know," he replied, pulling his shirt over his head. I had a lot less to do when it came to getting naked, so I just enjoyed the show for now while I smoothed my hands over the quilt he had on his bed.

"Why does it feel like no time has passed from that night until now?" I asked.

"Don't know that, either."

I smiled wickedly, "What do you know?"

He grinned like the Cheshire Cat and said, "I know I'm going to make you feel so good…"

He dropped his pants and boxer-briefs in one swift single motion and I bit my bottom lip. Desire washed through me, stronger than it had that first night when I'd kissed him not knowing what I'd been doing, figuring, if anything, I could take his mind off his troubles and make him feel good for a little while, get him through to the next day and hopefully a better outlook on life.

I hadn't expected him to so thoroughly rock my world. Somehow, knowing just what I had in store made this time even hotter. He pulled the sash on my robe, unwrapping me like a present, and I stopped breathing for the nonce. I slipped my arms out of the sleeves and reached for him and he came to me, willingly, laying over the top of me but holding himself off of me just enough so I wouldn't feel crushed.

I'd forgotten how big he was, and the three or so years we'd been separated had been kind to him. He was in fantastic shape, and I didn't know how much of that was due to his job. He kissed me and I kissed back, letting my hands roam over his heated skin, fluttering over his shoulders and down his obliques.

"God, I missed you, Claire," he breathed against the side of my neck, and I shivered at the hot wash of breath over my skin.

"I missed you, too," I murmured, and I meant it. I had missed him so much. It was why, when I'd found the stray bullet in my pocket, I'd kept it. I'd wound copper wire around its base and threaded the black cord through it to wear it next to my heart as a necklace.

My circus family knew the meaning behind it. They'd been excited about our return to the US and Indigo City. We'd spent an evening in the bar in Prague laughing and imagining what it would be like to see my Angel again, making up stories about how we would be reunited.

They would be so disappointed when they found out how this had come to be.

I couldn't be sure they didn't know already, about my hospital stay. I didn't know how they would, unless Carter had told them but Carter had already made it pretty clear he didn't want to associate with 'those people'. That had hurt me deeply, compounding the stress, hurt, and heartache that I'd already been feeling. I mean, *I* was one of 'those people'.

I quickly refocused on Angel and left those thoughts to fall away, basking in the warmth of his body on mine as he kissed me, concentrating on all the sensations he woke in me. I reveled in his embrace as we made out like teens under the bleachers. His shaft pressed against me, at the wrong angle for penetration, but that didn't stop me from lifting and dropping my hips in a sultry rhythm to excite and entice him further.

He moaned into my mouth and I liked that about him. He wasn't afraid to be vocal, to let me know with sound, without words, that I was doing it for him. I wanted him inside me so badly, but I'd had my birth control interrupted…

"Condom?" I asked, breathy. "My birth control was interrupted."

"Mm, yeah, shit. Hang on." He jerked open the drawer by my head in the little night stand and rooted around it by feel. He cursed and dragged himself up so he could see and I laughed and giggled as he pressed down over the top of me.

"Sorry!"

"Don't be," I laughed, and he came back down to me.

"Got lucky, I had one from Lil's last thing."

"Lil?" I asked, remembering the name from dinner, but not placing it immediately.

"My buddy, Backdraft, the firefighter's girl. She writes the romance novels."

"Right! Sorry. I know I shouldn't be jealous."

He chuckled and unwrapped the condom, rolling it on, and my desire shot up a notch from where it'd cooled into a low simmer. What was it about watching a man make himself ready to take you that was so exponentially hot?

"You don't have anything to worry about," he said gently. "Been on a few dates, that's it, never made it further than a kiss at the door."

"What?" I asked speechless.

"They weren't you, *mi alma*."

Holy. Shit.

He hadn't been with anyone in the three years since our one night together? I stared at him speechless, mouth agape.

"What?" he asked.

"I…"

He leaned forward and kissed me and whatever I'd been about to say went clean out of my head. I pulled him down to me with arms and legs and he groaned into my mouth, lining himself up with my entrance.

I'd forgotten how big he was, but he was careful with me, easing his way into me slowly, letting my body adjust.

"Good?" he asked, his voice low and soft, carefully controlled, as he strained against becoming too passionate and hurting me.

"God, yeah," I whispered back and kissed him. He started to move again, slowly, like I was fragile and prone to breaking, and it was something I loved about him. He was so considerate, so gentle with me despite his sheer size and I couldn't ever remember anyone being that way with me before.

He made love to me. A slow burning passion sweeping through my body, turning up the heat incrementally, until I came to a slow simmer with pleasure. The euphoria swirled through my blood, starting some-where at my back and rising slowly to burst over the surface of my skin in wave after wave of goosebumps.

I wrapped my arms around him, sheltered beneath him, clung to him as my last hope that there was hope for me and it was beautiful, touching, one of the most profound things I had ever felt.

I had been living my dream but that dream had been so lonely, and for the first time in a long time, I didn't feel alone anymore. I could reach out and touch Angel and that he was real, genuine in a way that anybody else hadn't been, or couldn't be, around me.

He worked his way in and out of my body and I climbed him like the silk I so loved performing with, wrapping myself in the comfort his body and soul provided.

He stared me in the eyes from inches away, and I felt like I was home.

I WOKE BRIEFLY the next morning when he kissed me good-bye, a brief and gentle press of lips against my cheek. I breathed in his clean, masculine scent and opened my eyes to see his back as he retreated down the stairs.

His jacket had a large grey shield emblazoned across it, a knight chess piece picked out on it in darker blue thread; above it a ribbon emblazoned with *Indigo Knights;* beneath it, another ribbon with *Indigo City;* and below that, *Nomad.* I didn't know what it all meant, but the visual was powerful and I would try to remember to ask him about it later.

A few moments later, the strong sound of a motorcycle starting split the morning air. It revved once, then twice, and faded into the distance. I cuddled down into Angel's big bed and breathed him in, and slept some more.

When I woke for real, I sat up and stretched. I found my bathrobe on the floor and pulled it on, pulling my hair from the collar. I padded barefoot downstairs and found a note and a set of keys on the dining room table beside a French press loaded with dry coffee grounds and an empty mug.

Good Morning, mi alma,

Have some coffee. Here's a set of keys in case you get home first. You have my number but I don't have yours, so give me a ring when you get up, okay? Please, make yourself comfortable. Put your things away.

This is your home, too. I hate leaving you this morning and I can't wait to see you again. Try to have a good day.

Yours,

Angel

I closed my eyes and looked around feeling a little foreign being alone in his space. I went to my purse on the bench seat and pulled out my phone, powering it on.

While I waited for it to boot, I put the kettle on to make my coffee. He was so sweet, thinking of everything like he did. While I waited for the water to come to a boil, I added milk and sugar to my coffee mug and stared at the bathtub, deciding 'What the hell'.

I started the bathwater and went back to my phone, picking it up to a slew of messages from my circus family. Most were from Aleksi and Giada, wondering why I wasn't answering them, demanding if I'd found my Angel yet.

I couldn't bring myself to text back the news, deciding instead that I would see them in a few hours and that I would tell them then.

I didn't want to lie about it. I already felt guilty enough over the whole thing. I knew it would be worse seeing their faces, harder, but it was no less than I deserved. I had a feeling their disappointment, much like my brother's, would be palpable.

I fixed my coffee, took it and my phone over to the bath, and shut off the water and got in. I took in the view and sipped, letting the peace of the water out there soak in, and after a little while, and with most of my coffee gone, I set the mug aside and picked up my phone.

I called Angel because one, I wanted him to have my number, and two, I wanted to hear his voice. While he had been sad, and while he had been disappointed, he had this way about him that didn't make me feel like he was disappointed in *me*. It was like he was disappointed, but he was disappointed in everyone and everything else that had led up to me feeling like death was the only option left to me to stop the pain.

I was uncomfortable with that because in a lot of ways, that still felt like a true sentiment. I still hurt. I didn't hurt any less, I just had someone and something to hold on for at the moment.

I wasn't one to pray, but I was beginning to pray that things would get better somehow, some way, soon. I wanted my staying here to be more than just a short reprieve. I wanted desperately to begin feeling like I was normal again, like I was worth something again.

"*Mi alma*, are you okay?" was how he answered the phone.

"Yes, I'm fine," I said with a smile, thinking *If fine meant fucked up, insecure, neurotic, and emotional.*

"You sure?" he asked carefully, and it was like he knew.

"Struggling a little, but I'm okay. I just wanted to hear your voice."

I could hear him smile on the other end of the line. "I'm here if you need to talk about it. At least for the time being, can't promise we won't get a call."

"It's okay," I said. "Really, I wanted to say thank you for the coffee and for everything this morning."

"You're welcome, baby."

"I have a feeling I'll be getting back before you, any ideas you want for dinner?"

"No, not particularly. Just whatever you feel like cooking. What's your favorite thing to cook? Let's do that."

"To be honest, I don't do that much cooking. Not that I don't like to, it's just not something I get to do a whole lot of when I'm with the Night Circus."

"That's fair," he said.

"I'll think about it," I promised.

"Okay. I miss you," he said simply, and I smiled and shifted in the bath.

"I miss you, too," I whispered, and I heard him laugh.

"Taking advantage of that tub and the view, huh?"

"Yeah, I think this could be my new favorite thing. Although depending on how hard I push today, I might need an ice bath when I get home."

"Don't push too hard, stay hydrated, and call me if I need to bring home some ice."

"You're kind of amazing, you know that?"

"Back at you, Claire."

The radio crackled to life behind him. I couldn't make out what it said but after a short pause, Angel said, "I gotta go."

"Okay, be careful."

"Should have told that to the guy we're going to go rescue."

I laughed a little, and the call ended as the siren kicked up on the other end. I set my phone aside and rolled my head on my neck and shoulders. I didn't have a lot of time if I were going to make it to the big top that had been erected in Ridgeview Park, so I reluctantly finished the dregs of my coffee, let the water out of the tub, and got moving.

~

"DON'T you ever answer your phone?" Giada demanded, her rich Italian accent making every word that fell from her full lips sound like they'd been dipped in pure sex.

Aleksi raised an eyebrow, and I chewed my bottom lip and said, "I was in the hospital. I only got out yesterday and they wouldn't let me have my phone. I wanted to tell you in person."

All activity on the stage stopped and you could hear a pin drop. Giada and Aleksi looked horrified and I felt my eyes well with tears. I looked around at every one of the performers gathered on the round center stage and sniffled.

"What happened?" Thierry, one of our French acrobats asked. He was frowning and I sniffled again and wiped at the first tear as it spilled free.

"You guys, please don't be mad at me. I don't think I could take it if you were mad at me."

Aleksi and Giada moved in and wrapped me into a group hug. The rest of the troupe filtered across the stage drawing closer, realizing something was really wrong.

"Why would we be mad at you, *Kotyonok*?" Alexsi asked, calling me by his pet name for me, 'Kitten', because he'd told me that I reminded him of one when I started to climb my silks.

"I tried to kill myself. My heart stopped and everything," I sobbed.

The entire troupe looked stricken, everyone shuffling across the stage until I was enveloped in so many bodies, arms and hands going around me, that the guilt was overwhelming for a moment before it was crushed under a veritable wave of love.

"What's going on here!" I jumped and the troupe held me tighter, filled with silent support as Milo came out from backstage. I swallowed hard and Giada swore in Italian, rattling off an impressive angry spiel.

"Why does everyone act as if someone has died?" Milo demanded.

Oksana, Alexsi's partner in the contortionist act spoke in her thickly accented English.

"Because Claire has, we are lucky she is home."

I closed my eyes as Milo scowled at me. I shrank inside, but stood a little taller, wiping my face.

"What is the meaning of this?" he demanded and I shook my head.

"Nothing," I lied and the rest of the troupe stood with me, unease sweeping through them.

"Then get to work," he demanded, and tapped that damn cane that he always carried but never needed against the stage. The sound boomed like a cannon in the quiet space.

We all broke apart, and drifted to our respective positions in line.

Let the fun begin, I thought unhappily, and I went through the motions, my heart sinking, while I clung to thoughts of Angel, and just how much I wanted to see him when I went home that night.

7

*A*ngel...

I'd texted Golden and told him I needed to talk to him as soon as was convenient. He'd asked what was up, but I told him this was an in-person kind of talk. He'd said sure, he'd see me when he dropped off Manolo the next night.

I made it through a pretty busy shift and thought about getting take-out from the *10-13*, but Claire had messaged just as soon as I clocked out to let me know she was home. I texted back and said I would be right there and she had texted back a simple 'okay.' I could almost feel her exhaustion through the letters on the screen. I was right there with her.

I messaged asking if I needed to stop and get ice and she messaged back, 'No, just come home.'

I just went home.

She was in the small kitchen washing vegetables in the sink when I came in. It smelled fantastic in the houseboat and I set down my shit inside the door. I went to her immediately and pulled her into my arms.

63

She tilted her face up to mine and our lips met in a kiss full of fire and need.

"I missed you," she said against my mouth, her hands pulling my shirt out of my waistband, ducking under the hem to get skin-on-skin.

"I missed you, too," I breathed and let my eyes roam her face. It was pale, pinched, and etched with tired lines under her eyes. I frowned slightly and said, "You look exhausted."

"I am."

"Dinner almost done?" I asked.

"Mm-hmm, just fixing a salad. It comes out of the oven in about ten more minutes."

"Let me take over; go sit down and tell me about your day."

She nodded and let me go, drifting over to the dining room table. I fixed her something cold to drink and took it to her first, then shrugged out of my jacket and cut and hung it on the back of one of my dining room chairs.

She eyed it and said, "I thought I saw something on your back this morning as you went down the stairs. I meant to ask what it was."

I smiled and went to work, cutting up salad into a bowl to toss it. I told her, "Yeah, I belong to an MC. A bunch of cops and first-responder types."

"Oh?"

"Yeah, there's about a dozen of us. My brother Golden is one of us. Then there's Youngblood, he's a homicide detective. Poe is another beat cop. Backdraft is a firefighter; he works out of the same house I do, and then Blaze is another. Reflash is retired, and is the head cook at *The 10-13*, the bar we all hang out at. Reflash is our DC and runs the *10-13* with our chief, Skids. Skids is a retired cop, too. There's Narcos and Driller, they were undercover out of ICPD's Narcotics division but are looking at reassignment, and there's Yale, he's one of Indigo City's ADA's. Last but not least, we've got one of the jailer's, a guy we call Oz, you know, like the TV show about the prison. Not like the Wizard of Oz."

"Wow, will I get to meet them?" she asked.

I smiled at how unfazed she was and nodded, "As soon as I can arrange it. I'd like you to meet Golden, first. He'll be by tomorrow night with Manolo. I planned on talking to him then about us."

She nodded carefully and said, "Okay." I could tell she was nervous about the prospect of meeting my family, and with family like her brother, I couldn't say I blamed her.

"I should tell you, Angel is just my road name, not my real name. My given name is Ramiro Martinez."

She smiled again and she just looked so damn tired, still, gracious as always, she said to me, "I never would have guessed, but thank you for telling me. You'll still always be my Angel, though."

My Angel, I like the sound of that.

I used the salad set and tossed the greens and veggies in the wooden salad bowl that'd belonged to my mama. I turned things off of me and back onto her.

"How did it go today?"

She let out a breath and gave a bit of a broken laugh that told me just how overwhelming the day had been.

"Well, I came clean to the troupe about why I wasn't answering their calls all week. They took it pretty well. I think they ran interference with Milo for most of the day, but he'll be back at me again, soon."

I frowned. "'Ran interference'? How do you mean, and why would they have to?"

She took a sip out of her glass and sighed.

"Oksana and Aleksi made stupid mistakes, things that I know they wouldn't ordinarily do, to draw Milo's ire onto them. Giada gave him a little hell, too." She shook her head. "It's only temporary."

"You make it sound like this guy has a hard-on for you," I said, bringing the salad over to the table.

"He sort of does. I refused to date him in Russia. He's been getting steadily worse ever since."

"How old is this guy?"

"Forty-three, I think?"

"Huh, I don't know why, but with a name like 'Milo' I pictured some sixty-year-old dud. Like some kind of Anthony Hopkins dude. All accented and super-proper."

"Well, the attitude is pretty spot on when he's pandering to the board or investors or whatever it is he does when he isn't lording it over the performers."

"Small-man Syndrome?"

"Yep."

"You complain about him?" I asked, and before she could answer, remembering that fierce, in-control woman from that night three years ago, I said, "What am I talking about? Of course you did. What happened with that, though?"

"I was basically told that personality conflicts happened all of the time and that he was doing his job as the director of the show and I needed to get over myself." She rolled her eyes. "At least, that's the way I interpreted it, anyway."

"Let me guess, the treatment got worse shortly thereafter?" The timer on the oven went off and I shut it off and got whatever she had going in there out. It smelled divine and looked to be some sort of chicken with rice and wild mushrooms.

"Not right away. It was little criticisms at first, things that he had a point, but I didn't think they were that serious. It got progressively worse. Instead of one-off lectures, they became more regular, then it turned to shouting, then it turned to embarrassing me in front of the rest of the troupe, then it turned to actively trying to turn the rest of the troupe's attitude towards me, to the point that they were invited to take it out on me, too."

She got really quiet and I could tell that the systematic abuse had been going on for a while. I pulled down plates and dished up food, trying to figure out what I could do, and I finally settled on asking her what *she* wanted.

"What do you want me to do, *mi alma*? Just name it."

She smiled and it glowed with love and sadness. I sank into the seat beside hers and set plates in front of both of us. She took my hand in hers and ran her thumb lightly over the back of my fingers in a light caress and I felt my dick start to stir.

"Nothing," she said quietly. "I don't want anyone to fix this for me, I want to fix it myself. I just don't know how. If you want to help, you can tell me what gym you go to and take me with you. This level of fitness doesn't maintain itself and I need to be at the top of my game, in peak performance all of the time. That means cardio and strength training."

I nodded slowly and told her, "I go where the cops go. I get in as Golden all the time unless he's with me, then he guests me in. I can guest you in under his name."

She smiled and said, "I didn't know you and your brother looked so much alike."

I laughed and said, "We constantly forget to mention that part. We're identical twins."

"Oh, wow. That's unexpected," she laughed. "I guess I just assumed that you were a year or so apart like me and Carter."

"Ah, nah, more like seven-and-a-half minutes."

"So who is the oldest?" she asked, putting air-quotes around 'oldest' with her fingers.

"That would be Golden and he never lets me forget it, either."

She laughed and speared some salad with her fork. The more we talked, the more she relaxed, and I was glad for it. Her job should have brought her joy as something she loved to do. It wasn't like mine, it shouldn't *be* like mine, *at all*. The stress was killing her, literally, and I could see her self-worth had dwindled in our time apart. I wasn't sure how to build her back up, but I was here for it. I was all the way here for her.

We cleaned up together, put the leftovers away, and went up to bed. She put some of her things away in the dresser while I went down and took a quick bath. When I came back up, she was in one of my tee shirts, and I couldn't tell you the swell of pride and lust that overtook me when I saw it.

"I probably could have dug deeper and found one of my nightgowns. It probably would have been sexier, too, but –"

"Hey, no, *mi alma.* I don't think you could be any sexier to me if you tried right now."

She gave me a twist of lips and tried to suppress her smile but couldn't. I went to her and pulled her into my arms. She lay her head on my chest and I felt the tension drain out of her.

"I like sleeping with you," she murmured.

"Yeah?"

"Yeah, it feels safe."

I chuckled a bit and said, "It *is* safe. I would never let anything happen to you."

She looked up at me and touched the side of my face. I kissed her gently and pulled back before we could get too involved. I smiled and said, "You get me started, I may not be able to stop."

"Mm, that would be a shame." She rolled her eyes and I laughed. She fitted herself to the front of my body and I felt myself rise to attention for what must have been the fifth or sixth time since I'd come home. I was like a horny teenage boy around her, in a constant state of arousal and I couldn't say I held a single regret when it came to it.

I certainly didn't stop her when her mouth went from mine, to my chin, to my chest, as she lowered herself to her knees in front of me.

Last night's sex had been deep and emotional, but hadn't felt like us, not like that first time. It had felt more like the sex was to ground her, to bring her back to me, and I was okay with that, but I was overjoyed, as she slipped my boxer-briefs over my hips and freed my cock, that the feeling this time was that slow, intense burn of our first time together, a reconnection on that soul-deep level that I seriously craved with her.

She traced her tongue lightly in a velvet touch from root to tip along the underside of my shaft. Those lovely dark eyes of hers met mine as she looked up my body and took the head of my cock between her lips, suckling gently. I closed my eyes and breathed out, lacing my fingers behind my head as an electric frisson of sexual energy traveled through my body.

"Oh, God, Claire…" I whispered and she took more of me into her mouth, plunging over the top of me, down the shaft, nearly to the root. I gasped and forgot what it was to breathe for a moment as she gripped the outsides of my thighs with her hands for balance and delicately bobbed her head, sucking me off with sensuality and passion.

My knees were weak, my heart raced and my balls tightened all too quickly in that familiar way that said I was going to come.

"Shit, Claire, baby I'm gonna come, I can't help it."

She didn't let up, plunging all the way down my length, her lips meeting my body as I groaned and spilled down her lovely throat. Jesus, it was like she had no gag reflex to speak of!

"Oh, God," I cried and it was like a prayer, but not any kind I should make to Him.

She waited a moment before pulling back off of me and smiled, pleased with herself that she'd satisfied me. I shook my head and held down my hands to help her to her feet.

"Your turn," I murmured, and grasped the hem of my tee, pulling it over her head. She raised her arms and let me take it, and I was pleased that she wore no panties. Her sex was lightly perfuming the air and I was happy to know I aroused her as much as she did me.

I led her to the bed, where I lay down on my back, urged her to straddle me. She did, and as soon as she was on her knees, I dipped down between her thighs, and kissed the slick folds of her sex. She leaned forward and grasped the headboard, and I wrapped my hands over the tops of her thighs, pulling her down, meeting her pussy with my mouth, gently separating her labia with my tongue and trailing a line up to her clit, which I took my time to suckle and tease.

She arched, riding my face gently, her hips making uncontrolled movements in her desire. I slipped my hands up her body to cradle her breasts in my hands, flicking my thumbs over her pert nipples as she fought to hold still as I licked her.

"Oh, God!" she cried, and shuddered above me, and I pulled her down again from where she'd moved her body just out of my reach.

Her breath came sharp, punctuated by long pauses where she held it. She was close, so very close, walking the edge of the cliff, balancing delicately until I found the key, that last push of whatever to send her over and plummeting into the shining fall of orgasm. I was hard again already, my recovery time near superhuman with how enthusiastic my body was to be inside of her.

She gave a ragged scream and jerked away from my mouth, her legs shaking. I sat up and spilled her onto her back with a surprised yelp.

"God, I want you so bad," I growled, and she panted, trying to catch her breath.

"Then take me," she said.

"No condoms, forgot to get some."

"Ohhhh, God, why?" she cried, but there was no accusation to it, merely a lament.

I laughed and said, "I promise not to forget any tomorrow."

"You better not, or I'm gonna die."

"Pretty sure you can't die from lack of sex," I said, laughing.

"Pretty sure you can," she countered, and I laughed some more.

"Who's the medical professional?" I asked, and she smiled faintly.

"Fine, you win. Now kiss me."

"Hold on, I'll go brush my teeth first."

She dragged my mouth to hers and whispered, "Don't you dare."

I could do this every night. Be like this every night. I wanted her like this, every night.

God, let us figure out a way that she can stay with me that brings her happiness and no regrets, I prayed.

8

*C*laire…

    I hung from my silks by my feet like a bat and Giada called up from where she practiced her fan dance below me, "So, did *anything* good happen while you were away from us?"

"Oh, my God! I can't believe I didn't tell you yesterday–" I sat up, and unwinding my feet, climbed the red silks. I didn't even do any of my tricks to get down. I simply wrapped one leg and let the material slide through my hands in a controlled descent, much like sliding down a fire pole; if they still had those anymore. I didn't know.

Aleksi and Giada gathered around the base of my silks and several other people looked on curiously. It was a practice day blessedly free of Milo, his attention elsewhere on some dispute with the city and where our big top was placed in the park.

"I found my Angel, or rather, he found me."

"What?" Giada demanded as I turned around.

"Trust me! This is so crazy, I couldn't possibly be making it up."

They listened intently as I told them about how it was Angel who had responded to my brother's call for help.

"What are the odds?" Callie asked, and I shook my head.

"Like I said, it's so crazy, there's no way I could make it up."

"We must meet your Angel, *Kotyonok*." Aleksi was smiling and I nodded.

"I'll bring him around, I promise."

"Soon," Callie said with a bright smile, but Giada remained uncharacteristically silent on the subject and I could see the wheels turning in her head.

"I promise," I said. "Soon."

Before anyone could start to pester me, I gave a leap, grasped my silk, and turned myself upside-down. I used my legs and skittered up the red practice silks like a spider up her web. It was the fastest way to climb and I still had to do a full run-through of my almost-eight-minute routine.

I SIGHED and finished getting dressed in my street clothes after yet another long day of practice. I should have sensed the ambush, but honestly, I was just too tired. Aleksi threw an arm around my shoulders as I exited the women's lockers in one of the smaller side tents and Giada's arm curved around my waist from the other side.

"Okay, what's this?" I asked smiling.

"We are going home with you, my little darling," Giada declared.

"Yes, we must meet this Angel of yours," Aleksi agreed.

I rolled my eyes and said, "Fine. He should be home. Let me let him know you're coming with me."

I pulled out my phone and went to send a text, and saw that I'd missed some from him.

Angel: Grabbing dinner from the 10-13 and condoms. Don't want to make that mistake again. You might beat me home. See you when I get there.

Damn! I hoped it wasn't too late; I sent a text to him to let him know we would have company.

Me: Aleksi and Giada are insisting they come meet you.

He surprised me by getting back to me right away.

Angel: Cool. Got a bottle of wine in the fridge, will have Reflash make up some extra food. See you when I get there.

God, he was incredible.

"Okay, I guess we're having company, come on."

I ordered a car through the rideshare app on my phone and we all went outside, laughing and talking, to wait for it.

"So, where does your man live?" Giada asked.

I said, "You guys, I can't wait for you to see this. It's beautiful. He lives on a boat, but it's a house. Just wait. You won't believe it."

"A boat?" Aleksi asked.

"Yes, but it's not like a boat-boat. It's a house, but it floats. We call them houseboats, obviously, but that doesn't really help describe what it is. You'll just have to see it."

I tried explaining it the whole ride to the marina that Angel lived at. They followed me through the locked gate and followed me up the dock close to the end.

I took the three steps to the front door and unlocked it, while Aleksi and Giada exchanged a look.

"Okay, this is it," I said excitedly, and both Aleksi and Giada took off their shoes and left them by the steps on the dock. I took mine off just inside the door and said, "I'll be right back." I ran them upstairs and to the tiled sunroom, leaving them on the little mat I laid out for them. I set my gym bag on one of the iron chairs and hung up my coat and scarf. Aleksi and Giada were hanging their coats on the backs of the dining room chairs, looking everywhere.

"The bathroom is strange," Giada commented, but more in a curious way than disparaging. She could be a queen bitch with the best of them, but she typically reserved it for people who deserved it.

"Sit," I waved a hand at the wing-back chairs in the living room. "Wine?" I asked.

"Please," Giada said. Aleksi smiled and nodded.

"Today was nice," I said.

"Only because Milo was not there," Alexsi commented dryly.

"Right?"

We commiserated over what a dick Milo had become and I poured three glasses of wine, two liberal for them and just a little for me. I brought the three glasses over and set them on the coffee table. I took a seat on the bench seat and we talked, waiting for Angel to arrive home.

About ten minutes later, he walked through the door, scowling. My face lit up and Aleksi and Giada stood smiling, but Angel just scowled more. I was jarred, but I went to him and it was as I drew near I realized the problem, just as Angel's twin growled out, "Who the fuck are you people?"

"Ah, you must be Golden," I said, and his posture eased.

A little boy popped out from around his back and demanded, "Yeah, who the fuck are you people?"

"*Hombrecito!*" Golden barked, and railed off at the kid in Spanish.

I bowed at the waist to bring myself eye-level with the kid and said, "You must be Manolo." I straightened and addressed Golden. "I'm Claire; this is Giada, and Aleksi." Giada and Aleksi each nodded in turn, but Golden's scowl deepened.

It was Angel to the rescue when his calm and even voice said, "Ah, shit, my bad. Move aside, bro."

Golden stepped further into the house and Angel came in behind him, Giada exclaiming in Italian, *"Buon Dio, ce ne sono due!"* or 'Good God, there are two of them!'

"Don't get too excited, both of them are taken," I said with a smile. Golden didn't look amused, while Angel handed me take-out bags around his brother. I took them into the kitchen.

"What the fuck?" Golden demanded.

"Manolo, behave, I need to talk to your Tío Rodrigo."

Aleksi, who adored children, stepped in and contorted backwards, his body folding as if it was made of paper and creased by God's hand. He ducked between his own legs and held out a hand to Manolo.

"I am Aleksi," he greeted, and Manolo reared back, his eyes going wide.

"How do you *do* that?" he demanded, fascinated.

I took down plates and got to work plating food while Angel took his brother outside. I was nervous. Clearly, he hadn't had the chance to tell Golden about me.

9

*A*ngel...

"What. The. Fuck?" Golden demanded quietly.

"Dude, I need you to listen to me, and I need you to not be pissed," I told my twin.

He stared at me for several heartbeats and said finally, "Just by you saying that, I'm already pissed. You know that, right?"

I put my hands on my hips and hung my head. I'd kept this a secret from my own twin for three years and it'd felt fuckin' horrible. I think the only thing that felt worse at this point was the not-knowing how he'd handle it when I came clean. Fear was a powerful fucking motivator and it'd motivated me to keep my fucking mouth shut for far too long. Well, fear, shame, and guilt. A lot of guilt.

"Just listen, please?" I asked him and it must have been the dismay in my voice. He held his hands out and didn't say anything, but it was a clear *'Proceed, motherfucker'* gesture if I ever saw one.

I told him, all of it, and his expression grew ashen. He stared at me in disbelief and demanded, "Why didn't you talk to me?"

"I wasn't in my right head back then, bro and I never thought I would see her again. I mean, it's a fuckin' miracle she's here." I crossed myself out of habit and he stared at me, mystified. I'd just dumped a lot of heavy shit in front of him. I expected him to take a minute to sort through it.

"So you mean to tell me, she tried to kill herself, hell, she *succeeded* in killing herself, less than a week ago and she's in there right now with our nephew? Shit, Angel! You don't even know this bitch –"

"Hey!" I barked, and he stopped and looked at me, his hand half-way through raking back his hair.

"I wouldn't say it about Lys; don't you *dare* say it about Claire."

"You're really serious about this bro-"

He changed tack immediately when I gave him a look that said, '*If you finish that word, I'm going to lay your ass flat.*'

"Woman," he said, finally.

"As serious about her as you are about Lys," I told him.

"Why?" he demanded and I could tell he didn't understand, but that was fair. I didn't quite understand it, myself.

"I wish I could tell you, but Golden, brother, it's unlike anything I've ever experienced. It's like, the moment she walked into my life I found my other half, and I *know* it's the same for her."

He shook his head bewildered and asked, "What the hell does she even do?"

"She's some kind of acrobat and dancer hybrid with that circus up in Ridgeview Park."

"Wait, do *what* now? The circus? Are you fucking kidding me?"

I grinned and shook my head.

"No."

"Jesus Fucking Christ, Angel…" He mirrored me, his hands on his hips. I scowled at his blasphemy and he grinned at my look. "I don't know what to say," he said and I blinked, taken aback, when his eyes got wet. He came over to me and hugged me tight.

"You ever feel like that again, you *gotta* come to me, bro. I don't care what the fuck your brain is telling you about me. It wasn't fuckin' true. I *always* got you."

I hugged him back and felt my own nose start to tingle. I cleared my throat, which suddenly felt too thick to speak, and said, "I know, man. It's why I didn't tell you even after I was doing okay again. I didn't want you to feel like this. Besides, it was three years ago. I'm fine now, dude. I promise. I mean, I'm better than fine!"

"Man, I don't know about this," he said, and I reminded him.

"She's why I'm still here."

He took a step back and looked through the window through the slatted blinds at Manolo and Aleksi. Manolo was stretching while Aleksi showed him how; Giada looked on and Claire had got down on the floor with them.

"You're sure?" he asked one more time.

"I'm sure. I'm more sure about this than I have been about anything in my life, dude." He searched my face and nodded, seeing the sincerity there.

"I love you," he said and it took me back a bit. Golden wasn't sentimental like that. Or, at least, he hadn't been until Lys.

"I love you, too."

"Don't you ever fuckin' scare me like this again," he said.

"Promise," I told him. "I won't have to."

"Anything else I should know about?"

I laughed. "Gonna be you a little more often at the gym unless you can get me and Claire signed up. Her job is pretty demanding and she needs to stay fit."

He nodded. "I'll get you set up. Pretty sure they don't really fuckin' care at this point as long as you're related to me and keep it to the one guest."

"Thanks."

"Don't mention it, and you better bring her around the *10-13*, and *soon.*"

"Yeah, definitely. I missed this week; next week for sure."

He shook his head and said, "This is so weird. I'm not used to you being the one with poor impulse control."

I laughed and went for the door. He turned and fell into step beside me and I slapped him on the back.

"*Hombrecito* seems to like her," I pointed out and he laughed.

"And that kid don't like anybody," he agreed.

We went inside and Golden said, "All right, kiddo, I've got to go. Be good for Tío Ramiro, 'k?"

"*Bueno*," Manolo said distractedly, intent on what Aleksi was showing him.

"All right, I'll see you, man. It was nice to meet you, Claire."

She looked up and smiled, her dark eyes full of light and murmured, "You, too," but I could tell she was apprehensive and we would need to talk. My guess was she was upset that I hadn't told Golden about her before he arrived, but to be honest and fair, I'd completely forgotten about Manolo staying the night. I think she had, too, but that was no excuse for any of it.

I had to give myself a little forgiveness. We were still on a learning curve with each other and she'd been through a lot and had just sort of been thrust into my crazy life.

Golden left, and everyone got up and went to the table. I told Manolo he could eat upstairs and watch TV, if he kept it down, and he jumped at the opportunity.

"Behave, keep it down, I mean it! Or it's right back down here and you can eat at the coffee table."

"Okay, okay!" he called back, exasperated and Claire smiled a secret little smile at his sass.

"Sometimes I think his living with Golden was a monumentally bad idea." I laughed.

"I think it might be good for your brother, no?" Giada said taking a sip from her wine glass.

"If you're thinking it's because little man is *exactly* like my twin, yeah. You'd be right."

Claire and Aleksi chuckled.

Dinner was nice, her circus friends were good people, and I suddenly longed to bring her to the *10-13* to meet mine. There was a Thursday meet planned for the next week for those of us that couldn't get the weekends off. Considering Claire's line of work, she'd definitely be busy on Friday and Saturday nights, so that suited.

I was on day shift for now; we tended to rotate, so things would change at some point but for now, this worked out. I didn't know what things would be like when she started performing for real instead of just rehearsing, but we'd cross that bridge when we came to it.

The night flew by, and it felt like Giada and Aleksi had only been there moments instead of hours. They rose and gathered their things and I saw them out to the parking lot to wait for their ride.

"You are a good man to our *Kotyonok*," he said in his thickly-accented English. He held out his hand and I smiled and took it. "Thank you."

"She's amazing," I said. "No need to thank me."

Giada stepped in and kissed both my cheeks. I laughed a little awkwardly at it and she winked at me.

"*Ciao*," she declared as their ride pulled up. "Come see us at the Night Circus."

"I will! I'll try and bring the club and their families."

"Perfecto!" Aleksi opened the back door to the rideshare's car for her and she ducked in. He winked a blue eye at me, his teeth straight and white in his grin, and got in behind her. I got the distinct impression they weren't a couple, just really good friends. I waved and watched my breath plume the air as I sighed.

I found Claire in the kitchen loading the dishwasher and she put a finger to her lips and winked.

"He out?" I asked.

She nodded and I went to her, pulling her into my arms. She looked up at me questioningly and I smiled.

"I didn't tell Golden about you because I wanted to tell him the whole story and I needed to do that in person. I never told him about that night, at all. I didn't want to freak him out or upset him."

Understanding and relief washed over her face.

"I see," she murmured.

"I'm sorry," I said. "I should have, but I couldn't."

"No, no! I understand," she said.

"Yeah?"

She nodded. "Look what happened with me and Carter."

I felt my shoulders drop and whispered, "Give it time." I kissed her forehead and she sucked in a brave breath and kind of shuddered in my arms. I hated how much she was hurting and I wanted to take all of that pain away.

I held her close to me until she felt strong enough to pull away. We finished cleaning up together.

"I'll go bring him down," I said and she nodded and went over to the bench seat, pulling back the blankets.

Manolo was out, the TV playing the *Desperado* DVD's menu screen on loop and I had to smile. He must have smuggled it over from Golden's collection because I didn't own it. I lifted him and carried him downstairs and he didn't so much as stir. I tucked him into his makeshift bed and Claire stood by smiling.

"He's a great kid," she said softly and I smiled and nodded.

"We're going to the first Mass tomorrow, so we're going to be up early."

"I don't exactly have anything that can pass for Sunday best. I'm going to have to go shopping."

I put my arm around her shoulders and guided her to the stairs, switching out the lights as we passed. She went up before me and I lusted after her ass. I wanted her so bad I ached, but I wasn't about to go there with little man in the house.

"I think you need to sleep in tomorrow."

"I could probably use it," she confessed.

"You practicing tomorrow?"

"Is it a day that ends in 'y'?" she asked.

"Seven days a week? Really?"

"If Milo had his way it would be eight days a week, but no, we just don't really get a day off until he deigns to give us one. Even then, I take myself to the gym and do basic workouts."

"Claire, this guy sounds nuts. Somebody is going to get hurt if you all keep at it like this."

"According to Milo, we must all suffer for our art," she said and huffed out a miserable sigh. I shook my head and we got ready for bed.

"I don't know what to say, *mi alma*."

"There's nothing *to* say, love. It just is what it is," she said softly.

I stared across the bed at her and tossed her one of my tees. She put it on and pulled back the blankets, getting into bed. I climbed in on my side and pulled her against me. She settled and rested her head on my shoulder. I held her tight and smoothed a hand over her hair. She sighed and it sounded measures more content.

"Just promise me you'll be careful," I murmured.

"That I can promise you. This art form is my life; I'm not about to subject myself to a career-ending injury."

"Good," I whispered and settled down to sleep.

10

*C*laire…

"Claire, come on! We're gonna be late!"

"Whoa, buddy. Let's let Claire sleep, okay?"

"But I thought she was coming with us."

I was laying on my stomach and I pushed myself over onto my side to see Angel leading Manolo back down the stairs.

"Next week, buddy, I promise, okay?" I asked.

He looked over at me, frowning, and said, "Okay, but who knew circus work was such hard work?"

I smiled and said, "You'll have to come see us practice and perform and then you'll know why."

"Really?" he asked excitedly.

"Really. I'll get a bunch of family passes for the family performance night."

"You have those?" he asked curiously.

"We do. It's one of the final dress rehearsals and we want to perform in front of an audience and make it feel as close to the real thing as possible."

"Cool!"

"All right, *hombrecito*, go on downstairs. I'll be there in a sec."

"Cool, I don't want to watch you guys make out anyway." He trotted out of sight and Angel hung his head. All I could do was laugh.

"Mass is a couple of hours, then I take him over to his paternal grandmother's. Golden picks him up from there."

"Okay."

He bent down and kissed me soundly.

"See you when I get home, and then we can go to the gym."

"Sounds good, then you can drop me at the big top."

He nodded carefully. I could tell he didn't want to, but it was what it was. He left and I cuddled back down into the still-warm sheets. I couldn't go back to sleep, though, so instead I got up, limbered up, and practiced some yoga in the sunroom.

It was perfect. Tranquil and peaceful, surrounded by all that green, the warm sun through the glass, with the near-endless view of water outside the window. I felt refreshed when I finished and took myself downstairs to fix coffee and breakfast.

I bathed with my coffee and chatted with Giada and Aleksi via a group text. They liked Angel, and they were happy for me, glad the way I wished my own flesh and blood could be. It hadn't quite been a week since Carter walked out of the family-day group session and the sting from his rebukes still felt like a third-degree burn on the lining of my heart.

I sighed and put together what I would need for the rehearsal today, which was really just an athletic ensemble, tight and close-fitting, more skin than not. I put on more athletic clothing in preparation for the gym. I had no idea what police gym facilities looked like, but I was about to find out.

Angel came home right when he said he would and said, "Let me grab a change of clothes and we can go."

"We going for a ride?" I asked casually, hoping that the answer would be yes.

He grinned at me and asked, "Thrill-seeker?"

"Which one of us works for the circus?" I asked, and he laughed.

He ran upstairs and changed, when he came back down, he said, "I'm still not exactly clear on what it is you do," he said.

"I'll have to show you. I could explain it, but there's really nothing like experiencing it firsthand."

"Well, then…" He came to me and pulled me close by a hand on my ass, giving it a squeeze, he kissed me before finishing his sentence, "I can't wait to see it firsthand."

I smiled and bit my bottom lip as a golden glow of happiness suffused me.

He asked me, "Have you ever ridden before?"

"Yep, all over in Europe, it was nothing but motorbikes and scooters."

He chuckled and said, "The Harley's no scooter."

I grinned. "Must go faster!"

He laughed and went into the little closet by the stairs and brought down an extra helmet and held it out to me.

"Come on, I can't wait to have you on the back of my bike."

"Oh? And here it was I thought *I* was your favorite thing to ride."

"Oh, trust me, *mi alma,* you are."

I laughed and followed him out onto the dock. It was a nice day. Crisp, but beautiful. We drifted out to the parking lot hand in hand, our gym bags slung across our chests. I wore my leather jacket which was more fashion statement than actual 'biker bitch' but even though it was form over function, it was indeed functional, too.

His bike was kept in a small garage that he had to unlock and open up, which is why I hadn't seen it before.

It was beautiful, with a sleek, glossy midnight tank, and when I say that, I mean it was a deep and somber black – until the light hit it. Then, it was swept by brilliant deep-blue fire. The paint contained some sort of metal flake to make it happen.

The seats were butter-soft leather and the whole thing was edged tastefully in chrome. The whole effect one of a sleek, glossy, gorgeous piece of machinery that was sure to turn heads wherever it went.

"Wow, Angel, this is beautiful."

He smiled with silent pride and said, "She's my pride and joy. Well, next to my house. I've worked hard for these nice things."

"You've outdone yourself," I told him and put the lid on my head. He smiled and swung a leg over the front seat and fired it up. I jumped slightly and laughed, and he winked at me. I got on behind him and held onto him as he steered us out of the lot and took us towards parts unknown.

We ended up on the other side of the city, close to Ridgeview Park and the big top, but in a more industrial-type area. He pulled into a small lot by a warehouse, a mural painted on the side of the building depicting a black-and-white American flag with one blue stripe. In front of it was a larger-than-life, incredibly photo-realistic police badge.

I gave a low whistle as he shut off the bike and I stood by, taking off my helmet.

"That's some serious artwork," I said.

"Yeah, we held a barbecue fundraiser to pay the artist," he said.

"'We', as in the police force?" I asked.

"Nah, 'we', as in the Indigo Knights."

I smiled.

"That's why I asked."

He took my hand and led me around the fenced-off lot, through the gate, and to the glass doors. He gripped the panel and pulled it open for me and I went through. He went to the front desk and the guy behind it said, "Hey, Rodrigo or Ramiro?"

"The former," he said, with a wink.

"Yeah, sure. Your brother said you'd be in with your girlfriend. Can we get you guys to fill these out?"

"Sure thing. I'm glad he remembered to call ahead."

"Yeah, well, wouldn't have made much difference. You're family and could have passed yourself off as him, anyways." The guy manning the counter winked and Angel laughed. Busted.

We filled out the paperwork and the guy made us up some membership cards. We paid the dues and he asked, "You need the tour for your girl or are you good?"

"We're good," Angel declared and held out a hand to me. I took it and he drew me further into the spacious warehouse.

It had a mix and match of equipment. Some traditional gym stuff, like weight machines, ellipticals, and treadmills, but it also had a big wide area that was more conducive to CrossFit training. The locker rooms were at the back of the gym and I followed Angel there, pausing briefly at the three widely-spaced climbing ropes attached high up in the rafters.

There were several heavily-sweating men in Indigo City Police Department issue dark blue gym shorts and grey tee shirts, all waiting their turn and shouting encouragement to the men climbing the ropes.

One of the men, with an obvious good ol' boy attitude, caught me looking and called out, "You think you can hang with us, sweetheart?"

I laughed.

"I don't know. The question is, do you think you all could hang with *me?*"

All of them had a really good laugh at that one. I winked, and Angel and I parted ways at the locker-room doors. I found a locker, fancy with the push-button locks: enter a four-digit code, wait for the light to flash, enter it again and presto, your things were secured until you entered the same four digits a third time.

I stored my things and met Angel back out front, and he asked, "Treadmill?"

"Yeah."

I lingered again, watching them all climb the ropes, and Angel watched me watch them, a mixture of fascinated and amused. He didn't know what I could do, either, and one of these days, I would show him. I would like to do it here, though.

Unfortunately, today wasn't the day I would be rehearsing on my silks. Today was the dreaded cast-wide dance number. I was a dancer, and a damn good one, but when Milo couldn't find any fault with me, it felt like he sometimes just made shit up. At first, I thought I was crazy, but after last night, Giada and Aleksi assured me I wasn't; that I was, indeed, doing just fine, and Milo was most definitely being unreasonable.

We did the treadmill at a flat run. I went for a couple of miles and felt pretty good. After that, Angel hit some free weights while I hydrated and watched him, talking with him for a while. My eyes kept drifting towards those ropes and I wondered if the hookups up top were the same type of hookup we used at the big top. Eventually, I stopped at the bottom of one and peered up. It looked like a U-bolt secured into the metal rafter by rivets, as secure as it could get. An industrial carabiner held the rope to the U-bolt. It was very similar to our setup.

That was good to know. I might be able to get some extra practice in here, if I asked nicely. It was just a question of smuggling some silks out of the prop room.

Angel dropped me off at Ridgeview and I got off the bike. He shut it off so we could talk but made no move to follow.

"If it's cool with you, I'm going to run home, grab a shower and a change of clothes, then come back."

"Absolutely!" I said.

I leaned in and gave him a kiss and heard voices cheering. I looked up and over to Oksana and Thierry cheering and waving.

Thierry shouted at us, *"C'est manifique!"*

Oksana cried, "So happy for you!" in her thick accent and both laughed and waved before disappearing inside the performer's entrance.

I shook my head and said wryly, "When you're here, you're family."

"That's a good thing, isn't it?"

"Only if you're okay with basically having close to eighty-seven Golden's in your life." I wrinkled my nose.

"Eee," he cringed. "I see your point."

"I'll see you later?" I asked.

"Time to face the music," he said, and I nodded.

"Certainly feels that way."

I leaned down and kissed him one last time so that I could carry it with me inside.

"You've got this, *mi alma*."

"Thanks."

I didn't feel like it. I didn't feel like it at all.

11

———————

*A*ngel...

"What the fuck am I hearing you almost offed yourself three years ago, and you didn't call on us?" Skids growled in my ear.

I took a deep breath and let it out slow.

"Golden told you."

"Yeah, he told me. He came in fit to be tied after he left your place last night and hit the old barstool confessional."

I hadn't been asking, more making a statement, but fair enough. I rubbed my forehead and shut my garage door, holding my phone between my shoulder and ear while I moved the hasp over the ring and slid the padlock home.

"It was three years ago, Skids, and that's exactly why I didn't tell any of you."

He gave a long suffering sigh and asked, "One-time deal?"

"Yeah, I promise."

"Don't you scare us like that, boy. The problem of suicide among our ranks is real."

I knew what he meant. He meant among first-responders, and he wasn't wrong. We had a tough job and it could wear on us. *Bad.* I heard Skids suck in a breath and let it out on the other end of the line. There was a pause and he changed the subject.

"So when you plan on bringing this girl around here?" he asked.

"Well, she's at one of her rehearsal things right now. I can bring her back to the house, let her get cleaned up, and we can do some dinner at the *10-13.*"

"Didn't you come in here last night?"

"Yeah, but I brought it home, not the same thing."

Skids laughed and said, "All right, then. We'll see you tonight."

"Okay, call it tentative, though. I'll call and let you know if plans have changed."

"You do that."

"All right now, talk to you later."

"Yeah, you better."

I laughed a little and the line went dead. I felt instantly bad. I'd rattled Golden's cage but good, which is exactly why I hadn't told him in the first place. I loved my twin, but he could let shit consume him and drive him crazy if he wasn't careful. I felt bad about it, so I tended to keep more than I should from him sometimes, as a mercy. I hated seeing him get wrapped around the axle like that.

I went into the house and got cleaned up. Took my time, too. Showered and shaved, went up and found the bed made already, which was nice. I got dressed with an eye towards comfortable and casual, and while I did it, set my phone on the charger. Before I left, I put a load of laundry in the wash, dinged out the fridge, and took the trash with me.

I knew her practice was likely to be hours long, and I was okay with that. As eager as I was to see her and just be in her presence, I wanted to play it chill. I didn't want to be a source of pressure in her life, I wanted to be her release. So, when I got back to the park, I found a place to park the bike and sat for a while, soaking up what sun was on offer this late in the fall day.

"Hey!"

I looked over at the approaching security guard in the yellow windbreaker and gave him a chin lift. I fished out one of the passes from the inside pocket of my jacket. It was around my neck on the lanyard it'd come on, but I hadn't wanted it caught by the wind. I held it up where the guy could see it, and he kept coming over.

"Wow, you actually know one of the performers, huh?" He raised his radio to his mouth and depressed the button, saying into the mic, "He's got a family pass."

"Yeah," I said. "Claire Montgomery."

"No idea who any of them are," he said.

"Oh, she's the silk dancer, whatever that is."

He laughed and clapped and said, "You don't even know what she does!"

I grinned and shook my head.

"No idea. I thought about YouTubing it, but I didn't want to spoil the surprise, you know?"

He nodded, "Well, I'm Demone, and when you're ready to go in, all you do is go to that entrance right there and show your pass to the guards there. Cool?"

"All right man, thanks, and cool." I flashed the dude a winning smile. He ran a hand over his bald head and gave a nod. "I'm about to go to lunch, yo, but if they give you problems, just have them radio me? A'ight?"

"Will do, thanks, man."

"A'ight, you have a good time."

He turned and looked both ways before jogging back across the asphalt driving track that cut through the park.

I stretched and got off the bike, locking my helmet in the saddlebag across from where I'd stashed Claire's. I drifted at a sedate pace to the entrance Demone had indicated and looped the pass off over my head and handed it to the guard there.

"Huh, we don't get a lot of these through here for the rehearsals," he said. He was a tall white guy, older and looked through his eyeglasses in a way that indicated he had bifocals. He noted the number on the pass down and asked my name. I gave him my legal one, because 'Angel' wouldn't be of much use, and he handed me back my pass.

"Keep that on yah, and it's right through there. I'd fly under the radar of that director, though. He's in one of his moods today."

"Thanks for the pro-tip, bro."

"No problem."

I went into the darkened – hell, I don't know what you called it. Foyer? Rotunda? Anyway, I went past darkened concession and souvenir booths, empty of goods and the people to man them, and ducked through one of the archways leading into the main tent. Risers full of theater-like hard-plastic seats had been set up and all of them led down, bowl-shaped, to the round stage in the center. There was a man standing on a platform in front of the stage, a silver-tipped cane in one hand, waving it around as he shouted over the loud music at the performers twirling and dancing, doing short vignettes of their performances as they leapt and danced across the stage.

They looked poised and collected, smiles splitting their faces in rictus grins that even from here looked painted on. Dude wasn't as old as I pictured. Not by a long shot. He couldn't be more than mid-forties, tops. His close-cropped dark hair was just beginning to frost with silver at the back as the spotlight splashed across him.

I crept as close as I dared and brought my phone out, just getting a feeling. He bowed his head and raked a hand over his face in frustration, and it reminded me of some of the tweakers we picked up and transported to detox. Something was just *off* about the dude, and whether it was drugs or crazy remained to be seen.

I started to record from my seat as he bellowed out, "Stop, stop, stop! That's not it at all, what are you doing, Claire?"

I thought to myself, *Aw shit, here we go,* and he leapt down from the platform and took the stairs up to the stage two at a time. Claire had frozen in among the people on the stage and he stood beside her and demanded, "Look, watch me!" and he went through a set of steps that looked, to me, just like what she'd done the moment before he started screaming.

"You can all thank Claire for having to do this again! If she would only get it right, we could all go home early, but at this rate we'll be here all night. Now do it once more. Music! Again, from the top!"

The performers, chests heaving, took their places, and I could see by the set of her shoulders that Claire was getting beaten down. I didn't say anything, I just kept recording, because I knew the only way to get something to change was by having irrefutable proof of this guy being a royal assbag.

They went through their steps and motions; Claire looked flawless, but again, he stopped the production and singled her out. I could see she was at the end of her rope. She threw up her hands and cried, "I don't know what you want from me!"

"Please," a red-headed girl said, another American by the sound of it.

"He wants you not to suck. You've been dragging us down for weeks." She was a real Regina George mean girl, that one.

"Oh, please, Gloria. The only person dragging anything down is Milo," Claire shot back and she'd clearly lost her temper and was at the height of exasperation. Milo stalked across the stage and growled, "What did you say?"

"If you're not screaming at us, you're berating us. If we spent half the time actually going through the steps rather than stopping every time you perceive an imperfection that isn't there, we might actually improve!" she shouted, and I was proud of her.

"You little –" His hand flashed out and Claire's head rocked back.

I leapt up from my seat and shouted, "Hey!"

All heads were suddenly on a swivel and turning towards me.

"You keep your hands to yourself, asshole!" I was already dialing 9-1-1 as I stood there, trying to resist the urge to pummel that fuckwit.

"9-1-1, what is your emergency?"

"Yeah, I'd like to report an assault. Ridgeview Park, inside the Night Circus tent…"

I got through the call with dispatch and waved at Claire to come down, away from that maniac. She was holding the side of her face, which was turning bright red, and I snapped pictures of the handprint left behind before it could fade. She hugged herself into my side and I put my arm around her. The production looked like it was split into two camps, Claire's supporters and a smaller knot of people that looked like they were either afraid, or clearly on Milo's side.

The police arrived and I felt my frustration grow. They were Blue Templars, another cop MC, but one with bad blood with my crew. It was mostly because we knew those fuckers were dirty. Not only were they dirty, they liked to provoke violence, race-bait, and generally were everything about cops that was giving cops a bad name, and this was no exception.

"Seriously, Martinez? Your girl got mouthy. I'm not hooking this guy up for what should be a complaint to upper management. They should handle this shit in-house."

"Think the brass is going to agree with your assessment?" I demanded.

Schwartz rolled his eyes at me, but in the end, Milo got hooked up and taken for a ride. It wasn't Schwartz's call anyway. It was the prosecutor's office's. Schwartz and his lazy-ass partner just didn't want to do the paperwork. I was betting they'd fuck it up intentionally, somehow. I was tipped off to that fact when I had to remind them to Mirandize the piece of pond scum.

"You're fired," he'd said to Claire. She'd held out just fine right up until he uttered those words, then her eyes glassed over and she fought not to cry, and I nearly went to jail for punching the motherfucker out, myself.

I'd already sent the video clip out to the rest of the club with a briefly-texted explanation of what was going on, so there was no getting rid of the video. That was probably the smartest thing I'd done.

"Can we just go home?" Claire asked tightly. I nodded, and led her out of the circus tent amid the rest of the production crew milling around talking in low whispers and tones.

"Don't cry, *mi alma.* This isn't over yet."

We emerged under a twilit sky and had got no more than twenty paces out from the place when a voice called out, *"Kotyonok!"*

Aleksi jogged out from the tent and held out Claire's gym bag to her. He touched the side of her face and said something in Russian. Claire gave him a weak smile and took the bag, giving him a startled look at the weight. He winked at her and jogged back toward the circus tent.

"What is it?" I asked.

"Nothing," she said, shaking her head. "I just want to go before I completely lose it."

We got as far as the bike when her tears started to fall like rain and wouldn't let up. My heart broke for her all over again, but I had a steel resolve. I *would* see this through. Nobody deserves to be treated like that, and Milo and the Night Circus had broken all kinds of labor laws. I'd see they paid for it, too.

I would need a lawyer's advice. Good thing I knew two of the best, who I knew for a fact were as connected as you could get. I was like a-thousand-percent sure they knew a labor attorney worth their salt, somewhere in this city.

12

C laire…

    I couldn't help but cry it out, but Aleksi's gift was giving me hope, bolstering my spirits. My bag was stuffed to the gills. The metallic click of the connectors was a dead giveaway. He'd brought me my things *and* had smuggled a set of silks out as well. I couldn't practice without them, and lucky for me, I knew of a place. Fired or not, I had to keep my skills up.

I was honestly weeping more from my incandescent rage than out of mourning.

Milo had gone too far, and I was prepared to wage an all-out war with the company running the Night Circus now. There would be a reckoning and I would fight. He couldn't be allowed to do this to anyone else, and now that I wasn't there, he most assuredly would move on to another performer.

Angel held me in the parking lot and let me cry it out for a minute or two before he held me at half an arm's length, looked me square in the eyes and said, "Get it together, they're coming out." I took a few deep breaths and locked it down, and he murmured, "That's my girl."

He got our helmets out of the saddlebags he'd stashed them in and handed me mine. I put it on and he got on the bike, I got on behind him, and he pulled forward over the painted line and steered us out of the parking lot and down the drive leading out of the park.

I held on and let the wind carry some of the tension away and cool the side of my face, which still throbbed from where Milo had struck it, though the sting had diminished by quite a bit.

Angel took us home and parked the bike out in the lot rather than the garage. He turned around on his seat and gathered my hands in his and asked, "What do you want to do?"

I sat still, searching his face as the engine of his motorcycle ticked beneath us intermittently as it cooled. I swallowed hard and said, "I want to fight, but I'm scared."

"Scared why?"

"I've been blown off so many times when it comes to Milo and I feel like this won't be any different."

"It better be or you've got some pretty solid grounds to sue, I would think."

"I just don't know, I have a paper trail, though."

"Do you?"

"Yeah, emails with the head office."

He nodded. "Let's get you cleaned up. We're going out for dinner."

"We are?" I asked, taken aback. That was a rather abrupt pronouncement.

"We are," he said, getting up and holding out a hand to me. I took it and walked with him back to the house. He drew a hot bath the moment we were inside and pulled me over to it, lifting my shirt over my head. I mean, I could undress myself, but it was just so nice to be taken care of. The emotional roller-coaster was taking its toll. I should be starving by now, but I wasn't the slightest bit hungry.

"Relax, soak, I'm going to go upstairs and pick you out some clothes."

"Okay," I murmured. He helped me into the bath and turned on the jets and I did as he suggested. I let the heat do its work, relaxing my muscles, and I simply soaked. He came back down a little while later and sat down at the head of the tub, his hand lightly tipping my chin as far as I could go. His lips descended onto mine and he kissed me tenderly.

"I'm tagging myself in on this one, *mi alma*."

"You can't save me from this; we're even and if you save me now, I'll owe you," I murmured. It was meant to be a joke, but his gaze was somber as he searched my face.

"You save me every moment of every day you're still breathing, Claire. I've only just found you again, and this shit…" He trailed off and swallowed hard. "I'm scared I'm going to lose you again if it continues."

I shook my head and reached up, laying my palm against his cheek. He turned his head and caressed my palm with a delicate kiss.

"I'm never leaving you again," I said. "I don't make the same mistake twice if I can help it. I let him get to me once. It's my turn to get to him."

"That's my girl," he breathed and we kissed again.

I couldn't get enough of kissing him. I couldn't get enough of the feel of him against me, inside me, and around me. I'd never believed in love at first sight, but now I had to. The depth of emotion I felt when it came to Angel was so beyond lust there wasn't any other word for it.

I loved him.

I knelt up out of the water and pulled myself to him. He made a slight surprised noise of protest against my mouth as I plastered my body to the front of his, getting his shirt wet, but then his stiffened posture eased and he laughed against my mouth. The sound sent a frisson of wanting down my spine and I suddenly just wanted to stay here, alone with him, making love all night.

"Can't we just stay here?" I whispered.

"No can do, *mi alma,* I already texted we were coming."

I groaned and asked, "So, where are we going?"

"The *10-13*. It's a cop bar and grill out in Old Town a couple of streets over from Bayside Park."

"The one your President and Vice President run?"

"That's right, just don't let them hear you call them that." He grinned and I smiled, too. He'd explained they preferred the rankings they'd been used to as cops and firefighters, so it was 'Chief' and 'Deputy Chief.' He looked me over and said, "The food we had last night came from there."

I sighed, and said, "Well in that case, sign me up. That food was amazing."

I finished washing up and he went with me upstairs to change his wet shirt and to watch me get dressed. He'd chosen pretty well for me, laying out selections from my meager wardrobe across the bed.

Most of my clothing was either athletic, or natural fibers that rolled or folded down small. I'd pretty much lived out of a suitcase, carry-on and a gym bag for the last three years. I needed to travel light.

I put on the olive green Cheema pants and slipped the simple black ladies' fitted tee over my head, pulling it down. I sat down on the edge of the bed and pulled on the athletic socks he'd put out and he brought over my Doc Marten's. I smiled and murmured my thanks, putting them on and lacing them tight.

"You need some jeans," he said, "or some leather pants; those would be good, too." He bit his bottom lip to try and contain his smile at that last thought and I felt my eyebrows go up.

"Most of my circus family are a bunch of naturalist, holistic, borderline-hippies who are full-time vegan, card-carrying members of PETA. Showing up in leather pants could ruin a lot of relationships for me."

He laughed and said, "Good point. You'd be screwed either way. You in leather pants would also ruin those relationships, in that I'd never let you out of the house again."

I laughed and stood up, and he held out my leather jacket to me with raised eyebrows. I rolled my eyes. I didn't typically wear it to work, and to be honest, on the rare occasion I did, no one had ever made any kind of deal over it.

"Fine, you got me," I declared.

He laughed and I put it on, lifting my hair out of the collar. I shook my head and said, "Just give me a few minutes to do something with my hair." I went downstairs feeling cool and confident in what I was wearing and took myself over in front of the bathroom mirror. I French braided my hair tight to my scalp and tied the end with the thin black hair elastic around my wrist. As a last touch, I put on some of the natural lip balm from my jacket pocket, the smell of natural peppermint, herbal and sweet, tickling my nose, with just a hint of beeswax underneath.

I dusted a stray eyelash off my cheek and gave myself a last going-over, and nodded. I looked good, despite feeling a little wrecked, still, sometimes looking good was half the battle. I went out to the living room where Angel stood in his jacket and leather motorcycle club vest, scrolling through his phone. He gave a nod and put it in his pocket.

"Everything okay?"

"Yeah, actually. Better than. Looks like most of the club is coming out to meet you."

"Really?" I asked, taken aback.

"Yeah, really. Come on." He handed me my helmet and we went out. He locked up behind us and I followed him down the dock, to the parking lot where his bike waited.

The thrum of the engine and the rush of pavement beneath the tires was soothing to my soul as we made our way through the city. We found ourselves on a one-way street and he followed it through traffic for quite a ways. Of course, it didn't help that we hit every red light the city had to offer.

Eventually, he thumbed on the turn signal, slowed his roll, and turned into an alleyway by a building whose old-fashioned shingle hanging above the door read *The Cormorant.*

"I thought you said this place was called *The 10-13*," I said hopping off the back of the bike and going for my chinstrap.

"It's a double play on words," he said. "The address is one-zero-one-three, or 10-13, and 10-13 is the call sign when it comes to police for *'Officer in need of assistance'.*"

"Ahhh, clever!"

"Yeah, Skids thought so too when he realized the happy accident that was the address after signing the papers. He pointed it out and the name stuck."

"So where did '*The Cormorant*' come from?"

He laughed a little and I realized I was probably peppering him with questions, but I couldn't help it, I wanted to know everything when it came to him and the people in his life. It was important to me.

"*The Cormorant* has always been *The Cormorant.* When Skids and Reflash bought it, one of the contract provisions was that the space kept its name. They didn't have a problem with it. They were determined to build something here and when they took over, *The*

Cormorant was in serious trouble. The place had hit the skids in a bad way – no pun intended."

"How so?"

"Well, for one, when you walked in the front door, you could smell the bathrooms. They closed it down for close to six months while they put it through renovations."

"Yikes! Also, that's disgusting."

"Tell me about it. A lot of us pitched in on getting this place up to code. It was a disaster."

He opened the door for me and I slipped through with murmured thanks. I didn't know what I'd expected after the bleak origin story, but I was pleasantly surprised when we walked through the door.

"Hey, Angel. Go on back to the banquet room; Skids and Reflash are waiting for you," the hostess behind the podium said.

"Thanks, Kristy."

"No problem!" She beamed at him and smiled more when she saw me and gave me a nod.

I relaxed a little, the atmosphere was welcoming despite how packed the place was. Football recaps played on the televisions and there was more than a decent crowd for a Sunday night. I followed Angel, threading around two long high-top tables full of beer glasses and piles of chicken bones, past two dartboards and a couple of pool tables, to a switchback ramp leading up to a glassed-in banquet dinner room full of leather- and denim-clad men and women.

He dragged open the glass door, which squeaked as it scraped across the lintel, and the majority of the people in the room turned and broke into glad cries.

"Hey, bro."

I peeked past Angel and smiled at Golden, who gave me a serious, considering look, and then a nod that couldn't be interpreted as anything less than grateful. I smiled and gave a nod in return and then it was an absolute flurry of introductions.

There was another semi-familiar face in the room, although he was much more outlandishly made up than he had been back on the psych ward. I hugged the male nurse who'd delivered Angel's message, and he cried out, flustered, and waved me off.

"Oh girl, I do *not* know why you would think you're my type!" he declared and I grinned.

"I'm everybody's type."

He looked me up and down shrewdly and smiled.

"I know that's right. Welcome to the madhouse, baby."

"It's cool, I'm from the circus."

He grinned broadly and I think he could tell I was a kindred spirit. We theatrical-type kids always stuck together even through adulthood. I figured it was just that now, outside of the mental ward, he could see me. That more of my real personality could shine through. While I was stressed, I wasn't *as* stressed, or melancholy, or medicated to within an inch of my life… It made a big difference.

I met so many people I was a little worried I wouldn't be able to keep them all straight. There were well over a dozen people present, and even Angel remarked, "Added some leafs to the table and brought some chairs out of storage, huh?"

"Had to," a man that I could only assume was Reflash or Skids said over the dull roar of laughter and conversation.

"Skids, I'd like you to meet Claire."

I held out my hand and Skids gripped it firmly. I gave as good as I got and he smiled as we shook.

"It's nice to meet you, Claire."

"It's nice to meet you, too."

"So you really work for the circus?" he asked, and I kind of blushed a bit.

"Well, I did. I was fired a few hours ago."

"No shit?" Skids was loud enough that the rest of the room quieted down.

"I'd like to talk with you about that, if you don't mind," a short man with a small build said. He held a bubbly blonde out of a bottle against him; Aly was her name.

I had no idea why he would want to talk to me about it, but Angel jumped in with some clarification. "Yale is one of the city's ADA's."

"And Chrissy is one of my lead prosecutors," Yale said, tipping a glass in Chrissy's direction.

Chrissy gave me a little wave from where she was likewise cuddled up to her man, a shrewd-looking man who looked me over.

"Okay," I drawled. "What do you want to know?"

13

*A*ngel…

We set up shop around the big table and brainstormed.

It was a little weird having the girls in on it, but there wasn't anything even close to something they needed to be kept out of on this one. There was quite the layman's discussion about Maryland labor laws and thoughts on what could happen when it came to Milo's potential prosecution.

There wasn't much there, sadly. His first offense, likely to be pled down. Hell, it wasn't even fifty-fifty on if he'd even bonded out already – more than likely he *had*. It wasn't like he was a hardened criminal. Just an asshole.

Oz had given the dude a little bit of hell during booking in only the way that Oz could, mostly letting Milo think he could get his way, before pulling the rug out from under the guy with reality. It was one of Oz's favorite games and he'd gotten the dude a couple of times. It was good for a laugh, which Claire needed.

"So, do you know what you're going to do?" Lil asked, putting down her phone. She was the Google queen when it came to anything. Her author brain somehow tapped her into an extreme-research superpower that usually left the rest of us blinking stupidly, asking 'How the hell had she come up with *that*?' It was useful sometimes; sometimes she came up with some bizarre bass-ackwards way of doing things that left us howling before we could set her straight. Tonight she'd fallen on the side of mostly useful.

Claire pondered the question and heaved a heavy, slightly-over-whelmed sigh. She sat back in her seat and said, "I don't know. I'm going to email Milo's boss tomorrow, but I don't really expect to get anywhere. I mean, I definitely haven't gotten anywhere before."

"If they don't address this properly, you definitely have grounds to sue under U.S. labor laws," Chrissy said, wiping her mouth with her napkin.

"I don't understand how it would work out that way. I mean, most of this didn't happen in the U.S., it happened in other countries."

"Doesn't matter," Yale interjected. "You're an American worker working for an American company. They have to abide by the American laws *and* the labor laws of the countries they were operating in."

"I didn't know that," she said.

"Happy to help," Yale said, and I could tell he was looking forward to being an asshole about this. He'd been one of the guys I'd sent the video to for safekeeping. There wasn't a whole lot he could do, but he was more than likely going to follow up and make sure the dude was prosecuted and the deal put on the table wasn't the most savory for the defendant. He'd get his pound of flesh and pint of blood.

The rest of the dinner conversation was fluid, the club finding out more about Claire and Claire finding out about the rest of the club. My brother caught my eye; Lys wasn't here. Likely she was home with Manolo. He shot me a look in our secret silent twin code and I gave him a chin lift. Claire was laughing at something Oz was saying and I leaned in and whispered I would be right back. She turned to me, smiling, and gave a nod.

I kissed her to a round of good-natured harassing 'Awww's' and got up. Golden came around the table and followed me out.

"You need to bring her over for dinner with us at my place," he said without any preamble.

I grinned.

"You like her."

He sniffed and looked past me, peering through the glass of the fishbowl up at Claire where she laughed at something someone said.

"She's all right. Can't really get a good feel for her with the big crowd."

I kept my smile to myself. I didn't want to antagonize him. I loved my brother, but he might take a dislike to her on principle if I pushed it. He cracked a smile at me and I laughed a little.

"You asshole."

"Legit, bro. She's all right, but I'd like to get some family time."

"Fair enough. How about Saturday night, we can come by, have dinner, take Manolo back with us so I can take him to Sunday service."

He nodded. "Good deal. It's a date."

He turned to head back into the fishbowl and I sighed, "Hey, Rodrigo."

He froze and turned back. I didn't typically use his given name like that, but what I had to say, it was important.

"Yeah, what's up?" he asked.

"What I did, you know, me not telling you? It's not your fault, bro. It's nothing you did. I'm serious when I say it was all me." I swallowed hard and he cocked his head. I pushed on before he could say anything.

"I was scared you'd be pissed, sure, but I think I was more scared that you'd be disappointed. I didn't want you to look at me that way, you know? I didn't want you to ever think you couldn't count on me and –"

He came over to me and pulled me into a fierce hug and pounded me on the back.

"You're the only motherfucker I got in this life that I can count on. I never, not once in a million fuckin' years, thought there would ever be a time you weren't there, man. I always thought it would be me to go first, and facing that possibility? That I almost lost you? Dude, it sucks… but you're still here and that's all that matters."

I hugged him back, and I said, "I swear to God, bro. The only reason I'm still here is because of Him and that woman right up there."

He put enough distance between us to keep shit from getting awkward and said, "And I'll thank Him every fuckin' day of my life for that. You have no idea. Even though He and I ain't seen eye to eye in a minute, I'll fuckin' thank Him for that."

"And Claire?" I asked.

"Let me warm up to her, dude. You know how I am."

I laughed a little and nodded. "Yeah, I know how you are." A silence stretched between us, and I had to ask, "We good bro?"

Golden nodded and said, "We always good." He knocked me in the shoulder and I nodded. We went back up the ramp and into the fish bowl to a riot of laughter.

Oz was tellin' stories again.

"So, what'd you think?" I asked around an hour later, as Claire and I strolled up the dock arm-in-arm.

"I think I like your family, both biological and chosen," she said.

I couldn't help but smile. "Good way of putting it."

"I know what that's like," she said quietly and the mourning in her tone was unmistakable.

I sighed and felt the weight of her pain when I did it. Wishing I could unburden her from it, knowing that I couldn't, I said, "Give him some time, *mi alma.*"

"Yeah, no, I know…" she trailed off and I stopped in front of our door. She faced me and looked up questioningly and I cupped her cheek. I drew a deep breath of the cool night air and bent, laying my lips over hers carefully.

Her dark, liquid eyes fluttered shut and she returned my kiss, melting into me, and I held her close. It was moments like these that the troubles surrounding us in their maelstrom of drama and bullshit just fell away and it was just down to me and her. When it was like this, nothing else mattered and it was like we could breathe and take a short reprieve from all of the bullshit.

I was so down for that, and I could tell Claire was positively eager for it. I broke the kiss so I could get us inside and shut all the drama outside to drown in the bay, for all I cared.

No sooner had I shut and thrown the lock on the door, Claire was dipping to her knees in front of me, looking up in adoration, her hands drifting over the soft tee covering my body, beneath my jacket and cut, and going to the belt holding my jeans.

I smiled and leaned back against the door, letting her have her way. She didn't hesitate, her hands undoing my belt, her fingers nimbly undoing the button and zipper of my fly. I watched her, the first stirrings of desire making my cock grow warm even as she lifted it free of my pants and underwear and slipped it into her mouth.

I was still soft, just starting to grow hard, and the feel of becoming fully aroused in the soft, wet, warmth of her mouth was a new sensation. It was one that I had to admit I liked. I closed my eyes and tipped my head back against the door and half-sighed, half-moaned as she worked me, carefully with her lips, tongue and hands.

"Shit, Claire…" I lost my voice to a shudder as she brought me from zero to sixty faster than I thought I was capable of. The friction of her velvety soft tongue against my shaft was outstanding and I was finding it hard not to thrust.

I looked down, straight into her dark eyes which were glittering with mirth, a playful smile turning up the corners of her mouth around my cock. Somehow, the whole effect of watching her blow me and enjoy it put me on cloud fucking nine. Legit, if I could hold out and watch her all night, I would, but as good as her mouth on me felt, I just loved being inside her pussy. There was something about listening to her moan, watching her arch beneath me, her body fluttering around mine where I penetrated her… God, the whole package put me into seventh heaven.

"God, yes," I growled and felt my legs shake.

It was just me and her, and we had all night. I wasn't about to waste a minute of it sleeping, either. Not if I could help it.

*C*laire...

I think I completely undid him because one moment I was blissfully sucking his cock and the next I was being hauled to my feet, his mouth crushing over mine. He spun me around and shoved me against the kitchen counter, bending me at the waist, pressing me flat against the cool stone.

"I think you're asking for it, little girl," he breathed in my ear, and I pressed my ass back against his cock.

"I'm most definitely asking for it," I answered and he growled, this low, guttural, and completely erotic sound that made me four times wetter than I already was.

He ripped open the junk drawer I'd stashed the condoms in last night and pulled out the bag. He thrust his hips tight up against my backside and pinned me against the island counter, the edges of the stone digging across my hips. That helpless feeling was delicious, mostly because I knew I could trust him to just make it feel good.

"Get your pants down, Claire," he ordered and let me up just enough to comply. I did as I was told while he put a condom on himself, and no sooner did I have my pants and underwear off my ass then he was back. He kicked my feet apart and bent me forward over the counter, his big hand buried in the collar at the back of my neck.

"Touch your pussy, baby. Touch your pussy while I fuck you."

Oh, God. My body clenched at his words, desire coiling low in my belly like a snake about to strike. He shoved himself inside me and I cried out, both hands flat against the cool stone countertop as my hipbones barked against the counter's edge. He stilled, asked if I was all right and once I gave a breathy "Yeah, don't stop," he was back at it, his intensity, the frenzy, not one bit diminished.

He reared back and slammed back into me and I tightened around him, reluctant to let him withdraw. Withdraw he did, though, and then he was back, surging forward, each thrust powerful and possessive in all the right ways. He claimed my body and I didn't need to touch myself to get the orgasm to grow.

A sharp smack landed on my right ass cheek and he barked, "I said touch yourself!"

I slipped a hand between me and the counter and pressed fingertips to my clit crying out, "Oh God, Angel!"

"That's it baby, don't stop. Don't stop until you fucking come for me."

I arched provocatively, thrusting my hips back, tilting my ass up like an offering, accepting the punishing rhythm of his cock into my body. I welcomed the pleasure that was so strong, so intense, it bordered on pain, an exquisite pain that was a much-needed catharsis with everything I had going on. I begged for it, I needed it, and he was perfect, he didn't relent, he was everything I needed and then some, and I reveled in this.

It wasn't long until I exploded around him, a sexy wailing scream of delighted release escaping my throat making me wonder for a second *was that even me?*

He shoved into me repeatedly, his even strokes breaking up, stuttering as he lost his pace to his own release. He shoved into me one last time, touching me soul-deep and bent, collapsing forward over my body, sheltering me and protecting me, his hot, panting breath teasing behind my ear and making me shudder, my pussy rippling with aftershock around his thick shaft.

His breath caught, and he gave a spasming cry of pleasure. His dick was still way oversensitive from his own orgasm. I clenched around him again, this time on purpose and he sucked a breath in, hissing between clenched teeth.

"Fuck, you feel so good, baby."

"So do you," I said. "I really hope you're ready to go again soon, because I am *so* not done."

"Gimme five and a change of position and I'll fuck you all night if you want. Just, this angle? My thighs are screaming."

I laughed and said, "Let me up and let's get naked."

"Ooo, I like your style."

He straightened and I cried out, a little oversensitive myself, as he pulled out of me. My body throbbed, an angry, pleasure-filled ache that was like an itch that just hadn't been scratched to satisfaction. I wanted him, no, I *needed* him inside me again. I needed more, and I needed him not to stop until we were both too exhausted to continue.

We moved slowly, still half-basking in the afterglow as we pulled off the rest of our clothes, leaving them littering the kitchen counter and floors like casualties of war. *Love is a battlefield,* I thought to myself, and suppressed a giggle.

He hauled me to him and we pressed skin-to-skin, our mouths clashing, each of us vying to dominate the kiss, the heat between us shimmering like wave patterns off a summer sidewalk. He bent, cupping my ass and hauled me up his body. I gave a little leap into his arms and twined my legs around his hips. He snatched the remaining condoms off the counter where they'd been abandoned and murmured against my mouth, "Hold onto me, baby."

He carried me bodily through his house and up the stairs to the bedroom, laying me back against the covers, kissing down my body far enough to worship my breasts. I moaned and melted into the cloud that was his bed, clutching my fingers in his hair as he worked first one then the other nipple, his hands tearing open and rolling on another condom. I was so wet, so slick and ready for a second round, I could feel it coating the insides of my thighs. The sex was getting messy, but then again, that was the best kind.

He teased my pussy lips with the head of his cock, rubbing the head through my wetness, teasing my clit with it, slapping it against my body to cause pleasurable vibrations. I writhed and demanded he fuck me and he laughed and shoved himself inside me to the root. I was open and ready for him, so all that resulted was a pleasant, full feeling. I put my hands around his neck and wrapped my legs back around his hips and pulled him all the way back in when he pulled back to thrust.

He laughed and I let out a pleasure-filled hum and drifted a hand down my body between my breasts.

"Just stay there, just like that," I said, and worked my clit in circles with my fingertips. He pressed tighter against me and watched me masturbate with his cock pressed deep inside me, a small smile playing on his lips with his amusement. I didn't care, I was glad he was enjoying the show as I ground against him, my other free hand gripping one breast, pinching the nipple. He grinned and bowed over me, pressing in harder, his mouth engulfing my other nipple as I drew tighter, my pussy giving that first blushing, trembling throb.

I was close, so very close, and I wanted to come again so bad. He mumbled against my breast, "That's it, baby. Come all over that dick," and I did. I arched, a thin wail escaping my throat that dove to limitless depths as the last drop of whatever caused the vessel of my body to overfill, spilling over and across his bed.

He leaned over me as I shuddered and jerked as if electrocuted, and moaned out, "Mm, yeah; you feel so good. Keep coming, keep coming just like that."

God I loved how sensual, how erotic his deep voice in my ear was as I pulsed around him. The sound alone drove me into another smaller, but no less pleasurable, orgasm as he began to move again, rolling his hips, starting slow at first before picking up the pace. I gasped for breath but had trouble sitting still. I wanted him, I needed to move, I wanted to be on top, to writhe for him, to dance for him in that way that gave us both pleasure because I was addicted to him and his love and I wanted, needed, to come for him again.

"Stop! Stop, stop, stop! I want on top, let me fuck you!" I begged, and he obliged, helping me up so I was riding him halfway. He stood back up, turned around and let himself fall back onto the bed. I fell too, laughing, shrieking with joy until we landed and he thrust impossibly deep, to the point where pleasure met pain.

I shuddered and sat up, pushing against his chest to give myself leverage, getting my knees under me before I rolled my hips, rising and falling, his cock impossibly deep at this angle and touching off a euphoria I don't think I had ever felt with another human being. I watched him through eyes hooded with passion. He looked up at me like I was his personal goddess and I felt powerful, beautiful, and in control. It was intoxicating. I was pleasure-drunk and looking for more, and his hands smoothing over my hips only encouraged me to go find it.

I leaned back, changing angle slightly and that was the key that unlocked the door for both of us. His eyes slipped shut and he cried out, breathless with enjoyment, as his hands returned to my breasts, fondling them, pinching the nipples and rolling them between forefinger and thumb as I joyfully fucked both of our brains out.

I came again, only this time he came with me, and I shook so hard, I couldn't get enough control to keep at it if I wanted to. He lay beneath me, my body over his, rising and falling with his short but deep breaths, his arms around me, his cock softening inside the condom inside me and all I knew was bliss.

"You're something else, you know that?" he asked later. I lay back against his chest, the warm water of the bath we shared swirling around raw, sensitive bits and causing little intermittent aftershocks.

"Why do you say it that way?" I asked, laughing a little. His arms tightened around me and he chuckled with me, holding me tight.

"What way?" he asked.

"Like you're surprised."

"Pleasantly surprised, but yeah, I guess I am kind of surprised."

"Why?" I asked.

"Most people fall in love but they have to work at it, you know? They love their wife or girlfriend, but they compromise, or have to settle on some things. It's not like that with you. I don't feel like I have to compromise on anything. I don't feel like I have to settle. You just feel that fuckin' good. You do everything I like. You're just amazing."

I cuddled back into him and said softly, "So you think you love me, huh?"

He barked a laugh and kissed my shoulder, up to the side of my neck, nuzzling behind my ear he whispered into it, "I don't *think* I love you, *mi alma*, I know I do. I've loved you from the first moment you looked into my eyes back on that dock, that sliver in your hand and the heel on your shoe broken. There's never been anyone else but you, babe."

I felt my lashes collect tears, the sparkling lights of the arching Bay Bridge to the side of our view from the tub out the houseboat's bay windows, blurring and turning to stars. I tipped my head back and begged for his lips with mine and he kissed me.

There had been a few lovers since Angel in my life. Aleksi was one of them, but he was gay and the best thing I could do for him while we were in Russia was fuck him and sing his praises to cast off suspicion. He'd honestly been the most awkward fuck of my life and we'd laughed about it afterwards. He'd told me he loved me, but not in that way. More like a sister, and I'd begged him to never, ever say that again, considering we *had* fucked.

It'd been a deal. We'd kept up the ruse, until we hit a country where it'd been safe to be himself. Then it'd been a gentle, mutual break-up, and he'd come out of the closet to the rest of the company, and that had been that.

I told Angel the truth, all of it, and we'd laughed and laughed over it, my relief palpable when he promised he wasn't jealous or upset that though I'd missed him, I hadn't exactly stayed celibate. I felt a certain amount of guilt that he had.

"I love you, too," I whispered and I could feel the glow of his happiness even at my back.

"Yeah?" he asked.

"Of course!"

"You have no idea how happy that makes me, *mi alma.*"

I chuckled and asked, "What does that even mean?"

"What?"

"What you keep calling me, *mi alma...*"

He smiled against the side of my neck and said, "It's Spanish for 'my soul', which you are."

"You believe in soulmates?" I whispered.

"I didn't, but then I met you."

He cradled me against his body, rocking me back and forth gently in the tub as rain began to patter outside on the roof. I sighed and closed my eyes and sank gratefully back into him, my body loosening, an unknown tension easing from my muscles.

"You're my everything now, Claire," he whispered.

I smiled, and said with absolute conviction, "You're mine, too."

He sighed out in contentment, a sentiment I echoed, and we lay sated and comfortable in each others' arms in the warm bath as the rain pattered down outside. I didn't think there was anything that could be more perfect about tonight, after what a disaster the day had been.

Of course, that was before we got out, he built a fire to warm the place, and we went to bed. I slept so soundly cuddled in his embrace, and I felt so alive.

Angel's presence in my life was making all the difference.

15

*A*ngel...

I was first to wake the next morning. She was so peaceful when she slept. No trace of sadness remained when she was like this, and I just lay beside her for what must have been an hour or more just watching her. Her dark lashes quivering faintly against her freckled cheek, the dark circles beneath her eyes all but gone, the faintest of shadows left behind. She was so beautiful, with her long dark hair down, brushing her forehead. I could stare at her for hours more if she would let me.

Of course, this was Claire, and I was learning that, similar to me, she had to always be moving at a thousand miles an hour.

She sucked in a tremulous breath and her sleek body stretched and shuddered. She yawned, pressing the back of her hand over her mouth to cover it, before she opened her eyes and caught me staring, memorizing every line, every curve, every freckle of her beautiful face in this most intimate of moments.

"Were you watching me sleep?" she asked, laughing at me.

"Yes."

"Oh my God, why?" She covered her face with her hands and I pulled them away.

"Stop that, you're beautiful when you sleep."

"You think I'm beautiful all of the time," she said accusingly, and I smiled.

"Guilty as charged."

"Mm, that's okay," she said softly. "If I woke up first, I would probably be doing the same thing."

"Oh, yeah?"

"Mm-hm."

"Why?" I asked, and then I wished I hadn't; her eyes lost some of their sparkle.

"Because I still keep expecting to wake up and find out that this was all some sort of terrible but beautiful dream. It just doesn't at all seem quite real…"

I palmed her cheek and smoothed a thumb over her soft skin and smiled at her.

"This is as real as it gets, *mi alma*."

"Promise?"

"I swear it."

She leaned forward and kissed me, and I smiled against her lips. She drew back, enough to speak but not enough for me to really look at her; her voice was soft as her insecurities came out to play.

"Even with as broken as I am?"

"We all break sometimes, it's part of life." I drew back to look at her and she gazed at me, her luminous dark eyes, so lovely in their contradiction, held worry and concern. I cocked my head and asked, "What do you know about martial arts? Specifically, out of ancient Japan?"

She laughed, amused at my abrupt change in topic, before saying, "Nothing, why?"

"Well, did you know that some ancient Japanese warriors used to break their arms and legs on purpose?"

"No, why would they do that?"

"To become unbreakable."

"I don't understand."

I cuddled her into me and she laid her head on my chest.

"When a bone is broken, it heals stronger than it was to begin with."

"Really?"

"Yep. They figured it made them better warriors. My point is, that the theory holds true for more than bones. We all break sometimes, but once we recover from that break, we're stronger, and harder to break a second time around. You've been through a lot, baby. You're still healing, but when you're there, you'll be stronger; better than you were before."

"You really believe that?"

"I do."

I didn't exactly tell the whole truth when it came to the bone thing. It was true that it was stronger after healing *initially*, but things eventually evened out and the site of the break was just the same as the surrounding bone after a while. Either way, the same was true. 'Time heals all wounds' was a true statement for a lot of things.

We were quiet for a time and eventually she sucked in a breath and blew it out.

"What's wrong?" I asked.

"I want coffee, and I need to pee, but I don't want to get up, I'm too comfortable."

I laughed and said, "Coffee and taking a piss are definitely on my list of things to do, too, doesn't matter which order, though. Up you go. Let's get this party started."

She groaned and whined playfully, but got up. We padded downstairs in our bare feet wrapped in our bathrobes and I let her use the bathroom first while I got coffee going. She came out, and finished what I started so I could take care of business. We didn't have to ask each other, we didn't even really speak, instead maintaining a close and comfortable silence. It was the closest I had ever felt with anyone other than my twin, and it felt good, this sharing my space and the mundane little pieces of life with her. I would hate to go back to work the next morning.

"So, what did you want to do with your new-found freedom today?"

"Never give up and never surrender," she answered. "I want to hit the gym and I want to start sending emails."

"Which one first?"

"Ugh, I *want* to do the gym, so that means I should probably do the emails first."

"Fair assessment," I agreed, laughing a little.

"I'll go get my laptop," she said sulkily.

"Keep it up there, take your coffee in the sunroom. What do you want for breakfast? I'll make myself useful and bring it up."

"Really?"

"Really."

"You're the best." She stood up on her toes and kissed me. "And whatever is fine. I'm in one of those moods where food is just something you eat so you don't die."

I laughed. "Not a breakfast person?"

"No, not really, but I need to eat with as many calories as I tend to burn in a day."

"True. You may have to adjust for a while," I said and she made a face at me.

"You're right, damn it."

I was sorry I'd brought up the loss of her job again, but I knew she wanted to stay in peak condition and putting in as many calories as she was probably used to, without expending as much as she had been, could lead to a host of other self-image problems for her. Not to mention, when she got her job back or if she found another job performing, she would have a lot less to worry about when it came to getting back into top shape.

"Stop it," she said gently, and I scowled.

"Stop what?"

"Worrying that you offended me. I get it. It's not a commentary on me keeping my figure; it's you genuinely looking after my health, happiness, and well-being."

I smiled and asked, "That obvious?"

"You're like an open book, baby," she said to me and winked. She took a drink of her coffee and drifted towards the stairs.

A few moments later she called down, "What's the Wi-Fi password?"

I chuckled and called it up to her as I set about making us some baked oatmeal, mostly because it was still grey and dreary outside, and baked oatmeal was hearty, tasty, and just sounded amazing on such a cold and miserable day.

When I went up, she hit a few keys, looked over what she read, hit a final key, and leaned back with a gusty sigh. I set a bowl by her laptop and sat across from her with mine, laying down a napkin and a spoon for her. She picked up the spoon and said, "House smells great."

"Bonus feature."

She smiled and took a bite and I felt my own smile grow with hers. She nodded and finished her bite.

"This is fantastic."

"Yeah, just because it's something you eat so you don't die, doesn't mean it should taste like shit."

She laughed and it was a brighter sound than the sun outside, hidden by the clouds as it was. She nodded and said, "You got me there."

"So, now what?" I asked, glancing at her laptop by way of clarification.

She sighed. "Now, we wait, I guess. I don't really know. First time I've ever been fired from anything in my life."

"Really?" I asked. "Not even as a teenager, from your first shitty dead-end job?"

She laughed and shook her head. "Nope."

"Wow. I'm impressed."

She nodded and said, "What about you?"

"Never been fired, been laid-off before from a private ambulance company just before I got on with the city. Rage-quit the bodega I worked at when I was sixteen because Mr. Corleone was a massive cheapskate, dick, but yeah, that's about the extent of it."

"Hmm." She chewed thoughtfully, and nodded, finally.

"You have anything else in mind for today other than the gym?"

She shook her head. "I was expecting to be at rehearsal after that, so, no, I have no idea what else to do."

"Weather is crap, you down to come back here, cuddle in bed, and watch some movies?"

Her shoulders dropped and an expression of longing crossed her face, "That sounds so amazing, actually."

I nodded. "We can stop at the store on the way back in, figure out what we want for dinner and snacks."

"Popcorn and Red Vines, if we're doing movies."

"Ooo, yeah. You know how to do it right, don't you?"

She laughed and nodded. "That I do."

We finished our breakfast and talked movies, what each of us liked and what was out at the box-rental kiosks around the city. She didn't get to see many movies when she was overseas, so she was really looking forward to this as a treat. Truthfully, so was I. It sounded like bliss to me. Just me and her, curled up in comfy clothes and relaxing.

"Well," she said, pushing her empty bowl to the center of the table. "Shall we?"

"We shall," I agreed and got up. We got dressed and carried the dishes down to the kitchen. We weren't in a terribly big hurry to get to the gym, needing to give ourselves time to digest. So, we cleaned up the place before we left, leaving the dishwasher to run and getting laundry separated and ready to do when we got back.

She grabbed her overstuffed gym bag and I asked, "Don't you want to empty some of that out?"

"Nope!" she declared and marched right out the door.

I laughed and shook my head.

"Okay."

The ride over to the gym was both damp and brisk, but Claire didn't complain. I was an all-weather, any-season rider, so it didn't bother me. She just kept impressing me, minute by minute, hour by hour, day by day. She'd really pulled herself up by the bootstraps, and I couldn't honestly be any prouder. I gave her a quick kiss and we parted ways at the locker rooms. I geared up to work out and went back out to wait for her. I had a feeling she would want to hit it hard today, as a means of compensation for her assured drop in activity level, thanks to that asshole.

I was a little surprised when she came out of the women's locker room in short little skin-tight black workout shorts and a matching black long-sleeved workout jacket, zipped all the way up. I mean, her attire wasn't all that surprising; what was, was the fact she had her gym bag slung across her chest. She stopped by the climbing ropes and lingered, looking at the center one critically.

"You good, Claire?" I asked, and she nodded faintly, clearly distracted.

McGowan, one of ICPD's training officers, and the one who'd given her a little flak the day before asked her, "How about it, sweetheart? Want to give it a go?"

"Sure, I'll give it a shot," she said cheerfully, and I detected some mischief. "I even bet you that not only will I beat you to the top, I'll do it with this on," she said shaking her bag. McGowan, the arrogant prick that he could be, laughed his ass off at her. A bunch of the other guys around the gym, taking notice that some shit was about to go down, started putting up weights or hopping off machines to come watch the drama.

"Oh, Lord," I muttered and put my hands on my hips.

"Bet you this crisp, one-hundred-dollar bill, you can't hang with me. Not even close. Not even a little bit." She pulled a hundred out of her pocket, and I blinked, wondering where the fuck she'd come up with that.

Laughter swept through the gathering crowd.

"Oh, you're on, sweetheart. Easiest hundred I'll ever make."

"Your girl isn't very smart, Martinez!" someone called out. I looked over, to a guy that used to work with my brother once upon a time.

"I don't know about that, Fitch," I said evenly.

"I do," someone called out with surety.

"McGowan has one of the fastest times in the rope climb in the department, little girl," someone told Claire.

She smiled carefully, stretched some, and said, "Oh, that's nice."

I just stood back as bets started getting placed and cellphones started coming out. McGowan let her have the center rope and went to the third one, closer to the locker rooms. He stretched, and someone stood in to officiate with an official start time, and he and Claire lined up and took positions.

I took a deep breath and let it out slow. The officer dropped his arm and shouted 'Go!' and – holy fucking shit.

Clair gripped the rope, *turned upside-down*, planted the arches of her feet against the rope, and hand-over-hand, foot placed over foot to either side of that rope, she skittered up that fucker like a spider up a web, reaching the top before McGowan got half-way up.

I felt my jaw drop, and I swear, you could hear a pin drop in that gym. Someone called out, "Please tell me you got that shit recorded."

A murmur broke out, but Claire, it seemed, wasn't done. She had righted herself, locking her legs around the rope and holding herself aloft by just her feet while she held onto the U-bolt set in the ceiling. Her other hand, she used to rummage in her gym bag.

"What are you doing?" McGowan called up, panting and sweating, while Claire was hanging up there like a monkey, cool as a cucumber.

"You'll see," she called down. She pulled a connector out of the top of her bag with some cloth attached and hooked it up. "Okay, look out, guys." She then looped the strap of her gym bag off over her head and dropped it.

A voluminous amount of cloth cascaded from the ceiling as the bag fell and struck the blue mats at our feet with a thwack. I was grinning like a madman and silently cheered her on as she transferred from the rope to the silk, holding herself aloft as she toed off her shoes, first one, then the other, to join her bag down on the floor.

She deftly twisted herself in the cloth and stood in two almost-stirrups, as she unzipped her jacket and peeled it off. It fluttered to the floor, and more phones went up to capture what she was up to. She was up there in nothing but the black little short-shorts and a matching black athletic bra, and she looked right at home.

She unfastened the climbing rope and dropped it, getting it out of her way. I went in and started gathering her things up, clearing out underneath her, kind of mesmerized by her level of skill and core strength to be doing some of what she was doing. A couple of the guys, and some female officers who had come in, stared up at her, while another joined me in coiling the climbing rope.

I don't know what I pictured when she said she was a silk dancer, but this isn't what I expected...

Holy shit.

16

*C*laire…

"Can somebody put on the radio or something?" I asked. I reveled in the feeling of the night silks against my skin. Aleksi had handed over the actual performing silks, a beautifully-dyed amalgamation of blues and purples with splatters of white dots across the material. Somehow the dying process used made the silks look like every beautiful rendition of a nebulous galaxy you'd ever seen. With the whispering flow of the material, it was quite beautiful, whether under a spotlight on a darkened stage or under the harsh fluorescent lighting of the gym now.

"Yeah, I got it. Hang on a second!" A woman I didn't know called out from below. She jogged over to the front desk wrap, and the gym's sound system gave a static crackle. She called out, "Any preference as to what you want?"

"Nothing too fast, otherwise I'm open!" I called back.

"How about some AWOL Nation?" she asked.

"*Sail?*" I asked.

"Yeah!"

"Perfect, give me two seconds." I twisted and set myself up for a drop, hanging upside down, holding myself up and letting the blood rush to my head. I took a deep breath, let it out slow, and called out, "Hit it!"

The first notes floated out over the silent workout equipment and I could feel the onlookers below hold their collective breath. I closed my eyes, felt the beat and the first vocals hit, and I let go and threw myself into the routine.

I dropped, plummeting halfway down the silks to cheers and applause, and couldn't help but smile. I danced, moving my body sinuously, winding it through the two hanging sheets of the night silks, twisting myself through them to the music, stretching, arching, artfully letting go and immersing myself into the act.

It was different, freestyling like this, no rigid choreography to hold me down. It had been a while since I enjoyed myself, unfettered by Night Circus company bullshit, and it felt *so* good. I tumbled, swinging the silks out from my hands, giving myself wings and letting myself fly, and the small crowd below went nuts, whistling and cheering.

Honestly, I couldn't care about the lot of them. I only cared about one, and what he thought. I was happy to finally be able to perform for my Angel, to let him see one of the best parts of me, after only seeing some of the worst lately.

I tucked and spun, rolled and stretched, displayed every bit of my athleticism and flexibility, and felt my confidence rise with every gasp, clap, and cheer.

Fuck Milo Sarkisyan and his bullshit unreachable standards. I had met or exceeded every one of them, but I didn't have to anymore. There was no point in me chasing the impossible. I knew I was good. One of the, if not *the* best to have held my position at the Night Circus, and the Night Circus wasn't the end-all of be-all's when it came to this type of performance, either. I had money, I had my name, and I would figure it out.

I did a final drop, the silks pulling tight around my hips as I flung out my arms and arched, looking up and straight into the eyes of the man who loved me as the last notes of the song faded over the gym's sound system. I crooked a finger at Angel to 'Come here' and he obliged, walking up to me casually and kissing me as I hung, suspended from the ceiling, wrapped in the comfort and freedom of my trade.

Everyone around us was going nuts, the applause loud; the ear-splitting whistles louder, and the cheering bolstering my confidence and spirits even more.

"That was amazing," he whispered.

I laughed and said, "That was just me going off the top of my head, I'm just getting started."

He laughed softly and let me go. I looked past him and straightened into a more vertical position, and asked the man who'd asked if I thought I could hang with them yesterday, "So, I ask you again, do you think you can hang with *me?*"

He laughed and hung his head, his hands on his hips, and then reached into one of the cargo pockets of his sweats. He opened up his wallet and handed me five twenties.

"You win, girly," he said, and I tucked the money into my sports bra.

I winked at him. "A pleasure doing business with you."

He laughed a little and I reached up, hand over hand, climbing back to the top. The woman who had set the music asked, "Do you want another song?"

I smiled down at her and said, "Not right now, thanks. I think, if it's alright, I'm just going to practice a few tricks and call it a day."

"You do you, just put the climbing rope back up when you're done," the man I'd won the money off of called.

"Sure."

"Babe, I'm going to get some cardio in," Angel called up.

"Okay! I love you."

He laughed. "I love you, too." He bowed his head and shook it, grinning, before heading over to one of the stair-climbers across the big room.

"How much core strength does that even take?" I heard one of the other guys ask, and I laughed, answering even though the question had been rhetorical.

"A *lot*."

"I wanna learn how to do it!" one of the female officers declared.

"It's not too hard to start; it's actually surprisingly easy," I said, hanging upside down. "Here, come here, I'll show you a couple of things."

"Seriously?"

"Yeah, come on over here."

She walked over, her short blonde ponytail bobbing, and I slid down the silks.

"First off, there's a lot more going on with your legs than you'd expect. It's easier climbing the silks than it is rope, watch me." I pulled myself just off the ground with my arms and layered one foot on the bottom, then, trapping the silk between the top of it and the bottom of my other foot, I stood.

"You can just almost stand here forever and just use the silk for balance so you don't go ass-over-teakettle." To make my point, I gently leaned into the silks and took my hands away, braced against the silks with my shoulder.

"Cool."

"Come on, you try…"

I spent the rest of my time transitioning from the joy of doing to the joy of helping others do.

I hadn't realized that McGowan was not only a part-time training officer, but was also one of five officers on the verge of retirement who owned the gym. He approached me as I was getting ready to put his climbing rope back up.

"Gotta say," he began, "you schooled me, but good, little girl."

I smiled to myself and said, "Sorry, you did kind of make it pretty easy for me."

"I did, I did," he said laughing. "I'll own it. Sometimes the good ol' boys club mentality gets the better of me."

I respected him for that. He itched the side of his face, which was scruffy with a few days' growth. I mean, picture a bald-headed Sam Elliot, fit and aging gracefully. That was this guy.

I was securing the climbing rope by tying the bottom of one of my silks around it so I could climb to the top and haul it up after me when he drifted closer.

"You ever put a mind to teaching this stuff for real? Like some actual classes?" he asked.

"I mean, I could instruct, but my heart is really in performing, why do you ask?"

"I'm about to retire and a cop's pension isn't what it used to be in today's market. This place is supposed to supplement mine and my partner's income, but there are four of us and the plan was to keep this a cop's gym for as long as possible, but lately we been getting too close to not making it with just cops comin' here and paying their dues."

"Ah, is that why you opened it up to family?"

"Yeah. We're probably going to open it up to the public, too, here, soon. Unless…"

"Unless?"

"Well, we been talkin' setting up specialized classes. Like CrossFit and, well, something like what you do could be a thing, too. We got some back rooms that are just being used as storage, collecting dust and the like. We could clean them out and you'd have your own space to practice whenever you like."

"In exchange for teaching some classes?"

"Well, yeah, but you'd be paid for those, too. Nothing like a salary, but we could maybe work something out on a per-class basis." I thought about it. "Think you might be interested?" he asked.

"I could be," I said. "I mean, it would just be a part-time thing, right?"

"Right. I'd need to talk to my partners, of course, before we could solidify anything."

"Yeah," I nodded. "Let me know what they say. I'd be down."

He grinned, "Okay then. I'll let you know. Let me get your information."

I gave him my phone number and email.

"Yeah, let me know," I said, and hoisted myself up the silks. It took effort, but I prided myself on making it look effortless. Angel had stood by silently, smiling to himself and I think he was as excited as I was about the prospect of not having to leave, that there might be money to be made with my craft while staying right here.

I put back up what I'd taken down and with a heavy sigh, clung to the less-forgiving rope and unhooked my silks. I looked down and Angel was there, gathering the bottoms of the silks into my bag. I hooked the top of them into my waistband and worked my way down the rope at a sedate pace so that he could gather them up, and by the time I hit the floor, all I had to do was drop the connections on the top until next time.

"Let's go shopping and let's get home," he said, hooking an arm around my shoulders and pulling me into his side. He kissed my temple and I nodded, bending to grab my shoes and jacket and walking with him towards the locker rooms.

Between the sex last night and the small performance, and the freedom to do what I wanted today, I was more relaxed than I had been in a long time.

I'd needed this.

17

*A*ngel…

When we returned home from the gym and our shopping excursion, she had an email waiting for her from the Night Circus telling her to basically stand by while they investigated the situation, and that they would get back to her as soon as possible. She said she'd give them until the end of the week, before she contacted them again if she hadn't heard from them. I figured that was fair.

In the meantime, I still had to work, which was where I was. That night was a total shit-show.

"Whoa, we got a ped's case. Fuck me and this city, this is gonna be bad."

I frowned and looked over from the driver's seat at Johnson, who was tapping around on the tablet, accepting the call. Tina came over the radio.

"Dispatch 641." I picked up the mic and depressed the talk button.

"641, Dispatch go ahead."

"Alpha 641 you have priority one traffic for a 34-S, male approxi-mately two years old, the scene is Code 4."

"Copy that, Dispatch. Alpha 641 en route." I hung up the mic, flipped the lights and siren and mashed down on the accelerator, kicking it into high gear.

A 34-S was a gunshot victim, Code 4 meant the scene was secured by ICPD. I was dreading this one.

"Who the fuck shoots a two-year-old, man?"

I shook my head. "You know how it goes. These bangers just start spraying bullets and don't give a fuck who they hit."

That was senseless violence that, at least, still made some kind of sense.

What we rolled up on, though? That was evil in its purest form.

"What the fuck is this?" Johnson asked, just as confused as I was.

"I don't know…" I trailed off.

There was a car parked, the driver's door hanging open, just chilling in the middle of the road, cop cars surrounding it, a regular blue-and-white-light disco party lighting up the night sky, strobing over the nearby buildings.

I got out of the truck and made eye contact with Poe. He shook his head and my heart sank. We weren't here to save anybody. We were here to put the call in for an official TOD, or Time of Death.

"What happened?" I asked.

"It's bad, bro. I'm so sorry it's you…" he said.

"Where?" I demanded.

"Still in his car seat." Poe fell into step beside me. "His mom stopped at a gas station over on Morley and 21st. She got out of the car and was headed around to pump her gas when this fool jumps in and takes off, her baby boy asleep in his car seat. Dude pulls a drive-by, kid wakes up and starts screaming, so he shoots the baby in the face."

I rounded the back door and looked in at the small body, its face a pulped and bloody red ruin, and I tried not to gag. My eyes watered and I straightened up immediately.

"Fuck me," I said shaking my head. There was a knot of officers standing off to one side, their faces wet with silent tears, and I was headed there myself.

Johnson shook his head violently and was like, "Nope," and just walked away, over to that knot of officers. I depressed the button on my radio and called into dispatch to relay me to the hospital.

It was Indigo City protocol, you had to have a doctor declare a time of death. We could relay the information, but the doctors had to make the final, official call. A lot of times, the PD would call EMS so that, by the time the coroner got there, they could begin investigating, dispensing with some of the formalities.

I got it done, but this was going to fuck with me, haunt me until the end of days. I crossed myself and prayed for the kid and his mother while I got the paperwork moving so the cops could do their job and catch this piece-of-shit motherfucker.

"Thanks, Angel," Poe said softly and I nodded.

"Welcome. Just go find him."

"Not going to be a problem. Homicide is on their way, but we got some ideas on what's what based on target, etc."

"Don't care; just get him off our streets and do it quick."

"Will do," Poe said, his jaw knotting with determination.

Johnson and I got the hell out of there.

He asked me, "Think this one'll make the news?"

"Hard to say," I said.

"Why?"

I sighed and shook my head. There was a lot of shit that went on in this city that should have been newsworthy. If the kid had been white, there was a better than good chance it would make the news, but it was a lot less likely to make it when it was a neighborhood like this and the kid was brown. The drive-by might be a footnote on the morning news. Maybe, if it was a slow news day, it would make the evening news the next night, but Indigo City was beginning to become desensitized to some of this shit.

Crime was moving out of Baltimore across the bay, had begun infecting Indigo City, creeping into our poorer neighborhoods like some blood-borne pathogen, sweeping through neighborhoods, carried by the network of veins and arteries that were our streets. And on nights like tonight, the pain was bad. Our city was screaming, the skies were weeping, and we were enveloped by a thick, wet blanket of despair.

Every time I closed my eyes I would be seeing the red, pulped ruin of that kid's head on top of his tiny shoulders, his small body still in its little blue jumper and his miniature little Timberland boots. This one was nightmare fuel for *years*, forget just days.

We made it through the last two-and-a-half hours of our double and I was honestly glad that I wasn't going home to an empty house; that Claire would be there. I needed something beautiful and alive, warm and inviting, waiting for me after that. Call me selfish if you want, but her words from our first encounter were echoing back to me.

You can't take care of anyone else unless you take care of yourself.

She was right, and tonight, I needed to practice a little self-care, starting with a little self-medication by way of a few stiff drinks.

I let myself into the house when I got there and she looked up from where she was curled in one of the wingback chairs. She had her laptop perched on her lap, thick socks on her feet and a steaming mug of tea on the little coffee table. She smiled at me over her reading glasses which were black-framed and very 'naughty librarian' but one look at my face and the smile slid right off hers.

"Angel, what's wrong?" she asked gently. She set her laptop by her tea and gracefully got up from her seat.

"Bad call," I said, and my voice cracked.

"Oh, my God, come here," she said, and she came to me.

My knees buckled under the weight of my sadness. This one was affecting me so damn much, and I couldn't hold it in anymore. I don't think anyone could hold it in after what I saw. At least, no one with a soul. She knelt next to me on the floor and pulled me against her, holding me, while I just let it out.

I let her be the strong one for a minute and prop me up, because sometimes as a first responder I encountered things so horrible out there… I needed it, like I'd needed it three years ago, like I needed it now. I'd gotten better about leaning on some of the guys in the club over the last few years, but always had the vague worry that when it came to some of the shit that got to me, they'd think I was some kind of pussy.

I didn't have to worry about that shit this time around. I'd seen the same haunted feeling, the indelible stain on our souls, reflected in Poe's eyes at the scene. I could have reached out to him. Hell, I expected he would reach out to me, and I wanted to be ready if and when he did, because he would need it. Just like I needed it right now.

So I turned into Claire, resting my head on her breast, and wept like a little boy who'd just discovered the monsters were real. I knew that they were. I'd known for years, and I guess it was the mark of a decent man that I could still be shocked this far into a life working the street by what people fucking did to each other, but damn… It was harder and harder to keep the faith.

Claire soothed me. Held me, rocked me, stroked my back and petted my hair, and the seething anger, the impotent rage, drained out of me. Some of the burden of my sadness slipping from my shoulders.

"What happened?" she asked firmly, and I drew back, shaking my head.

"You don't want or need that image in your head, *mi alma.*"

She brushed the moisture from my cheeks with gentle fingertips, her dark eyes deep pools of empathy and concern.

"Want it? Probably not. Need it? If it unburdens your soul, then yes, absolutely, I need you to talk about it, Angel. That's what I'm here for. You were there for me – you *are* here for me. Let me give back."

I sniffed and nodded, and I told her. I tried to keep it vague, tried not to paint too clear a picture, but she was a creative. It didn't take much for her eyes to well and the tears to crest and fall. I pulled her to me and we held each other for a time and mourned for not only the child, but his mother, his family.

"I'm so sorry," she whispered, and I whispered back, "Me, too."

She got me. I got her. We were two souls made one from the moment we met and I couldn't, I wouldn't, let her go.

This, more than anything, was proof that I needed her.

18

*C*laire...

We'd tried him leaning against me in the tub, but his larger frame to my smaller didn't quite work for us, so I had ended up back in front, wrapped in his arms as we sat in warm water, wine glasses at our elbows, champagne fizzing lightly in them. I'd curtailed getting into the whiskey, and the only other thing Angel had was a bottle of champagne in the back of his fridge. He couldn't even remember where it'd come from. It wasn't special, so we'd cracked it open.

"I've never had this," he confessed as we cuddled and took in the night-darkened view of the bay outside our living room window.

"Had what?" I asked.

"This kind of closeness with a woman."

I smiled, "What about with another person, period?"

"My twin, sure, but things changed after he went into the military. He came out more guarded than he went in. Even with me. Like there was some sort of a gap or a rift that wasn't there before. Like a cold glass wall separates us. We can see each other, talk and hear each other, but when we reach out, it's a cold thin layer between us that wasn't there before."

I heaved a heavy sigh and raised a knee, the water sloshing, tinkling gently where it beaded up and fell from my skin.

"I wish I had something I could tell you about that. A magic suggestion to heal you guys, but I'm afraid on the sibling front, I'm in far worse shape than you."

His arms tightened around me and I covered my face with my hands and said, "God, no, oh, my God, I didn't mean for it to come out like that."

He kind of froze, "Come out like what?"

"You are having a bad night, like *the worst*; it shouldn't be about me and my stupid brother at all. You've been far too focused on me the last several days. I want to focus on you. It's not all about me all of the time–" I stopped, his hand was over my mouth. I craned my head back and he looked down at me, his eyes nearly crossing to look down his nose to see me with the angle we were at. I laughed slightly from behind the cover of his mitt over my mouth, and he put it back down into the water.

"We're here for each other, Claire, and I wouldn't have it any other way. Besides, and honestly and truly, things between me and Golden have healed up some in the intervening years. I think it had as much to do with me festering over being mad he left in the first place as much as him having to re-acclimatize to civilian life. That, and he had a mountain of guilt to deal with. Our mother died while he was deployed, and Maria gave him hell about it for a long time."

"Oh, my God, that's awful."

"We aren't perfect, far from it, but we're family."

I laughed but couldn't hold back the bitter edge. "I know that describes mine except for the part where we're family anymore."

He wrapped his arms around me tighter and said, "It's still raw, baby. Give it some time."

I gave a shaky laugh, on the verge of tears again, and said, "Yeah, patience was never my strong suit."

"Hmm, I forgot to ask, anything yet?"

"Nope," I said, popping the 'p'.

"Still a few days left to the end of the week."

"I know, still I feel like climbing the walls when you're at work. I'm having a hard time sitting still."

He laughed some and it was a good sound after so many tears, "Now *that* I can believe. What do you think would help?"

"You know, I don't know, and even if I did manage to get my job back, I'd only have it through the winter while the Night Circus was here. After they go, I'll pretty much be right back to square one."

He kissed my shoulder, paused a moment, then kissed it again, and again, and climbed the side of my neck. I laughed and squirmed from the tickling sensation and he gave the happiest, most satisfied sound, robust and so filled with relief and joy I couldn't help but smile.

"So you're staying, then?"

"I can't leave you again," I said, softly.

"You're sure?"

"Oh, I'm sure. The joy and the thrill of the Night Circus is gone and I just don't think I could ever recapture the magic. You know?"

He nodded and sighed.

"I kind of figured."

"It's really time for me to find something new, and to be honest, I'm really mad at the Night Circus' board and upper echelon. I mean seriously… they ignored it. Let it keep happening, and he assaulted me." I shook my head. "Fuck that. No. That's not how this is supposed to work."

"Does that mean you're going to start looking for a lawyer?" he asked.

"Already started. If they give me my job back and fire Milo, if they do what's right, I'll leave it."

"Sounds like you don't believe for a minute that that's what they'll do."

"I don't. I've worked for them for three years; I know how they operate. If they side with me I'll be surprised, honestly. They had every opportunity to stop him long before it ever got to the point I would swallow a bunch of pills to make it stop." My voice got quiet at the last and he rubbed my shoulders. I closed my eyes and sighed.

"I never asked," he said. "Where did you even get those pills?"

I snorted, "Milo, actually."

I felt him go still and he asked, "Milo had enough opioids for you to OD with and *he gave them to you*?"

"Mm-hm. He doesn't care about whether we're hurt or not. He just pushes pills, tells us to get over ourselves, and either we power through the pain or he finds someone who will."

"You're fucking kidding me, right?"

"Nope. We had a dancer, Marion, from England. Kept complaining of knee pain after she came off a jump a little funky. He told her she was fine; it started to affect her dancing; he gave her the pills. Not only did she end up hooked, but she damaged her knee so bad and so permanently she'll never dance again. Which is why the rest of us are so careful with ourselves."

"Jesus. That's all kinds of fucked up, not to mention illegal."

"Yeah, he got a pretty stern talking-to after that one. He let the troupe's doctor look at us and followed his recommendations more closely after that. Hell, that's how we even got our own sports-medicine guy. Milo still handed out the pills if they were needed, though."

"And that's what happened with you?"

"Yep, I knew he had them, I lied about shoulder pain, and kept collecting them until I was sure I had enough."

"Fuck."

"I'm sorry," I said, suddenly guilty. "I shouldn't be talking about it so matter-of-fact like."

"Don't be sorry, you need to talk about it. I'm glad you feel safe enough to talk about it with me."

"You don't judge me," I murmured. "You never have."

"You didn't judge me, that night, back then…"

"Fair enough, but there wasn't anything for me to judge. I knew that. We all reach our breaking points. It's sad, but it's true. It's not something worthy to judge someone by."

"You are a wise woman, Claire Montgomery. Now if only you would take and apply that wisdom to yourself.

"Well, you know," I said lightly, "I'm more of a 'Do as I say, not as I do' kind of girl."

He laughed and rocked me side-to-side in the water a bit. "That is the God's honest truth!"

I smiled to myself, glad that he had found his smile so quickly.

"Come on," he whispered. "Let's go to bed."

"To sleep or..?"

He chuckled and said, "Sadly, to sleep, but there's no telling. I might poke you awake."

"As long as you poke me with your penis in my vagina, I am totally okay with you poking me awake in the middle of the night. I can't get enough of you."

He made a shocked noise, somewhere between a cough and a '*I can't believe you just said that,*' before saying, "Well, all right then! That's good to know!"

I stood up carefully in the tub, turned around, and dropped back down, straddling his waist. He had a mischievous sparkle in his eyes and his good humor was back despite the tragedy. I put my mouth to his and his hands drifted to my waist as a moan slipped past my lips. I swallowed his answering moan, which was decadent and rich with his lust, and I, of course, wanted more. Much, much, more.

His hands drifted over my skin beneath the cooling bathwater and I boldly reached between us and stroked him. He was already hard, and I had to fight the urge to put him inside me without protection and ride him. While I wasn't opposed to kids someday, I didn't want them right now, and I couldn't trust the effectiveness of my birth control for a month after its interruption.

"Okay, okay, okay!" he cried and I let his bottom lip go from where I'd bitten it, carefully and playfully. He put his hand around mine stilling it on his penis.

"What's wrong?" I asked, and the edge of playfulness came out in my voice.

"Nothing. I'm going to take you upstairs and give you what you want, even though I probably shouldn't, you naughty girl."

"Hm, but you like it when I'm bad."

"Oh, I do, I love it when you're bad."

We fell into kissing again and he finally pulled back and said eagerly, "Come on, up you go!"

I got up, he let the water out of the tub, and we both dried off quickly. I turned around to precede him up the stairs and he gave me a light smack on my ass. I jumped and squealed in surprise before I picked up the pace. He chased me up to the second floor where I pushed him down on the bed. He lay down, compliant, and put his hands behind his head waiting and watching what I would do.

I went for the condoms. I know he needed to sleep. He had a long day ahead of him in the morning. I rolled the condom deftly down his cock and chased it over him pretty quickly by sliding him into my body, sinking down slowly to let it adjust, my pussy giving a deep and throbbing ache like '*Yes!*'

"Shit, Claire," he said breathlessly, his hands cupping my breasts as I rolled my hips. I danced for him, working my body sinuously and sensually, rolling my hips and letting the motion carry up through the rest of my body, putting on an erotic show, just for him, as I made love to his body below mine. He reached up and dragged me down so that he could kiss me, his hips taking over where mine left off, rising and falling, his cock sliding in and out of me slowly but evenly.

I lost myself in his touch as much as he drowned in mine, and it was beautiful. I had never shared myself so completely with another person and had them do the same in return, and felt it like I did with Angel.

"God, Claire, I love you so much," he whispered and I glowed from it.

I rested my forehead against his and closed my eyes, and soaked in the emotion and sentiment, and whispered back, "I love you, too, so much… I don't know what I was thinking leaving you like I did." And it was true. Even after only one night with him.

We took ourselves past the ability to speak, our breath coming in sharp, passionate gasps and panting, the pleasure rising, climbing, taking us high and higher still, giving us wings and letting us fly until, in a beautiful tragedy, we lost our wings to the burning sun and plummeted back to earth, sailing down, down, down, and crashing back to earth, back to stark reality in each other's arms.

We lay panting on top of the covers, our bodies slick with sweat and sex, catching our breaths and remarkably, emotionally-healed by our physical exertions.

At least for now.

19

*A*ngel…

"Man, the weekend can*not* come fast enough," Backdraft said, flopping down into the seat beside mine at the dinner table.

"Yeah, I feel you," I said, and he eyed me carefully.

"Last night was a rough call, I hear."

I nodded. "Man, if I hadn't had Claire to go home to, it would have been a lot rougher."

He grinned and nodded. "I like her," he declared. "It's good you have that, bro. I feel the same about Lil. It's like, things were good before her but it was always like a piece was missing."

I nodded and said, "That's exactly what it feels like, dude. You took the words right out of my mouth."

He clapped me on the back.

"How's she doing, anyway?"

"Still waiting to hear back from the Night Circus but she's not expecting much on that front. An opportunity opened up over at the Thin Blue Line for her. At least, maybe. She's waiting to hear back from McGowan."

"Oh yeah, what's that about?"

"You haven't seen it?" I asked. "I figured everyone had by now, I keep getting texts and messages about it."

"Naw, man. What're you talking about?"

"Hey!" I called out and a bunch of guys who were talking in the station house's living room looked over. "You guys actually watching that over there?"

"No, we're just talking, why?"

"Cool, I want to pull something up on the TV." I brought out my phone. Some of the guys around here were tech-crazy and we all had our phones synced with the TV. One of the guys picked up the TV remote and flipped it over to the input and my phone's screen popped up. I brought up YouTube and punched in the search term that would bring up Claire's performance at the Thin Blue Line.

The sound blared out a little loud and I turned it down from my phone, but it captured a bunch of the guy's attention as she and McGowan squared off to climb. Backdraft lost his shit when she straight up smoked him.

"It gets better, dude, just watch."

We settled back and she dropped that gym bag and Barnaby, one of the guys, called out, "Angel, is that your new girl? The suicide call you went on?"

"Yeah, and don't put it like that, man. I don't want that shit to be what she's known for. I knew her a long time ago before that even came up for her. That was just how we reconnected."

"My bad," Barnaby replied.

"Jesus, Barn." Ripley shook his head.

"What?"

Barnaby wisely didn't push it, just went back to watching Claire sitting up in her silks, asking for music. Everybody watched appreciatively as she went through her freestyle routine, and no surprise, one of the first comments made was out of Johnson, saying, "Man, she must be fun as hell in the bedroom with all that flexibility." He gave a low whistle.

"Dude! Respect, that's Angel's woman. You talked about my Lil like that, I'd knock your damn teeth down your throat." Backdraft scowled at Johnson who immediately shut his skinny ass up. Johnson, in typical fashion, got butt-hurt and got up, moving away from us to sulk. I shook my head.

"Man, I miss my old partner."

"How she doing?"

"You know, I don't know. Haven't heard much from her since she hit Florida. Funny how that works out, some people you work with, you think you're tight, you think you're friends, then they move on and it's like you're forgotten. You really were just a job."

"Wow, that's seriously how you feel about that one?"

"I mean, yeah. I've sent her messages and she's read 'em. It's said she's read 'em, but she don't answer back."

"Now, that's some bullshit. I'm sorry, man."

"Tell me about it. I hate to sound like a pussy, but that hurts."

"Maybe she's got something going on."

"Maybe, but is it really so hard to say so?"

"You've got a point there." Backdraft heaved a sigh and looked around. "Johnson getting on your nerves?"

I nodded. "It's not a good fit. I think he doesn't fit with anybody, to be honest with you."

"That's why they put him with you," Backdraft said dryly. "You've got God's own patience, bro. You *do* fit with anybody."

"Yeah, well, I guess it's saying something that I don't fit with him."

"Yeah, yeah it is. Gonna request a different partner?"

"Thinking about it."

"Hey, Angel! Let's go, man we got a call!" Johnson called from down below.

I heaved myself to my feet and said, "Duty calls." Backdraft and I grasped hands and I pulled myself down to tap shoulders.

"Be careful out there."

"Always."

"You should bring your lady for dinner. That was some impressive shit," Ripley said, as I passed him.

"Yeah, I'll suggest it to her," I said, and took the brass pole down to the first floor. I jumped into the passenger side of the rig and Johnson pulled out of the open garage door, tripping the lights, but waiting until we hit the end of the drive to hit the sirens.

I didn't really speak to him, still pissed about his inappropriate comment about Claire. It just wasn't something you said to a man about his woman. Not when it was serious.

By the end of the shift, I had put in my request to be partnered up with someone else. I didn't throw him under the bus and say why I wanted to be swapped, and I had a feeling it was a question I was going to be asked. The sad reality was, I had a laundry list of reasons. I didn't want to see the guy lose his job, and I was afraid for him on that front. It wasn't a good situation to be in, yet there I was.

I just hoped that Claire's night was going better than mine was.

20

Claire...

I skipped down the steps and went down into the urban market. I'd had to get out of the house. I was someone who constantly had to be moving or doing something and there were only so many books I could read without starting to climb the walls. We needed some things around the place, nothing super-essential, but enough to warrant a trip to the store.

It was a ways away from the marina, but a familiar market to me, being close to my brother's. I had walked there, and planned to take a car back. Rideshare apps had made city life so much easier in that regard, and I loved that.

I picked one of the little double-decker half-buggies out of the line of them. I liked those, too. Bigger than a basket, but smaller than a traditional shopping buggy, they seemed more efficient and less wasteful. I took a deep cleansing sigh and headed into the store, starting with the produce section. It felt good to be doing something even as mundane as grocery shopping. Especially, after the news I'd gotten, which had been expected, but still hurt.

I was still fired and Milo still had his job.

They were circling the wagons around him, and no, I wasn't going to go quietly. I'd already spoken to a lawyer, and after listening to all I had to say? He was already drawing up paperwork and seeing dollar signs. I hadn't told management everything – why would I? They had every opportunity to do the right thing, and had taken a pass. All bets were off, now.

Still, I felt down. I felt shitty, and for some reason, it seemed the universe just wanted to pile it on.

"Auntie Claire!"

My little niece's exuberant voice broke me out of my sightless staring at the carrots. I looked over as she broke free from her mother and came bounding over. She was wearing her little tap shoes, and her light pink tights peeked out from under her heavy, brighter-pink winter coat.

"Heyyy!" I cried, laughing nervously as she threw her five-year-old self into my arms. I picked her up and hugged her, because it wasn't her fault the adults weren't getting along. Still, I looked for Carter and didn't find him. When I didn't see him, I relaxed a little.

"Urgh! You're choking me!" I mocked, and laughed as her grip got just a little bit stronger where her arms were behind my neck.

"Gracie, come here, let's give Auntie Claire a bit of a breather, okay?" Mallory, her mother, called out. I set her down and tried not to cringe on the outside. She hadn't said so, but I heard the 'crazy' in Mallory's tone just the same; as in *Let's not agitate crazy Aunt Claire.'*

Of course, it could just be me projecting. I hadn't spoken to Mallory at all, not since before I'd taken all those pills. I also had no idea what Carter had told her. The whole thing left me feeling embarrassed and like I was standing on shaky ground. I didn't like the feeling at all.

Mallory took Gracie's hand and smiled at me, asking, "Claire, how are you doing?"

"Fine," I said, nodding. "Surprisingly, everything is good."

"Yeah?" she asked, taken aback, and it flipped the switch on my suspicion.

"I'm doing everything I should be doing," I said, nodding again. That wasn't exactly true. I was taking my medication they'd prescribed and I *was* feeling better, but I hadn't followed up with any therapy once I'd been released. I probably needed it, but I felt okay. Solid again. I had to credit that to Angel more than anything, for giving me someone to talk to, for loving me when I felt unlovable, and for providing me a safe, quiet place to heal.

She sighed and looked at me, a worried expression on her face. I shifted uneasily on my feet, unsure what to say. She broke the awkward silence first.

"I really wish you would reconsider and come back home, with us," she blurted.

I frowned.

"What?" I asked.

Her expression went from sympathetic and concerned to bewildered. I turned my head slightly and let out a sigh of pure frustration.

"Carter said —" and I raised a hand to stop Mallory in her tracks.

"I don't know what Carter told you, Mal, but I promise you, me not coming back wasn't *my* choice. What really happened was, he didn't care. He didn't want to know why. All he cared about was whether or not you and Gracie would have been the ones to find me like that, and he said he'd bring my stuff and that was it. I had to go. He wasn't about to have me back in your house to try again." I shook my head, tears stinging the backs of my eyes.

"Oh, my God, Claire…" Mallory looked stricken.

"Don't be sad, Auntie Claire," Gracie begged and I sniffed.

I knelt down and told her, "It's okay to be sad sometimes, Gracie. Just not all of the time, okay? If it's all of the time, you need to talk to somebody, okay?" She nodded and I smiled. "Come give me another hug," I said, before I lost it.

She hugged me tight around my neck again and said miserably, "I miss you."

"I miss you, too, little girl."

"Claire, I don't know what to say," Mallory said and it was true. She looked as speechless as anyone could get.

I stood up and shook my head, "There's nothing *to* say. I'm gonna go. It would probably be best if you didn't tell Carter you saw me."

I left abruptly, overwhelmed and fighting back tears. I loved my sister-in-law, adored my niece, and even though he was a total asshole now, I missed my brother. He was the only family I had left, so this was hard. Incredibly hard.

"Claire, wait!" Mallory called out, and I stopped outside on the sidewalk when I heard Gracie's running steps, her little tap shoes clacking against the pavement.

I didn't want her to get hurt, so I turned around and caught her as she flung herself at me. She was fighting back tears and cried mournfully, "Don't go! Not like that, don't be sad!"

"Gracie's right, Claire. Come inside, finish your shopping and *talk to me*. We're your family, too. Even…" she faltered a bit, then made up her mind and said resolutely, "Even if Carter isn't acting like it."

I sniffed and stared at my sister-in-law, my niece hugging me around my waist, looking up at me hopeful, and I couldn't resist that face even if I tried. I felt a deep concern of my own over her and Mallory's well-being, stemming from Mallory's siding with me over my brother. The fact she even remotely believed me over Carter spoke volumes. There was trouble with my brother's marriage, but I couldn't say I was totally surprised. Carter had turned into a control freak. The problem was, how to stop it? He lived for Mal and Gracie. I may have been hurt by my brother, but I still loved him and I didn't want to see him lose his family.

"Have things gotten that bad?" I asked Mallory, sensitive about asking something like that in front of Gracie, but my curiosity was over-whelming at this point.

"I *didn't* think so," she said, drawing near and hooking her arm through mine to guide me back down the stairs and into the market. Gracie echoed her mom on the other side, her little hand in mine. I realized my typically-exuberant niece was being uncharacteristically quiet and reserved and I knew she was a smart girl. I shot Mallory a pointed look and looked down at Gracie. Mallory nodded and gave a big sigh.

"I didn't think so, but apparently so," she supplied and I nodded and had to read between the lines. I assumed she was talking about Carter lying to her, which he clearly had about me. We went through the grocery's sweeping automatic glass doors and headed back in the direction of the colorful fruit and vegetable displays.

"We should have dinner," she said after we found our abandoned buggies, right where we'd left them in the produce section.

"Oh, I don't know…" I said.

"Seriously!" she cried.

"Yeah!" Gracie echoed enthusiastically.

"We could even have dinner wherever *you're* staying if that would make you more comfortable. Speaking of, I really hope you'll let me drive you home after we're done here."

"Oh, I really don't know…" I trailed off.

"Pleeeease?" Gracie begged. "I wanna see your house!"

"Oh, honey, I don't have a house," I said.

"What hotel are you staying at?" Mallory asked.

I shook my head. "I'm not staying at a hotel. I'm staying with someone."

"Oh." She looked at me, her eyes widening a little and she blinked, surprised, the sentiment echoed in her exclaimed, *"Oh!"*

I blushed and put some carrots into a bag, weighed them to make sure I had enough, added some more, and, satisfied, put them in the buggy.

"What does that mean?" Gracie asked.

I laughed a little and said, "It means that it's not my house, it's my friend's house; I'm just staying there."

"Oh. Well then I want to see her house!"

"It's not a she, honey. Angel is a man."

"His name is Angel?" Gracie asked, scrunching her nose.

"Well, no, his name is Ramiro, but all of his friends and family call him Angel."

"How come?"

Because he is one, I thought, but I didn't know how to explain that one. I looked to Mallory for help, and she just looked at me, amused, like I was on my own.

"That is a very long story for another time."

"When?"

"When you're older," I said, and Gracie rolled her eyes and gave an exasperated sigh.

"That's what Daddy tells me when he doesn't want to tell me."

Mallory chuckled and I fought not to smile. I knew she was smart for her age. I also knew she was about to be six, going on thirty-six. Gracie had my brother's habit of wanting to know everything, even things that were no five-going-on-six-year-old's business. Like trying to put herself in the middle of her parent's issues.

Genetically, she had a lot of her father in her, and as a result, I had no worries for my niece. She would go far and be quite successful in life once she got to be old enough to put that moxie to use. She would be just fine.

As long as she's not like you and tries to join the circus.

God forbid she become passionate about something other than a strait-laced job that would earn her money and praise. I already knew how that would go over with my brother. Something like a balloon filled with lead.

Nothing seemed good enough for Carter other than what his idea of success was. I'd learned that the hard way and I hoped that Gracie never had to.

We finished our shopping and I followed Mallory and Gracie to the garage. Gracie got herself settled in her booster seat and Mallory asked me where she could take me. I directed her to the marina where Angel's houseboat was moored, and Mallory asked, "When would be a good night for the four of us to have dinner?"

"Four of us?" I asked, unsure if she meant me and her little family of three, or if she were including Angel.

"Yes," she said evenly. "You, your man, your brother, and I."

"I didn't know if you meant Gracie," I stammered.

Gracie piped up from the back.

"Yeah, mom! Why can't I come?"

"Because the adults need to talk, baby."

Gracie harrumphed and went back to her tablet and whatever little game she was playing that had frogs' ribbiting all over the place.

"I really don't know how I feel about the whole idea, to be honest," I murmured. "When were you thinking?"

"How about Sunday?" she asked, and I shook my head.

"Angel and I already have dinner plans for Sunday night. He's a devout Catholic and takes his nephew every Sunday. We're supposed to go to his brother's for dinner that night."

"Oh, well, scratch that, then." Mallory laughed, and it held an edge of something I couldn't define but it almost sounded like nervousness. I guess the whole thing was really awkward. I mean, they'd never heard of Angel before. I hadn't talked about him.

"Let me call you," I said gently, as she pulled down into the lot of the marina. "Something next week maybe. I would like to talk to Angel about it first."

"Okay," Mallory said, a bit dubiously. "Just promise me that you *will* call."

I nodded and said, "I can at least promise you that."

She leaned across the center console and hugged me and I thanked her for the ride. A little, solemn voice came from the back seat.

"Auntie Claire, when will *I* see you again?"

"Soon," I said. "I just need to sort things out with your daddy."

"I don't know why he doesn't like you," she said sadly, and I felt my eyes mist. I exchanged a look with Mallory, who looked like she was on a slow simmer.

"Your daddy loves your Auntie Claire," Mallory said.

Gracie looked up at her and said, point-blank, "He doesn't act like it."

I tried not to laugh, and I almost felt sorry for my brother with the sour look Mallory had on her face. It was a bad sign if Gracie were picking up on the strife between us. Of course, I had no idea what he'd been saying or how he'd been acting in my absence, but I definitely knew it wasn't good. I think Mallory was on the verge of killing him between that and the bald-faced lie he'd told her.

I got out of the car after a few more careful words with my niece, and they watched as I keyed myself into the gate and walked down the dock. They watched all the way until I disappeared into Angel's houseboat, and when I shut the door, I finally felt like I could relax.

"*Mi alma,* are you okay?"

I jumped and let out a shriek, dropping the groceries and clapping my hands over my racing heart.

"You scared the shit out of me!" I cried.

He laughed and came to me, putting his arms around me and holding me tight. I held to him, waiting for my heart to settle, the adrenaline surge from the fear, to dissipate.

"You're home early," I murmured and he chuckled.

"Had some stuff to deal with."

"Oh, no… I'm sorry, I didn't mess anything up by not being here, did I?"

"Oh, no. It's nothing like that. I actually just walked in the door a minute or two before you, so it's all good. We were talking about *you,* though. What's going on?"

I told him about running into Mallory and Gracie at the store, about how Carter had lied to Mallory and told her that I had been the one to make the decision to cut ties, and about Mallory's suggestion that the four of us have dinner.

Angel put a hand to the back of his neck and said softly, "Son of a bitch…"

"I wish I could disagree on the sentiment, but I can't. Still, our mother was actually a fantastic woman and it's not her fault."

"No, babe, of course not. I didn't mean it like that, I'm sorry." He crushed me to his chest, burying his hand in the back of my hair and kissing the top of my head. I cuddled against him and marveled at how safe and just warm everything was when I was in his arms. The world made sense to me from here, and it was a feeling I cherished. I swore I would never take it for granted.

"I know that," I said, giggling. I sighed and looked up at him. "I don't know what to do. I wanted to talk to you and see what you thought."

"I think it's a good idea."

"You do?"

"Yeah. It sounds like your sister-in-law is on your side. You know *I'm* on your side. I think it's high time your brother got called out on some of his bullshit."

"Why do I feel queasy even thinking about it that way?" I asked.

"Because you want him to love you and approve of you, and he doesn't. That won't ever stop you from wanting it, though."

"Well, gee, look at you being all profound… You're right, though."

"Mm, I know I'm right on this one," he said smacking a kiss on my forehead and letting me go so we could pick up the groceries starting to roll across the floor. I realized the house was rocking and frowned. I couldn't ever remember it doing that before.

"Is the houseboat *rocking?*" I asked.

"Yeah, storm is coming in."

"Bad?" I asked.

"Not bad enough that I want to go to Golden's. At least, not yet. Let's get this stuff put away and I'll turn on the news."

"Okay."

He helped me get the two canvas grocery sacks reloaded and over to the kitchen counters.

"I think we should have that dinner with your family here," he said.

"Are you sure?" I asked.

"Yeah, for a few reasons."

"Okay, like what?"

"One, so they can see you're safe. Two, because this is your house. You live here and if your brother gets too out of line you can tell him to get the fuck out."

I blinked at him stupidly and asked him, "You haven't even met him, and you *really* don't like him, do you?"

"Nope. He's being a total asshole to you, and I think it's bullshit. I'm actually pretty pissed at him, but I can be cool and bite my tongue. At least, until you tag me in, babe. Then I can't promise anything. All bets are off."

I sighed and leaned a hip against a counter. The houseboat shifted again and Angel and I traded sharp looks.

"I'm going to turn on the weather channel. I'll be right back."

"Good idea," I said. "I had no idea a storm was supposed to be coming in. I walked to the store just fine and there was a stiff breeze when I got out of the car, but it seems like it's picking up fast out there, now."

"Yeah, and I don't like it much," he called down from upstairs. I heard the TV come on and he flipped channels. I put the rest of the things I'd bought at the store away and went up to join him. He was frowning slightly.

"Yeah, get a bag together, with a change of clothes for both you *and* me. Don't forget something to sleep in. I'm going to go out and shutter the windows."

"Okay," I said carefully.

"It's going to be a cold ride, possibly wet. I think we may have waited too long for it to be comfortable."

He shut off the TV and went out the sliding glass door and onto the top deck.

I set about getting the things he asked for together and let out a heavy sigh. Good Lord, it felt like the hits just kept on coming, lately. If it wasn't one thing it was another. I mean, I was used to living life at a hundred miles an hour but this was ridiculous! I just wanted everything to slow down for just five goddamned minutes! Was that too much to ask for?

It had been overcast and grey and heading into evening twilight when Mallory had dropped me off. It was getting dark *fast*. I worried a bit when the houseboat shifted noticeably again, but it honestly wasn't too bad. I was just so used to it feeling solid I sometimes forgot it was a boat at all.

When Angel came back inside from letting down the last shutter downstairs, he had to wipe the rain from his face.

"That doesn't look good," I commented dryly, setting the two gym bags I'd packed on the dining room table. "Grabbing toiletries," I called and went into the bathroom.

"I don't need any, I've got a set over there."

"Okay," I called back. I threw mine together and brought them out, tossing them into the top of my bag, zipping it closed.

"Come on, I don't want to be riding out in this for long. I just want to get over to Golden's and call it good."

"Guess we're getting that family dinner early," I said, dryly.

"With Lys and Manolo, maybe. Golden is probably at work and I am probably going to have to go back in. Medical emergencies don't give a shit if it's storming."

"Wait, so you came home just to seal this place up and take me someplace safe?"

"Yeah," he said with a reckless grin. "I love you."

"I love you, too, but you could have just called me, told me to seal it up and get a hotel for the night."

He shook his head. "No need for you to do all that. I could get the shutters down in half the time and you're family. We look out for our own."

He held out his hand and I took it. I smiled and shook my head and with a gusty sigh asked, "Shall we, then?"

"My lady." He held out his arm and I took it. We went out into the rain and dashed up the dock, our bags slung across our chests, bouncing against our hips.

The ride was cold and miserable, but mercifully short. He pulled into a driveway and down in front of a garage door, and revved his bike loudly, twice. The door raised and his twin stood in the recess of his garage looking amused. He pulled his motorcycle in alongside Golden's, which was much drier, and cut his engine.

"What are you doing here?" Angel asked, as the garage door trundled closed, shutting out the pounding rain. I felt like a wet cat, and stood by, taking off my helmet.

"Meal break: cruiser's out front, Pruitt's upstairs. Hurry your ass up, and we'll drop you by the station house."

"Dude, bro, you're saving my life," Angel said.

"Hey, Claire. Lys is upstairs waiting to give you the grand tour."

"Hi, and thank you." I ducked my head and Golden grinned.

We followed him upstairs and back to the kitchen.

"Oh my god, you poor drowned thing!" Lys cried. "Come on, I'll show you up to your room and bathroom first, so you can get a hot shower and into some dry clothes."

"I've got to get back to the firehouse, so I'll be back here later."

"Okay," I murmured. I was a little freaked-out at being left alone with his family. I think that had more to do with my earlier interaction with my own, though. I'd met Golden before, and I had been looking forward to meeting Lys this Sunday. So what if it was a few days sooner?

Angel leaned down and kissed my fears away, and his brother broke it up by clapping loudly.

"Okay, okay, okay! We get it. We gotta get going. Claire, make yourself at home. Y'all have free run of the guest room when Angel gets back tonight." He turned to Lys and said, "Baby, I love you, save me some dinner." He leaned down and gave her a quick kiss and a smack on the ass. She yipped and jumped and laughed, turning scarlet. Angel spared me the indignity of the ass-smacking in front of people I didn't know and handed me his gym bag to take up for him instead, with a final quick smack of lips onto my own.

"Be careful!" I called after the three of them as they went for the front door and the police cruiser that had been parked at the curb when we'd pulled in.

"As a virgin on her wedding night!" Golden's partner called back. Lys and I exchanged a look and rolled our eyes.

"Come on, I'll show you upstairs."

I followed her up to the second floor and she flipped on a light to a bathroom saying, "Please, grab a hot shower, by all means. I still have a ways to go on dinner."

We passed the open door to Manolo's room where he sat on his bed, a comic book open on his lap.

"Hi, Manolo," I called out.

"Hey, Claire…" he said, his voice sort of far-away. Whatever he was reading, he was really into it. Lys smiled and shook her head.

"That boy and his comic books," she said with a gusty sigh.

"Could be video games!" he shot back, and Lys rolled her eyes.

"Those, too!" she returned, and opened the door to a guest room. The bedroom set was masculine and blocky, not what I would have expected for a guest room.

She smiled a little wryly and said, "It's Golden's old bedroom set. When we first lived together it was as roommates. When we moved in together, we picked something for the master bedroom that was more… 'us.'"

"Too many conquests?" I asked, and she smiled, amused.

"You said it, not me. Don't let yourself get grossed out; the mattress is new. His old one went out with the trash."

I laughed and shook my head. "I could tell you how it goes when it comes to living with a bunch of other circus performers."

"Oh?"

"Mm, most of the time, you don't lose your guy or your girl. You just lose your turn."

"Ew! Gross!"

"Tell me about it. That's why I would either get them fresh or keep my happy ass single."

"Right, well, you get comfortable, I'm going to go pour some wine, and we can carry on this conversation while I finish up supper."

I laughed and set down my bag on the footlocker at the foot of the bed and set down Angel's bag next to it.

"Wine sounds fabulous," I said, and she ducked out the door. I pulled out dry clothes and went and took a long, hot shower.

21

*A*ngel…

It wasn't too bad. The calls, not the storm. The storm was a beast, but we only had to go out in it twice. Once was to give oxygen to a woman whose power went out; her travel tanks were low, and with the power out, her home unit couldn't run. We did a quick-and-dirty and swapped out the truck's full travel tanks for her empties and just refilled them from the big tank back at the house.

The second call was a heart attack. That guy made it to the hospital, but passed before we could get done with the paperwork. That was a bummer, but it was also one of the tough realities of being a medic. We'd done our job. We'd done a great one. We got him to the hospital. If Trinity Gen couldn't save him, then there was no saving him. Period.

Golden swung by in Lys' cage to pick me up after his shift and we rode over to his place together.

"So, given what she's been through, she doing okay?" he asked when we got through our usual chit-chat.

"She's had a real shitty day," I said. "I'd be lying if I said I wasn't worried."

He grunted an affirmative and said, "I kind of figured that. She looked a little wrung out."

"Yeah, well, between her job and her brother, it feels like I'm the only thing holding her together right now."

"Eh, that's not good, bro."

"Oh, shit, no! It's fine. I'm not worried about it at all," I said. "I can do it. I know I can, and I will for as long as she needs it. That part is all good. I just want to fix some of it for her, you know?"

Golden nodded carefully, his eyes on the sheeting rain coming down the windshield, the wipers going full bore and still having trouble keeping up. The only good news? The streets were fucking empty, partially from the time of night, but mostly from the storm.

"I can imagine, bro. You just can't fix everything, you know?"

"Oh, I know, trust me. I totally get it, G. That's what's driving me nuts about this whole thing. I mean, the job is a bit of a mourning period because she's leaving behind a bunch of people that were like family to her, but she gets another one and moves on. I think what's really killing her is her brother." I shook my head. "I can't imagine what I would feel like if you did something like that to me."

Golden snorted like I was some kind of epic dumbass and said, "You don't have to imagine that shit. It would never happen."

I stared out the window, quiet for a while, and said quietly, "What would have happened if she hadn't come along, G? What if I'd suck-started my gun that night?"

"Truthfully?" he asked.

"No, fuckin' lie to me."

He laughed a little, "Well, in *that* case, I probably would have thrown an epic party and invited all of the guys to roast marshmallows over your barbecuing corpse."

"Vivid picture," I said and snorted.

"Seriously, though," he said, without even acknowledging my comment. "I would have been pissed, I would have been hurt, but I wouldn't have been able to lie to myself or anyone else and say I didn't understand." He was quiet for a second, the sheets of rain drumming across the roof of the car and spattering across the windshield as we waited on a red light. A gust of wind rocked the car and I winced, trying not to think about my houseboat.

"Angel, you aren't the only one to go through rough times like that, man. I can't judge. I just dealt with it different."

"Yeah, like how?" I asked. I didn't believe him. He was always the stronger of the two of us.

"Like instead of suck-starting my service weapon, I took my happy ass out and drowned myself in meaningless pussy, hoping one of them would be my Claire." He shook his head, the light turned green, and he accelerated through the intersection.

"I never thought about it like that."

"Well, now you know my secret. I wouldn't want to burden you with my shit, just like I guess you didn't want to weigh me down with yours."

"Fuck me, we need to knock that shit off, huh?"

"Well, it's easier for the both of us now," he said. "But, yeah. We need to go back to our roots sometimes, dude. Those times where it was you and me against the world."

I gave a rough chuckle, choking up a bit and said, "It'll always be you and me against the fuckin' world, Man. Except now it's a little bit more than that. It's you and me, and Claire, and Lys."

"And Manolo, and Maria, and the rest of the guys with the club," he reminded me.

"And everyone on the ICPD."

"And ICFD."

"Shit." We said it in unison.

"I mean, we always wanted a big family," I said, laughing.

"Yeah," he agreed.

"Remember how we used to get fuckin' jealous of all the other Mexican and Dominican kids in our classes when they'd come back and talk about all their cousins and cousin's cousin's cousin's…"

Golden laughed, "Shit, yeah. We were like aliens from another fuckin' planet, just being us, Abuela, Mama, and Maria."

"Yeah, we laugh about it now, but back then it sucked balls."

"You always want what you can't have," he said with a shrug.

"You know, you're right," I said.

"But?" he asked, knowing one was there.

"Except, I don't really want anything except for shit to get straight so Claire can be happy."

He nodded. "I can't say there's anything I want either. I kind of have it all."

I grinned. "Yeah, you do."

He grinned back and pulled up to the curb in front of his place and threw it into park.

"Yeah, I do," he echoed. "You will too, bro. Just give shit time to settle. She's still in the thick of it."

"Yeah, I know," I said, staring up at his darkened windows. There was a glimmer of light on the top floor, which meant Lys was probably still up, but all I wanted was to go in and crawl into bed beside Claire.

"Come on, man. It ain't gonna dry out any out there."

"Fuck me, that's the truth."

"Hell of a lot warmer and dryer between the sheets," he declared, going for his door handle.

I smirked. "Then you're doing it wrong."

"Ha ha, fuck you," he said, deadpan.

"Not into twincest, how many times I gotta tell you that?"

We dashed up the steps and he went to unlock the door saying, "I should leave your ass out here."

"Better not, mofo. Nobody gets between me and my woman."

He laughed and said, "You don't know how long I've waited to hear you say something like that, man." He shook his head and shoved open the door. "I'm really happy for you."

"Yeah?" I asked.

"Yeah."

I followed him up the stairs and when we parted ways at the second floor, he gave a little salute and made his way up to the top floor and the master suite where Lys waited. I grinned and crept quietly past Manolo's room and went to the guest room, where I found Claire fast asleep despite the storm outside.

I didn't wake her. Instead, I grabbed out a clean pair of underwear from the bag I'd packed and went for a hot shower to warm up. Last thing I wanted to do was get into bed and put my chilled skin against her. Actually, it was the first thing I wanted to do, but I didn't think Claire would appreciate it much, so a hot shower first. I rushed through it, wanting her so badly I sported a hard-on through the whole shower, and the closer I got to getting into that bed with her, the harder I got.

I dropped off my damp uniform and things by the chair my bag was sitting on and shoved them out of the way up under it to keep them from being a tripping hazard. I tried to keep quiet, but Claire was out, so fast asleep she was dead to the world. I stood back up carefully and went around the bed to get in with her, lifting the blankets and easing in behind her.

"Huh? What?" She woke with a start, her tone startled and demanding, and I chuckled.

"Just me, baby."

"Hmm." She snuggled back into the curve of my bigger body and I spooned her, the rub of her ass against my cock tantalizing, to say the least.

She wriggled again a moment later and I kissed her behind her ear, growling into it, "Do it again, you're getting fucked."

"Hmm." She made that noise again, sultry and rich, her slight laugh throaty and sexy as she ground her ass against me one more time.

"Fuck me," I murmured.

She laughed again, a lighter, more amused noise, and murmured seductively, "Don't mind if I do."

I was already raising her leg, lifting it back over the top of mine. I'd already freed my cock by shoving my boxer briefs down and out of the way. I laughed a little, in a *'You've got to be kidding me'* sort of way when my fingertips delved along her front and found she didn't have any panties on… just one of my shirts.

I didn't think about anything, forgot a condom completely, and slipped inside of her. She gasped and drove her hips back and down to meet my thrust as my hand skated under my shirt that she wore and grasped the soft mound of one of her perfect tits.

Her body wrapped around mine like hot, wet silk. Slick velvet heat stroked up my shaft and teased the head of my cock with a warm press of her walls. She was getting wetter, slicker by the moment, and I loved how enthusiastically her body took me in.

While I loved to talk a good game, tell her things like how much I wanted to fuck her, I never really did. No matter how passionate it got, no matter how hard I thrust, no matter how much her nails bit into my back or my ass, we never *fucked*. We always made love, but right then had to be my favorite time with her so far. I loved her, low and slow, thrusting sensually, listening to her soft panting breaths in the close dark. Her body, moving in rhythmic counterpoint to my own, met me with an easy sinuous roll of her hips, stroking down to meet my every upward stroke into her.

It was calming, soothing, and utterly hypnotic, and I couldn't tell you how long we were like that together, making love. Minutes or hours, it was like time stopped, for us to have this eternal moment together and I loved that about her, too. I loved that we lost ourselves in each other so completely that time just stopped making sense and neither of us cared.

"Oh, God, Angel." Her voice was a low whispered caress in the dark as she writhed against me. Her orgasm caused her to shiver, her legs trembling uncontrollably as her body milked my cock for everything it was worth. I couldn't hold out against that if I wanted to, driving into her one last time and letting her have all of me.

Shit! No condom.

"Fuck!" I muttered aloud, and she stiffened and I felt our first fight may be on the horizon and she had every fucking right to be pissed the fuck off at me.

It was like she read my mind. She went very, very still and asked, "You didn't put a condom on, did you?"

"No, I meant to stop, to –"

"Angel," she said gently, "You're a medical professional, since when is pulling out a responsible method of birth control?"

"No, you're right, I… *fuck*! You're totally right."

She shuddered with an aftershock and moaned a little and it was torture waiting for the lecture or dressing down that I knew I richly fucking deserved.

"It's too late to really be mad about it," she said after a minute, but I could tell she was disappointed, which fucking killed me.

I sighed and kissed the back of her shoulder. She cuddled back into me and I was swept with a modicum of relief. She was pissed, she had every right to be pissed, but she wasn't so pissed that she didn't want me touching her. She still wanted me close.

"I'm not sure I could feel like any bigger of a steaming pile of dogshit if I wanted to, right now," I told her.

She chuckled softly, "You kind of deserve it just a little, but I think I knew somewhere that something was missing and I didn't exactly stop you." She shivered again and said, "It is what it is, now. What will be, will be and we'll cross that bridge when we come to it."

"You're sure?" I asked.

"I'm sure that if we aren't pregnant I should probably get an IUD until we want to be."

"You'd want that?"

"What? Kids?" she asked.

"Yeah." I swallowed hard. I'd always wanted kids. It would be a bit of a blow and take some adjustment if she didn't.

"With you? Someday, maybe. I mean, I never thought I would be in one place long enough to make having a child a thing I should do. The circus life isn't exactly child-rearing friendly… but yeah. If it happens, it happens, and I can't and won't be sad about it."

Her voice was so very serious, the veracity of her words ringing clear in my skull and I loved her so fiercely then, was so moved by her and those words, I couldn't bring myself to speak. I simply wrapped both my arms around her and dragged her back against my body, kissing every available inch of her that I could reach with my lips until she couldn't help but giggle and laugh.

"I love you so much, *mi alma.*"

"I love you, too," she murmured and leaned so she could kiss me back. Which, of course, eventually led to more of that timeless love making of ours, only this time she initiated it, turning in my arms and straddling my hips, peeling my shirt off over her head as she slid down over my cock.

"Babe!" I cried softly and she shushed me.

"Too late now, might as well make the most of it," she whispered in my ear before capturing the lobe lightly with her teeth.

Fuck, she drove me wild.

22

*C*laire...

I leaned back, his cock deep inside of me, as much to change the angle of penetration to get him stroking over that spot deep inside that woke up my insides, as to give better access to my clit from the outside. He licked the pad of his thumb, all the while keeping direct eye contact with me, and went for it.

That first electric jolt of pleasure when he made contact with the sensitive bundle of nerves at the top of my sex sent me to heaven. I rolled my hips, getting it going on inside, and I was afraid I wasn't going to last very long like this. That was a small tragedy, but at the same time, not too terrible, it just meant I got to ride this ride all over again.

One of the things I loved about Angel was that his sex drive was just as high as mine. After he came, just give him a few minutes and he was ready to go again, and could go until we were both exhausted and satisfied. Sometimes, that could take some doing for me. Pleasure was one of my favorite drugs, and Angel could keep me high for days.

"That's it, baby. Just like that," he said, his voice strained and on the edge. I loved that. I loved that I had that effect on him. I loved that he wasn't afraid to express how good I made him feel, that he gave himself over to the sex and the energy we raised between us just as readily as I did. I ground on him, and the feel of him against my walls, hot and stiff and touching every bit of the most intimate, sensitive, and sensual parts of me, had me unraveling in no time.

It was hard to keep my voice down; in the end, I bit my bottom lip to keep myself from crying out. The orgasm that swept through me was so strong that the added little edge of pain enhanced it, and when I found myself laying over the top of Angel, his hands smoothing over my skin, stroking every bit of my exposed body that he could reach, I realized I could taste the sweet copper tang of blood. I'd bitten my lip so hard it'd split slightly in all the excitement.

Angel reached up and drew me down, kissing me, then grunting and pulling back slightly, asking, "What'd you do?"

"I bit my lip," I said, with a slight laugh. "Sorry."

"Does it hurt? Are you all right?"

I gave a sultry little purr and said, "Mm, I'm better than alright," and giggled when he sucked in a sharp breath as I contracted my pelvic floor muscles around his cock.

"Do that again," he all but begged, and I did. I don't think he even had a chance to go completely soft yet, and he was already twitching, growing inside me again.

"Round, three?" I asked.

"And four, five, and six – if not more," he said with a dark little chuckle of his own. My pussy throbbed of its own volition at that sound and I felt my own breath rush out in a sigh, but then his mouth was on mine and we were making love all over again.

～

"THERE SHE IS," Golden declared from the kitchen table when I made it down the next morning. I'd woken up to an empty bed and was so tired, all I wanted to do was go home and sleep for real.

I'd showered and dressed before going downstairs and honestly? I felt like I'd been fucked on horseback, with how sore I was. My abs hurt from all of the orgasms and my legs felt like I'd had them ripped out of the sockets and popped back in on the wrong sides. Sometimes, there was such a thing as too much of a good thing. I'd sailed right on past 'deliciously sore' and was just plain sore this morning.

I sort of hated how Angel looked up from his cup of coffee and looked perfectly poised, like absolutely nothing was wrong with him at all. *How did he get off so easy?* I wondered. *Because you were on top most of the rest of last night*, another inner voice chased the first and then yet another was like, *Oh, yeah.*

"Oh, my God, I want it, I need it, put it in my mouth," I groaned and Golden started laughing, while Lys blinked at me with a look like she really wanted to know what the hell just happened. Angel handed me his cup of coffee and I swallowed some.

"Oh, *yes!*"

Lys, finally catching onto the joke, laughed with Golden. Angel just sat there shaking his head with an amused smile on his face and a levity I rarely got to see in his deep brown eyes. He was usually so serious.

I smiled from around the rim of his coffee cup and said, "A suitable sacrifice has been made."

"Does that mean I just lost my coffee?"

"It does," I affirmed, and he got up to go make himself another. To carry on the tradition of stealing things, I took his seat. He huffed a laugh and shook his head.

"I love you," I declared and he smiled softly and said, "I love you, too."

"Oh, please!" an exasperated voice declared. I turned to Manolo entering the kitchen, rubbing sleep out of his eyes as he proclaimed, "You guys are gross."

Golden went off in a litany of Spanish. I'm afraid my Italian was better, and my grasp of the Spanish language came from Spain more than it did Mexico. Still, my understanding between the Spanish and Mexican dialects of the language was that they weren't much different. The pronunciation being key and the fact that Mexican Spanish pronounced the letters 'Z' and 'S' the same while in Spanish Spanish, they were differentiated.

Mostly I was just having trouble with the speed and fluidity with which Golden and his nephew communicated. Still, it didn't take a rocket scientist to figure out that Manolo was getting a lesson in respect. Parenting translated clearly and quickly across a litany of languages. Manolo tried to defend himself and looked to Angel for help. Sadly for him, he wasn't getting any.

"What your *Tío* Rodrigo said."

"Aw, man!"

"Hey!" Lys barked, and Manolo came up short. She raised an eyebrow at him, and with all three adults in a unified front, his slim shoulders dropped in defeat.

"Now, what do you say?" Golden demanded, gently but firmly.

"Sorry I was rude, Claire." Manolo's apology was as sullen as any nine or ten-year-old's when forced to apologize when they weren't really sorry.

"Hey, it's no problem. I usually can't deal before my first cup of coffee either."

"I don't drink coffee, that stuff is nasty."

Golden snorted, "Wait 'til you get to be our age, kid. You'll change your tune."

"That's if I even get to live to be your age," he said, getting onto his own chair at the table, rolling his eyes and huffing out a sigh.

"Manolo, why would you even say something like that?" Lys demanded, bringing over a plate of a steaming stack of pancakes.

What followed was a stark conversation about his latest active-shooter drill at school, the happenings on the nightly news, and some very adult anxiety for a kid his age to have. It was a fairly heavy conversation for the breakfast table and a deeply uncomfortable one for the adults at that table.

When he went upstairs to get ready for school, the four of us exchanged some haggard looks.

I drew a deep breath and let out a cleansing sigh, and said with a heavy heart, "We need to do better."

"Shit, Angel and I are out doing what we can every day," Golden said, leaning back in his chair. Lys and I exchanged looks.

"I don't think she was saying it like that, babe. Correct me if I'm wrong," Lys said. I shook my head.

"You're not. I mean 'we' as in 'we the adults of this nation' period. We *all* need to do better than what we're doing."

"Yeah, we all do, we all see that we do, but good luck getting people to do it," Golden said bitterly.

"Amen," Angel said with a heavy sigh of his own.

"Well, that was a perfect way to start the day," Lys said flatly.

"If it's any consolation," I said, "you guys did good."

"Thanks," Golden said. "I think we always worry we aren't doing enough or right by that kid…" he trailed off, his gaze keen on the hall Manolo had disappeared through to go back upstairs. I smiled a bit sadly and thought about my mom and her own struggles when it came to us.

"I think when you *stop* worrying about things like that is when you've lost your grip on the whole parenting thing." I know, that was rich, coming from me, she who was childless and spent like zero time around kids unless they happened to be in our audience. Still, my mom had never given up worrying about Carter and me. Never. She'd worried about us right up until the bitter end. Some of her last words to Carter were about making sure he took care of me.

"Right, well, I'm going to get Manolo to school and then I need to open up the shop." Lys got up and kissed Golden on the way by. "See you guys later," she said with a smile.

"Thank you for breakfast. Have a good day at work," I murmured.

"Thanks for taking us in, Lys." Angel's thanks echoed not far behind mine.

"Yes, that too," I agreed, slightly mortified I hadn't thought to thank her for that first. I mean, geeze.

"You guys headed to the gym?" Golden asked.

Angel and I exchanged a look. I really didn't want to go, but at the same time, I did.

"I didn't think to bring my silks," I murmured. It was a lame excuse, but it was the best I could think of without out-and-out blurting that I'd had too much good sex the night before and wanted to do as little actual walking today as possible. I might be flexible as all get-out, but even I had my limits!

"That's okay, get some cardio in, it's good for yah," Golden said with a grin, and I just got the sneaking suspicion that somehow he knew.

I snorted and said, "More like cardi-*no*. I hate cardio."

His grin grew. "Then consider me your accountability buddy."

Fuck. He really wanted to go with us this time. Fine. Okay. We'd have it his way.

"Just let me digest some, we can go."

Angel was trying not to laugh the whole exchange and I was trying to think of a myriad of ways to get back at him. Truthfully, he'd made me feel so good last night, I couldn't get a single idea to stick.

Oh well, I guess I should consider this karma cashing in for every time I'd done a little shit kind of a thing to someone else. *Your brother, perhaps?* Except I literally couldn't think of a thing I'd done to him, except maybe not call as often as I should have for a good sister. To be fair, though, I hadn't wanted to listen to the oftentimes thinly-veiled criticism and little jabs at my profession. The, 'Have you decided to come home yet? and the 'You're still going strong in this phase, aren't you, Claire?'

He really hated my job and I was beginning to think that, by extension, he held a seething hatred for me, and I couldn't understand why. What had I done?

My thoughts were interrupted when I heard Angel talking with Golden and Lys and tuned into the fact he was trying to weasel us out of Sunday dinner with them so that we could have dinner with my brother and his wife. I knew I needed to do it but…

"Oh, are you sure?" I asked, when they acquiesced to Angel's request to get out of it with far too much grace. I mean, his logic was sound. We were here now, and dinner to get to know me in two days' time was more than a little redundant, considering Lys knew everything there was to know, thanks to last night, and Golden was about to catch up with the curve by learning more about me at the gym.

I met Angel's eyes and saw everything in them and thought to myself, *Oh. Oh you're good!* I didn't think that the gym suggestion was a happy accident. I think Golden was coached into asking, now. Sneaky, sneaky. Angel was not-so-gently steering me into a confrontation with Carter and I didn't like it. I didn't like it one bit. *Even if it's being done for your own good? With your best interests at heart?*

Nope. Not even then, I wanted to fiercely deny, but that light note of pleading in Angel's eyes pulled the ribbon on the neat little package of my anger and the paper fell away. The emotion, no longer contained, evaporated rather smoothly and I realized I wasn't angry at Angel at all for the tactic because he did love me, and he was trying to fix it. I was angry at my brother that there was anything that needed fixing in the first place, because he really was acting like a jackass. I knew that. I had known that. But I still didn't want to lose the only family I had left.

Fuck.

I felt my anxiety coalesce and rear its ugly head, and it made me unsettled and jumpy enough that suddenly cardio sounded like a really good idea.

"You mad at me?" Angel asked when we were back upstairs, gathering our things.

"I want to be," I said honestly, "but no. I'm more angry with Carter. I realize my brother has been acting like a real jackass and it hurts. I've always looked up to him, all the while growing up," I said, dropping onto the edge of the bed. "So I really wanted to believe it's my fault somehow, but I keep analyzing it and looking at it from every angle and all I can come up with is he's pissed at me because I'm living my life the way I want to live it, and for some reason he just can't deal with that."

"You know, I'm really proud of you, *mi alma*," he said and the comment caught me off-guard and warmed me all at once.

"Why?" I asked. "I mean, I guess I don't really understand." I didn't either; it would be easy to believe it was because despite my brother's wishes and emotional blackmail, I'd stood my ground and lived my life anyway, but with the way Angel was looking at me, I couldn't be one hundred percent sure that was all it was. He came to me and rested his hands lightly on my hips.

"For refusing to be gaslit by your brother, for one. I can tell you've struggled with it, but you're absolutely right. You're not dealing with *your* issues, no matter how much he's tried to make them your issues. You're dealing with *his* issues, and its high time he put on his big-boy pants and looked at himself rather than putting everything off on you."

"I almost feel bad for him," I confessed with a sigh.

"How come?"

"Well, I don't think I'd be half so willing to believe it's really not my fault what's going on if it weren't for you and my sister-in-law. You guys both have been really strong and steady that this isn't my fault. I mean, sure, I've probably done plenty that is my fault in the past, but this time, this thing, it's all Carter, not me."

Angel nodded and looked about as sad about it as I felt, and I hugged myself to him tight.

"What?" he asked with a slight laugh and I just let myself hold him and be held in return for a minute before I could get it out.

"I love you." I settled on that first. "For pushing me to get better, for understanding that I won't do it overnight, for holding my hand and taking much-needed steps forward and even taking the necessary steps back with me without ever judging... You've been everything I've needed lately. Selfless, trusting, and you're one of the most beautiful souls I've ever met. I am so lucky to have met you."

He chuckled and said gently, "All of that is like looking into a mirror, *mi alma*. Your soul is the very same." He kissed my forehead and hugged me tight.

I didn't know what to say, it was a pretty profound moment. The kind of moment that held gravity and weight, like speaking your marriage vows. Except it was just the two of us and whatever powers-that-be in the room... I guess that made it more special, more profound in some ways.

"I love you," I whispered again, and I don't think I'd ever meant those three little words as hard as I meant them right then.

"I love you, too, my heart, my soul."

And there he goes one-upping me yet again... I thought with a smile.

THE RIDE to the gym was damp and chill but not totally unpleasant. Golden rode beside us and it was a different experience riding when it was just me and Angel versus with another bike sharing the lane. Also, it made my thoughts drift to what it would be like to ride in a pack with the entire club once the weather got warmer. Angel had told me there wasn't a scheduled club ride until spring, that for now, the only way one would happen were if it was an impromptu decision.

I'd been vaguely disappointed by that. It was something I was definitely looking forward to experiencing. We parked in the fenced-off lot next door to the gym and went inside, where we found McGowan gathered with three other men at the counter.

"Speak of the devil!" he cried when he saw me. "We were just talking about you, little lady."

"Me?" I asked.

"Ah-yup. I'd like you to meet my partners. That's Jefferson, Colt, Ringold, and Reynolds."

He introduced each man in turn and I gave a meek little wave. "Hi, I'm Claire."

"Nice to meet you, Claire." Jefferson, a man as old as McGowan, stuck out his hand. I shook it with a firm grip and we ended up going down the line.

"I was just talking to them about using that back store room as your space for those classes."

"You can really do what McGowan here says you can do?" Ringold asked.

I nodded. "I can, and more."

He shook his head and said, "I don't believe it."

I didn't wait or try to explain, I just walked over to the climbing ropes, dropped my gym bag, did some cursory stretching, cursing my inner thighs, and kicked off my shoes. Without any discussion or preamble, I smoked their precious climbing times all over again in front of his partners. I locked my legs around the rope and even though it rattled my nerves because it wasn't as secure as doing it from my silks, hung upside down. It was then that I asked, "Any questions?"

McGowan laughed and clapped Ringold on the back who nodded and said, "All right, point taken. Get down from there, yah spider-monkey."

"I'd do it a lot more impressively if it were my silks, just so you know." I grasped the rope with my hands above my head and let go with my legs, flipping right side up and let myself down hand over hand, smooth, controlled, and measured.

"God *damn,* you got some strength on you," Jefferson said, admiringly.

"Years and years of practice," I said modestly, touching my feet to the floor.

Golden and Angel were having an entire silent conversation off to the side, and Angel interrupted, saying, "You do your thing, babe. We're gonna get it done."

I nodded and they wandered off to start their workout while I stood with the men to discuss what they wanted out of me. The five of them exchanged looks and Colt said, "Let's see what you think of the space."

We went to the back of the gym, through a set of wide double doors, into a dark back half of the warehouse. It was a lot bigger, more spacious than I expected and really only half taken up by a mishmash of defunct equipment and packaging, like they'd moved everything in out front and just forgot about back here.

"Oh, wow. You could do a lot more back here than just Tissu lessons." The ceilings in here were even higher than out where the climbing ropes were, by a good eight to ten feet, and the back wall was lined with huge bay doors, harkening back to when this place was indeed a shipping warehouse.

"In the summer, you can open those bay doors," Reynolds said.

"You could also run the silks up and use the space for yoga lessons when it's not in use for silks dancing. Have you thought about offering fitness dance classes?"

The men all looked at each other.

"Do what now?" Ringold asked.

"Like Zumba or belly dance?" I asked. "This space could be perfect for a multitude of things. Some chandeliers, mirrors all along that wall, some paint on the rest… You could really up your game and bring a lot of female clientele through the doors. You have something unique to offer them."

"Oh, yeah, what's that?" McGowan asked, shrewdly.

"You know any women who don't pursue their personal fitness?" I asked.

"I think we all do," Jefferson said, smiling.

"Why?" I asked. "What are their reasons?"

"Fear of judgment," Reynolds supplied.

"Hitting the gym after work is tougher for them, especially in the winter, because the city is dangerous," I said.

I saw the lightbulb come on.

"Hard to fear for your personal safety when you have a bunch of off-duty and retired police officers standing around and able to walk you to your car," McGowan said. "I like the way you think."

"Exactly," I said. "Make this a judgment-free space; crack down on the lunkheads that do come through that would say something – sort of a 'three strikes you're out'; advertise like crazy with fliers, postcards, on social media…"

"Holy shit, you've really thought all this through," Jefferson said with a laugh.

"I sort of lost my job at the circus this week and I've had a lot of time to think about it."

"What happened there?" McGowan asked, and as a prospective employee, I told them.

"You're joking?" Jefferson asked in disbelief, scratching the back of his head. He had brown hair and a hairline receding to either side of a wide swath up top in the middle. It didn't look bad, but much more he probably would have done better going bald. Of course, that was my personal judge-y preference and not one I would dare utter out loud.

"I wish I were. Angel has video of it and everything, but the owners of the Night Circus won't be swayed. They stand by his decision."

"I'd sue," Ringold said.

"I plan on it."

"Takes a lot of guts to come in here and tell us you're gonna sue your last employer while lookin' to work a deal here," Colt said.

"Hey, to be fair, it was my idea," McGowan said.

"I'd like to one-up your idea," I countered, looking at the five of them.

"Oh, yeah? This we gotta hear," Ringold crossed his arms over his massive chest and I smiled.

"I'm sitting on a pretty decent pile of savings," I said. "I'd be willing to put a chunk of it to use, buying the silks and some of the hardware to hang them. Paint, mirrors, basically everything needed to kit this back room out – including some advertising."

"In exchange for…?" Reynolds said carefully.

"A share in this place's profits until the loan is paid back, at say… six percent interest?"

"That's awfully low," McGowan said.

"I want this to succeed. I also want to do something that will keep me here in Indigo City with Angel. The loan and repayment would be on top of a regular wage, teaching regular classes."

"You want a job."

"I want a job. A real one. Not temporary, not a class-by-class under-the-table sort of thing. I want a real job, on the books, health insurance – the whole nine yards."

"You ain't asking much," Ringold said, his voice thick with sarcasm.

"Might as well make you a partner," Colt agreed, laughing.

"Up to you, boys. That's what I want, though. I'll even get this all cleared out and do most of the work in here myself. Save some money on having crews come in and do it.

"You, do all this?" Ringold demanded.

"I have friends in both high and low places," I said. "I'm betting Angel could get some of his club to help; I know I could get some of my circus people in here, too. I could do it. Don't sell me short."

"Seriously, boys. I learned that shit the hard way," McGowan said, laughing. "The hit to my pride still smarts."

I smiled at him and said, "You know where to find me."

"How much money you got put away?" Ringold demanded.

Colt shook his head.

"Jesus, man! That's not something you ask!"

"It's fine." I named the figure.

Looks got traded and Jefferson gave a low whistle.

"We'll get back to you," McGowan said, a bit of pride shining in his blue eyes. I winked and turned and walked away with my head held high even though I was a nervous screaming wreck on the inside. I mean, I'd just committed to something huge here, totally off-the-cuff. The risk to me was far greater than the risk to them and they had to know that.

Part of me was like *Oh fuck, oh fuck, oh fuck, what did I just do?*

I joined Angel and Golden, and about twenty minutes and three lifts into one of my sets later, the five of them came out of the back room. McGowan looked over at me and called out, "You got yourself a deal, sweetheart. Come talk to us when you're done."

My mouth went dry but I gave him a nod and kept at what I was doing, never losing count, never missing a beat. Confidence was everything, or at least the appearance of it. Angel looked at me questioningly and Golden's face echoed his twin's look down to the last detail. I shook my head and finished my set, winded. I caught my breath, drank some water and told them, "Later. Let's finish the workout and then I'll fill you in before I go talk to them."

"Okay. Everything all right?" Golden asked.

"May have just bitten off more than I can chew," I confessed with a reckless grin, "but yeah. I think everything is going to be fine."

"Whatever you've done, I'm sure it will be fine. In fact, I'm sure it will be great and I'm here for you no matter what," Angel declared. His tone was laced with approval and I smiled. I think he knew that I was trying to put down roots, to stay with him, and I knew that he wouldn't be disappointed by that. The rest was debatable.

We would find out.

23

*A*ngel…

I'd never seen her so nervous. Not even after she'd told my brother and I what she'd offered up to the men of the Thin Blue Line. That was a huge undertaking on her part, but one I was fully behind because it meant that she would stay, that she was trying to stay, and that was everything. Of course, with the money she was investing into the business and by extension her future, along with what it was going to cost for a lawyer to sue her former employer she was officially strapped, but I didn't care. I knew it would potentially take years for the lawsuit to be resolved, but I was proud of her for pursuing it, for not letting her poor treatment lie.

Now it was time to tackle her treatment closer to home. Her brother and sister-in-law were coming for dinner.

She'd tried to get out of going to church with me and Manolo that morning and I admit I wasn't gentle about pressuring her into it. I didn't want her around the house by herself worrying incessantly about tonight. She'd gone with us and had admitted afterward that the ceremony of it had calmed her nerves some. Still, she confessed that church wasn't always for her. I was a little disappointed, but I understood it wasn't for everyone. It wasn't a deal-breaker for me at all. Religious tolerance and diversity were more important. Claire had both so I could let it go. Besides, I got it. She was too free-spirited to be locked into something like organized religion. To her, it felt like a cage and I loved her as wild and free. There would be a sort of sadness about locking her into a cage, even one that I thought was as beautiful as my faith.

She was a good and beautiful soul, and that was enough for me. I refused to believe that my God would punish her simply for not attending his house once a week. My God was a loving and forgiving God, not a vain and vengeful one. It was something I deeply believed in and something that I was also deeply saddened by that more people didn't. After all, actions spoke louder than words when it came to any faith and a few bad apples really did spoil the bunch.

When we got home from dropping Manolo off with his paternal grandmother for the afternoon, Claire suddenly turned into a cleaning fiend. She went over everything from top to bottom, just to have something to do, something to occupy her, until her brother and sister-in-law arrived. We'd changed out of our Sunday best and she was suddenly off like a shot.

The damage hadn't been too bad from the storm. A few things had shifted on the kitchen counter; some books had fallen off the shelves upstairs. Enough had been disturbed to tell me that riding it out at Golden's had indeed been the better option. Still, she'd taken the opportunity, when putting things to rights with me, to do a lot of the dusting and cleaning then. She'd certainly gotten us all caught up on laundry. So this now was a pure frenzy of nervous energy and a bid at unparalleled perfection that her brother could find no fault in, and I let her have it. I simply did what she asked of me when she asked it, to keep her cool and keep her calm because she looked like a woman on the brink.

I did, however, have her take one of her anxiety pills when I caught her sniffing and tearing up while scrubbing out the bathtub which was far from needing it. She'd taken it and about an hour later, I'd asked if she felt better.

She'd nodded and affirmed, "Better."

Now we were dressed once again in some of our best, though quite a bit more casual than Sunday best. She paced between the living room and kitchen while she entrusted me to cook. It was more adorable than nerve-wracking how she back-seat cooked with me, checking and rechecking that I followed the recipe, making sure I'd added this, or had omitted that, because her brother hated that…

I could tell she really loved him despite how he'd treated her, and that all she wanted from him was one iota of approval. It broke my heart, but I got it. I really did. He was more her parent than her actual mom due to circumstance. Heartbreaking, but true. They'd been a close-knit family of only three, and she was the baby. I saw echoes of her dynamic with Carter in my own sister and Golden, but that was a challenge for another day, and Maria had genuinely fucked-up, so the situations were vastly different.

Granted, Claire had fucked-up too, by swallowing those pills, but I felt that was different. While my sister had support and help if only she'd set her pride aside and asked, Claire had felt, and to some degree had known, she had no-one. She'd been made to feel so alone, so isolated by her brother, and by that director, from her peers, that she'd genuinely believed she was. Her depression had convinced her unequivocally that the world wouldn't miss her, that it would have been better without her wasting space and sucking up resources, and I knew how that felt. I had been there myself. It wasn't pretty, and to someone who hadn't also been through such a dark place, there really was no explaining it, either.

You either knew, or you didn't and it wasn't a club I wanted to hand out memberships to just so the people who were in the camp who didn't get it, could. I wouldn't wish that kind of pain, that kind of having your thoughts and your brain on icy fire, on anyone. It was dangerous, too dangerous to wish on anyone, for even a moment, just for a life lesson in tolerance for the folks who would declare to one of us sufferers that something as simple as *Just think positive* would cure our woes.

Yes, I had managed to climb out of my deep dark hole with the help of Claire and without benefit of medication, or therapy. I'd managed to hold on until things had gotten better, but it wasn't a path I would recommend to anyone, and it also wasn't a path I would ever repeat, should I get that bad again. And if I were being honest, I was always low-level afraid of myself, that it would get that bad again…

Claire had done the wrong thing, but I worked in the medical field and could be the first to tell you – in order to get any kind of real help, unless you were very lucky, that was typically how far it had to go. Sadly, we usually didn't make it in time. By the grace of God we had this time and she was here. She was medicated and should be going to regular therapy, but those services were out of reach of her medical plan. The medication was helping, she'd gotten what therapy she could, and now it was one day at a time for us.

We were working on her issues together, now it was time to work on the issues outside her control that were negatively affecting her, and we could hear one of those issues coming. The footfalls on the dock, the low hushed tones of his wife scolding him, and the exasperated sound of his arguing with her were indistinct, but there, just before the blur of their bodies were visible through the frosted glass of my proper front door. Claire froze and the knock fell on the wood beside the glass. I raised an eyebrow at her when she looked at me, and stirred the pot on the stove. I knew I was stirring a very different kind of pot by making her answer the door, but it needed to be done.

Did I worry that it was too soon?

Yes.

Did I want to waste the opportunity that Claire's sister-in-law had presented, and that she was clearly going to be on Claire's side for this?

No.

If we had waited, there was a good chance that her sister-in-law would have become less sympathetic to Claire's side of the story, the longer she lived with Carter's excuses.

Although, judging by their expressions as Claire let them through the door, I had to guess that Mallory Montgomery was at the end of her rope when it came to her husband. My heart went out to her. Him? Not so much. I wanted to wipe that look of arrogant superiority right off his face, and with any luck, and God willing, I'd have the opportunity tonight before this family-drama shit-show was over – because make no mistake, Claire was my family now and I would fight to the death for any one of them, whether they had pissed me off or not.

You could hate your family, but they were your family, and when an outside threat came around, you fought for them because that is what family did. Carter had made himself an outside threat to the other half of my soul. It left a bitter, acrid taste in my mouth where he was concerned. I took a fortifying sip of my wine to try and wash it away, but it was so strong, I swear that it turned the wine to vinegar in my mouth. Still, I could handle this. I had diplomacy, and patience… typically, anyway. This, I was sure, was going to be harder than I was used to.

"Angel, I'd like you to meet my brother, Carter and his wife, Mallory," Claire said gently, and I wondered if her brother would recognize me from the night of Claire's near-suicide. He did, frowning as he stuck out his hand.

"Nice to meet you," I lied pleasantly, and couldn't get over how stiff Claire held herself.

"Likewise," Mallory said warmly and took my hand between both of hers to shake.

"Dinner will be up in just a few minutes; can I interest you in a glass of wine?"

"That would be lovely," she said.

Carter cleared his throat uncomfortably and said, "Yes, thank you."

"All right, then." I went and poured two glasses and brought them over. Claire took them from me and handed one each to her brother and sister-in-law as I began plating things up and getting them into serving dishes.

Uncomfortable silence reigned as everyone took a place around the dining room table and I worried about my girl. I had faith in her, believed in her, and I knew she would be able to handle anything that he threw at her tonight… and if she couldn't? I was right here to catch it for her.

24

*C*laire…

       When I had opened the door, Mallory had smiled warmly, but my eyes had gone straight to my brother, who looked positively dour.

"Claire," he intoned. That was it. Just one word, my name, the anger and derision with which he uttered it absolutely heartbreaking. I knew instantly that this was not going to go well and surprisingly, that didn't hurt. I mean, it did, but not as much as it made me angry. He was acting like a sullen little boy who had been forced to go to church on a Sunday when all he wanted to do was go play with little Johnny up the road who didn't go to church on Sundays.

Sort of like you were this morning, I thought a bit ruefully. I'd been glad Angel had slightly bullied me into going with him and Manolo. I'd needed it, as much as I didn't want to admit it. It helped that his church was so warm and welcoming for being Catholic. I'd always found their masses to be somber and almost melancholy, even when they were supposed to be celebrating something.

I let them into the house and it seemed that as soon as my brother stepped across the threshold, my bright little sanctuary became somehow darker, like using a filter on a photo in an app; everything just felt dingy all of a sudden. I thought it was just me projecting, I guess – or I don't know – maybe it genuinely *was* Carter and not me. I struggled with that. I really did. I couldn't fathom this bitter angry man as my brother but he was, and I loved him, and I couldn't give up on him. Not yet.

The walk across the short expanse of living room, past the dining room table, to the kitchen where Angel was felt like a walk to the gallows. I introduced my brother and sister-in-law, and Mallory was at least trying, warm and pleasant to my brother's cold and dark.

I brought them wine and we sat at the table while Angel finished some things up. Awkward silence descended on us as we waited for Angel to be seated and to begin dinner. Angel said a silent prayer, the rest of us bowing our heads in respectful silence for his faith. He crossed himself and looked up, brightly smiling at my brother and his wife.

"So," he said, "I have to admit, Claire hasn't told me too much about you yet, given the circumstances. What do you do, Carter?"

"Public school. I teach history."

"Oh, yeah? Where at?"

Carter cleared his throat and said, "Over at Bayside Jr. High."

"Oh, yeah, over in Old Town district."

"Yeah." My brother nodded and took another bite of his food. I swallowed hard.

"Mallory is in real estate," I murmured and Mallory smiled brightly, but her eyes held a bit of nervousness as she glanced at Carter. I was instantly angry for her.

"Yeah, my brother just bought a place last year. One of the old brownstones on Twenty-first."

"Oh, those were so nice! They weren't handled by my firm, but we did bid on the contract to represent the –"

"Mallory," Carter said with a bit of a derisive laugh. "Sorry, if you let her get started, she'll go on for days."

"I don't mind that," Angel said, sitting up slightly. "It's exciting when you encounter people who are still passionate and excited about what they do. It's one of the things I love about Claire."

Oh, he was trying to start shit, damn him. Although, chasing right after that same thought came *I need to remember to give him a high-five for that one, later.*

Carter cleared his throat and pushed his plate away from him a bit, and I thought *Here we go.*

"Mr. um…"

"There's no Mister anything, just Angel will do."

"Right, ah, Angel… I'm not sure how my sister tracked you down or convinced you to let her move in with you but –"

"First of all, she didn't track me down. I tracked her. Second of all, your sister saved my life three years ago, but I don't suppose you know anything about that, considering she's not the type to really brag about her accomplishments."

"Wait, um…" Carter frowned. "I'm not quite sure I understand. Claire did *what?*"

"She saved my life."

"How did she do that, exactly?"

"I don't really think we need to talk about that…" I interjected. I mean, I really didn't want Carter to know anything about that. I mean, that I slept with Angel and then bounced before he woke up. It was a total one-night stand, and not one of my finer moments.

"She happened to be walking by, just as I was about to eat my gun. She stayed with me all night, talking it out. She saved my life that night, three years ago, and we lost touch. I always hoped I would find her again, but I never figured it would be like that. You have to feel awfully alone and like a burden to everyone around you to pull something like that. I was glad I could return the favor and that we were able to reconnect."

Okay, he left a lot out, and pretty much made me sound like a saint. I so didn't deserve him.

"Ah-huh…" Carter's tone was skeptical at best, condescending and rude at worst, and my fuse was lit and snaking ever closer to the powder keg of anger I was barely holding onto.

"She's a good woman, your sister, and she's been through a lot."

Carter lost all sense of decorum at that point, crossing his arms and leaning back in his seat.

"Not how I would describe my sister," he said flatly. "Look, I don't know what line of… what Claire's fed you, but Claire does what she wants and damn everyone else." My jaw dropped and I know I made a sound because Carter looked at me and with eyebrows raised, said, "You do."

"Last time I checked, I believe your sister was an adult and capable of making those decisions for herself," Angel countered, and I was starting to get a little annoyed with the whole talking about me like I wasn't sitting right here.

I swallowed hard and forged ahead and demanded of my brother, "Do you really even care that I almost died, or was it just another inconvenience for you in a long line of them where I'm concerned?"

Carter actually had the nerve to roll his eyes saying, "Don't be dramatic, Claire. It's not always about you."

Mallory, who had remained silent to this point, drew back and leaned away from my brother, anger flitting across her face as she said, "Uh, do you maybe want to try that one again, Carter Montgomery?"

She used her Mom voice on him. She *actually used her Mom voice on him*. That was great. The three of us stared him down and he scowled.

"Oh, please, Claire! Don't pretend it was anything less than a cry for yet more attention. Haven't all of us already given you enough?"

"You don't," I said flatly, and leaned back. "You are literally so self-absorbed now that you seriously thought I tried to kill myself for attention?" I shook my head. "If I wanted or needed attention from you, Carter, that is certainly not how I would want to get it." I felt like he'd taken a hatchet to the center of my chest and had carved out my bleeding heart. I threw my napkin onto my plate, which I hadn't even touched and stood up.

"I think we're done here," I said. "I don't want or need to hear anything else." Tears coursed down my cheeks and I had a savage thought that if it weren't for Angel, I really should try again, that I literally was out of things to hold onto. My brother, my last flesh and blood, really didn't give two shits about me.

I went for the stairs, took them two at a time, and went to the sliding glass door. I felt hot all over, my face flushed as tears scorched lines down my cheeks, and I felt like I was suffocating. I needed cold, I needed air, and most importantly, I needed to *not* be inhabiting the same space as my damn brother.

Losing your family sucked, but at that point, it hurt so much, I think it would have been easier to take if one of us had actually died.

25

*A*ngel...

"I want a divorce." Mallory's voice was coated in a heavy layer of disgust, as she leaned as far away from Carter as her seat would allow.

Carter turned to her, scowling, and demanded, "What are you talking about?"

"I think she's talking about leaving your ass and I can't say that I blame her at this point," I said with a sigh.

"Excuse you!" Carter cried, indignant.

"No, excuse *you*, buddy. You're in *my* house, so this here is how this is gonna play out. You can either sit there and listen to what we've got to say, or you can get the fuck up out of here. I'm cool with either or, because you? The shit you're pulling on your sister? It has absolute sweet fuck-all to do with her and her decisions, and has everything to do with you and *yours*, and I'm not about to let you pretend otherwise."

To his credit, he shut the fuck up. Of course, his wife sitting there with her arms crossed, looking at him downright murderously, might have had something to do with it.

He looked at me, smug, and waved a hand in front of himself like I should be his guest in my own house and tell him what I thought. I took the invitation, but it was a close call between talking and putting my fist down his throat. He'd hurt Claire and I wanted so badly to kick his fucking ass for that. Still, kicking his ass would only make this worse on her, not better, and I wasn't about to do that.

"You know what? One day it's going to click how bad you've fucked up with your sister and you're going to regret it, and on that day, it's going to be too fucking late because Claire's going to have written you off in order to heal herself, and that's going to be all on you. I don't think there's honestly anything else I can say at this point because it's pretty clear you're not interested in listening." I shook my head.

"If you think I'm joking about that divorce, Carter, you have another thing coming," Mallory said. "I am not about to have Gracie grow up with a father like the man you are right now. What you just did to Claire was cruel. Unbelievably cruel. I think Angel hit the nail on the head. It's not her issue, or her issues. These are all yours, and you need to deal with them."

"Take all the time you guys need," I said throwing down my napkin. "I'm going to go take care of the love of my life. By the time we get back in here, though, there better be an apology waiting or you'd better be gone. Those are your two choices, man." I got up, and Carter looked a cross between angry and disbelieving, and I wondered if he'd ever really had to deal with any consequences for his actions. I mean, I knew his mom had worked a lot and left him pretty much in charge of Claire, something she idolized him for, but damn… I really don't know how he'd turned into this, where his line of thinking had gotten so warped along the way.

"Thank you, Angel, for the lovely meal," Mallory murmured, somber.

"*You're* welcome," I told her pointedly. "I'm sorry that we had to meet under such circumstances. I wish you all the best." She nodded.

"Are you fucking joking me?" Carter spluttered, indignant.

"Do I look it?" I demanded with an arched brow. I turned my back on them and went up the stairs, slipping out onto the top deck where Claire stood, facing the water, her fingertips pressed to her eyes, her shoulders shaking as she wept bitterly into the icy night.

I sighed silently, my breath pluming the air, and shut the slider behind us. She jumped at the sound it made when it clapped shut, and turned. When she saw me, fresh tears coursed down her cheeks.

"They gone?" she asked.

"Not yet, I don't think. I think your sister-in-law just drew a line in the sand, though."

"Oh, yeah? How's that?"

"Told him not once, but twice, she's lookin' for a divorce."

She took in a stuttering breath, sniffing as I pulled her against me and rested her head on my chest saying, "Poor Carter." Her tone held nothing but sincerity for the sentiment, too. She was far more amazing than her dumbass brother deserved.

"All the shit he puts you through, withholding love, approval, and just about everything a family member needs to thrive and you're worried about *his* feelings? God, I love you, Claire. I love you with everything that I am, with everything I ever hoped to be, and one day I'm going to marry you."

She tripped on a hiccupping laugh and asked, "Did you seriously just ask me to marry you? Now? At a time like this?"

I chuckled and leaned back so I could look her in her red-rimmed eyes. I brushed a thumb through the salty wet on her freckled cheek and said,

"No, there was no question mark there. Not yet. I just announced to the stars and sky my intention to ask you to marry me."

"You know, I always thought that if things got that far with anyone I would have to send them packing to ask my brother for approval. Now, I just don't know…"

"Trust me, baby. You've got more family than you know what to do with. You just can't see the forest for the trees right now, and that's okay." I sighed out and kissed her forehead whispering against it, "I'm so sorry he's such a douche."

"I don't know why. I don't know what happened to him," she said and rested her forehead against my chest.

I had some guesses, but I didn't know if I should share or not. I simply said, by way of open invitation, "I have a few guesses. Don't know how true they are, though."

"I would love to talk about it sometime, I just don't know if that time is right now," she said.

We heard raised voices from the dock side of the house that were clearly quarreling and Claire and I both closed our eyes. The voices were definitely Carter and Mallory, but neither was distinct enough to make out words as they faded up the dock towards the parking lot.

"I think your brother is getting divorced," I said and Claire sniffed against the cold and said, "I hope not. Sometimes I think Mallory and Gracie are the only things that hold Carter together and keep him from falling apart, you know?"

"Well, he's pretty well fucked it. I can see Mallory's point on that."

"What did she say?" she asked.

I told her everything while we listened to the water lap against the houseboat, joined by the subtle creak and clank of the dock. The night was still, otherwise. No wind off the water, just the pervasive biting chill as winter moved in to overtake fall and to likely overstay its welcome for another year.

Claire shivered in my arms and I said, "Come on. We can finish this discussion inside, where it's warm."

"Okay," she said quietly and let me lead her into the bedroom. She made to drift toward the stairs but I held her back. She looked at me questioningly and said, "We should clean up."

"Don't worry about it," I said.

"But the food will go bad…"

"Baby, this dinner was never about the food. It was about figuring out where you stood with your brother and about looking out for your mental and emotional well-being. Let it rot for all I care." I reeled her in and she put her arms around me, holding herself close. I held her to me, and pretty soon she shuddered and took another hitching breath.

"I don't deserve someone as wonderful as you," she said, and her voice was warped and strained by her sorrow and tears.

"Shut up," I said. "You deserved someone better than me a long time ago, baby. I honestly feel like a shitty consolation prize."

"No, you shut up," she said and a little titter of laughter made it through her sadness. We ended up on the bed, just laying together, holding each other and talking late into the night. It wasn't about sex. It was about intimacy. It was about being there for her as much as she was there for me and it was about communication which everybody on the planet always seemed to be sorely needing, yet never managed to get enough of.

Tonight, I was enough. Tonight, the story of what I'd said to her brother in her defense was enough. She must have had me tell her a hundred times and each time she lay quietly against me until the weight of the silence became too much and I asked if she was still awake. Finally she said, "I can't believe you said that to him. I can't believe you said all those wonderful things about me. I sometimes wonder if this is all just some beautiful dream."

"Me too," I confessed. "Every morning I wake up I expect to find you gone. I expect to find your drawers empty, and that anytime I speak of you, the rest of the people in my life ask 'Who?' as if you never existed."

She laughed slightly, and I suppose to her it sounded a little absurd, but she finally asked timidly, "Why?"

"Because if something seems too good to be true, it usually is, and you are so past too good to be true… I just don't know how you're here with me, Claire. I don't know how I got so lucky that you want to be with me."

"I think the same thing about you every day," she whispered.

I don't know why, it just felt right, so I whispered quietly, "Marry me?"

"You're proposing? Right now?"

"Yeah, yeah I am. Marry me? The engagement can be as long or as short as you like, I don't care, just say that you will."

"Yes, of course I will. As if there would be any doubt," she whispered fiercely. "I feel whole when I'm with you."

I closed the short gap between us where we faced each other, lying on our sides, and kissed her. She kissed me back and ceremony, pomp and circumstance aside, that was it. That kiss sealed the damn deal. Just her and I alone in our bed with the stars in heaven as our witness.

"You are absolutely insane, you know that?" she whispered.

"Good thing that your crazy matches my crazy so well, then."

She laughed and it was a good sound. Kissing turned to touching, the touching turned to petting and caressing, and pretty soon after that the clothes started to come off. I pushed her top out of my way, laying her back on the bed and put my mouth to her skin, kissing along her stomach, pressing open-mouthed kisses along her ribs until she yipped and giggled from a light touch against a ticklish spot.

I made it my personal mission to find every one of those, and to find every one of those spots that made her eyes drift closed and her body go lax as her breath escaped in a shuddering sigh or in a sultry little moan.

She arched beneath me and that allowed me to peel her out of more of her clothes. I unwrapped her like the gift she was, leaving a trail of kisses against her chilled skin, warmth and a trail of goose flesh left in their wake.

"Turn over," I murmured when I had her nude on the bed. She obediently turned onto her stomach and I marveled that she could trust me, or anything, after the amount of betrayal she'd been served up by just about everyone in her life. I stripped out of my clothes and rolled a condom on, even though I wasn't ready to use it; not just yet.

26

Claire…

"Turn over." The command straddled the line between a command and an impassioned plea and I obliged, turning onto my stomach for him and laying my cheek against the mattress. I could see him pull his shirt over his head out of the corner of my eye. I loved watching him do it, too. He just had this way when he pulled it off, like he meant business, like he was cool, calm and in control, and that he was determined to make us feel good and he always delivered. He finished stripping and I closed my eyes and felt my pussy tingle when I heard him open the drawer of the bedside table.

The sounds of him making himself ready always turned me on, my excitement for him climbing with the sounds of the wrapper, the delicate sound of him rolling the rubber down his length, hyping me up, making me wet, all in anticipation of his touch landing on my skin again.

He climbed up on the bed, bowing over the backs of my thighs and calves, his skin warm against mine as his hands found my ass and pried the cheeks apart. My hips rose off the bed, up and back in offering and he kissed my opening, his tongue lapping at me and I shuddered in surrender.

He could do whatever he wanted to me, anytime, anywhere, and he was the first and only man to hold such power, such sway over me.

He made love to me with his mouth, teasing the most intimate parts of my body, making me squirm with desire and need for a deeper touch. The slow climb of his lips up my back, the ladder of kisses, nibbles, and bites he placed as he stretched over me, was sweet torture, until he finally put the scorching head of his cock against my opening and forced his way in. I was so wet, so ready and he pushed me back down to the bed, his legs sliding to either side of mine, trapping me beneath him.

He laid over the top of me, and pressed me into the mattress, caging me protectively with the strength of his bigger body, driving deep, his mouth finding the side of my neck, his hand tangling in my hair and pulling my head gently to the side to give his lips better access as he pushed deep inside me.

It was powerful, left me feeling unexpectedly vulnerable, but safe and protected at the same time as he slowly began to thrust in short, slow strokes. I panted and gasped passionately as he set me on fire, one stroke, one lick, one bite, and one kiss at a time, turning up the heat gradually, always in control, always with my best interest and pleasure in mind.

I only hoped it was as good for him, because for me it was everything. He chased all the bad away, leaving nothing but good feelings, good vibes in their wake. He chased back the dark and filled me slowly, inexorably, with light until I shone like the sun, the pleasure intense, the stars just within reach, as I closed my eyes and just concentrated on the feel of him around me, inside me.

He whispered in my ear, "That's it, baby, just let go, I've got you."

His fingers found the spaces between mine, his hands covering the backs of mine, and I shivered, panted, and tried to hold out for as long as I could before taking the plunge. He thrust harder than any before, my clit rubbing against the comforter beneath us just right and I cried out and lost all control over my body. I jerked beneath him and he pressed me harder into the bed, holding me, keeping me safe from the overwhelming, and somewhat frightening, loss of control over myself, while wave after powerful wave swept through me, obliterating any last vestiges of worry, doubt, and fear I held onto about being abandoned by the one person who was always supposed to be there for me.

I yipped, a hysterical bubble of laughter escaping my lips as the orgasm seemed to go on and on. Swamped, overwhelmed by so many emotions and bodily chemical reactions that tears gathered at the corners of my eyes and leaked down my cheeks.

Angel didn't hesitate, he didn't miss a thing, he simply leaned over me and placed his lips lightly against the tears and kissed them away.

It was perfect. He was perfect, and all I could think was it was so nice to finally be home.

27

*A*ngel…

She slept soundly and I held her close. I stared out over the twinkling lights along the bay's surface from the bridge spanning it and cuddled her. She'd had a hell of a cathartic experience and I was glad that I could give her that emotional release. Still, something wasn't quite right for me. Wasn't quite there. It was like I was forgetting something but it was just out of reach and I couldn't quite put my finger on what it was…

It hit me, like I knew it would if I just pondered it long enough, and I smiled to myself in the dark of our bedroom, finally able to close my eyes and rest myself.

I was the first to wake the next morning and I put the last puzzle piece in its place. I slipped out from under Claire, who stirred but didn't wake, cuddling into the warm nest of blankets I reluctantly left behind. She lay on her stomach, the smooth line of her back inviting, begging to be kissed, but I resisted the urge. I was on a mission. I went over to the dresser, first pulling on a pair of cutoff sweat pants from one of the drawers. Then I went for my intended target, to the jewelry box perched on one end of the dresser's top.

I opened up the top of the box and I pulled out my Abuela's ring; Golden had our mother's. I went back to the bed. Claire's left hand lay on the sheets, lax, and perfectly placed and I prayed that the ring would fit and not need resizing at all. I slipped it gently over her ring finger and it was like Cinderella and her glass slipper. It fit, almost too perfectly. The diamond was small, barely a chip, but then again, when my grandfather had bought it, they hadn't had much. It was beautiful, though, the surrounding rose gold in a delicate filigree, making that small, delicate diamond something larger than life, a captured bit of star surrounded by flowering vines.

Claire sucked in a breath. She'd been facing her left hand and when she opened those gorgeous dark eyes of hers, they immediately fixated on her hand. She sat up abruptly and held it out in front of her and said, "Oh, my God!"

I smiled to myself and said, "Take your time, *mi alma,* I'm going to start cleaning up downstairs."

She sat on her knees, nude and perfect in the middle of the rumpled sheets, her hand splayed in front of her, gaze fixed on my Abuela's ring on her finger, her eyes wide, her mouth open in a little 'O' of surprise, and it was an image I locked in my heart forever, knowing that no matter how old we got, that this was how I was always going to see my Claire. The other half of my soul. Young, vibrant, beautiful, and perfect, her body fit and toned, the kind of perfection that famed sculptors could only hope to achieve once in their lifetime.

Her eyes met mine and I smiled and ducked down the stairs. I heard her feet hit the floor and a moment later, she came flying down the steps herself in that silk robe of hers. She ran to me, flinging her arms around my shoulders, leaping into my arms, and kissed me so soundly.

I kissed her back, and it was the most perfect kiss of my lifetime. More special, more precious than any that had come before it. Even with her.

"I love you," she breathed and I smiled against her mouth.

"I love you, too."

~

"You're serious."

"As a heart attack," I told him.

Golden looked at me from across the table, blinking stupidly as he tried to process what I'd just told him.

"I always knew you would get married before me, so I guess that part doesn't surprise me much but, bro… she's been with you something like two, three weeks, how the fuck…?"

He trailed off and I smiled and shook my head. "Physically, sure, but I've carried that woman in my heart for the last three years plus. I'm not letting her go and I know she feels the same. It's *right*, G. I can't even begin to explain to you just how right it feels. I didn't even hesitate. I gave her Abuela's ring, and it was like it was meant to be, fits like a dream."

"Holy shit," he said, shaking his head incredulously.

"I know you don't know her very well, and I know you're protective of us all, your family, I mean. I just wanted to tell you first before anyone else."

"When do you plan on telling everyone?" he asked, and I could tell he was still trying to digest everything.

"At the work party at the gym this weekend. It'll be the only time the majority of her people and ours will be under the same roof."

"Makes sense," he said, picking up his coffee and taking a careful sip.

"You're not pissed." It was a statement, not a question and he shook his head.

"There are some things in this life that just can't be explained. I don't know if it's God, or just – shit…" He groped for what he was trying to get across to me, but I held up a hand and waved him down. I think I knew. He shook his head and said, "You know I'm no good with the mystical mumbo-jumbo shit, but I get it. I don't know why, but I do. You take one look at you and her together, and it's like you were cut from the same cloth. You got the same kind of energy with her that you do with me, and truthfully, I'm a little jealous."

"Bro, not the same thing at all, I promise you," I said, laughing, and he scowled at me, his mouth flattening into a line of 'No shit, Sherlock' when he picked up what I was putting down. I loved Claire, but it most definitely wasn't the same kind of love you shared with your brother. Not even your twin.

"I'm happy for you," he said, smiling, and I raised an eyebrow.

"What about you and Lys?" I asked.

"Oh, yeah. That shit's gonna happen, bro. We're just not done bleeding her ex, yet. He had to sell their fancy condo. Between the alimony and the child support, it's a financial bloodbath." He grinned savagely.

"What child support?" I asked. I was confused; Lys didn't have any kids.

"Well, when the mistress somehow found out about what Lys' dipshit ex did to her, she dropped him like the bad habit he was. She damn-sure didn't let him off the hook where the bun in the oven was concerned, though. He's got some baby-mama drama, I'll tell you what."

"You can be a cruel son of a bitch," I muttered around the rim of my own mug.

He snorted. "God forgives so I don't have to," he said flatly. "That son of a bitch had it coming."

"I don't disagree with you there," I said.

"So what about the thing with Claire and her brother? How do you think he's going to take the news?"

I felt my face fall and I shook my head. Golden swore and sighed.

"Yeah, pretty sure Carter, Claire's brother, is headed the way of Lys' ex. You should have been a fly on the wall for that one."

"I don't even know how some dudes can even be like that, bro. I see this kind of shit day in and day out and it still blows my motherfuckin' mind."

"Tell me about it," I agreed. "I wouldn't be surprised if you and yours ended up at that apartment on a child-custody dispute call in the near future. She straight looked him in the eye and told him right there at my dining room table she wanted a divorce."

Golden inhaled some of his coffee and started to choke, spluttering at me, "How come you leave the good shit out?"

I laughed, "Sorry, trying to stay more focused on the good that came out of it all."

"I mean hell yeah, you got engaged! Weird fuckin' way to do it –"

"Eh, you had to be there, I guess." I waved him off and he laughed.

"Would have liked to, but you do all this shit on pure emotion."

I laughed and said, "It was a spur-of-the-moment decision. It felt right, like the pieces were all there and fell right into place and I just popped the question. I guess that's where the whole phrase comes from." I shook my head. "And I gotta say, you're taking this way better than I expected you to."

"Bro, I love you, and I know I don't say it enough or whatever, but I can see the way you look at her and the way she looks at you. I guess it's a good thing I found Lys, or Lys found me, or whatever, because I get it now. I see the same thing we got in you guys and at the end of the day, I just want my twin to be as happy as I am. I mean, are you?"

"Happy?" I asked. He nodded, worry wrinkling his forehead. I smiled and said, "Deliriously, man."

"Shit, then that's all that really matters. We have to get that shit where we can find it, sometimes we gotta make it what it is. We only got one life so we need to do our damnedest to live it right and leave the world better than we found it." He eyed me and added, "You're still whooping my ass on that front, Mr. Paramedic."

I smiled and shook my head, "You do a damn fine job yourself on that front, protector of the weak, defender of justice."

"Yeah, I'm a regular Captain fuckin' America," he said sarcastically and I laughed. "Seriously." The moment sobered and I looked my brother in the eye. I saw the fierce pride, deep love, and undercurrent of joy there and it warmed my soul. "I'm proud of you, Angel, and I'm happy for you, too."

"Thanks, G. You don't know what that means to me."

"Yeah, well, whatever," he said, shifting uncomfortably. My twin had never been awesome at his feelings, and today was no exception. Still, since finding Lys, he'd been doing a shitload better than he ever had before. His woman was healing parts of him that he never would have admitted in a million years were broken.

Claire did the same for me, and I was glad he could see that, because she wasn't going anywhere and I wasn't either. Things were changing for us, but they were changing in the best ways. I couldn't wait for what was to come.

It was a whirlwind week after that. Claire and I found ourselves ships passing in the night for the next few days. I was working; she was too. Planning, getting people together to clear out the space at the gym, ordering paint, talking with her circus people, and putting together work parties for the coming weekend. I was proud of her. It was like things had clicked and she was back.

It felt tenuous, though. Fragile. Like a blade that'd been freshly tempered. You didn't know if one misplaced strike was going to make it shatter or if it would hold true until the blow came. I worried, but I enjoyed her enthusiasm and excitement, her new lease on life.

We spoke in low and earnest tones at night, her head on my chest or shoulder, cuddled close in the dark. She whispered her secret fears and her close-kept secrets and it was everything. It was beautiful, how she shared with me, and I let her in, too. For the first time, I talked about the job, the heartbreaking calls as much as the triumphant ones. She listened and took some of the burden and we both found ourselves doing better. Healthier, for our midnight talks.

"What do you think they'll say?" she asked me quietly one night and I could tell by the lift of her hand, she was staring at her ringed finger. We hadn't told anyone other than my twin of our engagement, not yet, we planned on announcing it the next day during the first big work party at the gym. It would be the first time that both her world and mine collided. The guys and girls from the club and her circus people would all be under one roof, united in a common goal to make my woman's newest dream and ambition come true.

"Doesn't matter," I told her truthfully. "I know I'm pulling a page out of my twin's playbook, and I probably sound like a selfish asshole, but they can either get on board and be happy, or fuck off, for all I care."

She laughed and said, "I don't know, that sounds awfully harsh, but at the same time, I can see where you're coming from. Especially after..." she trailed off. She didn't need to say her brother's name. I could tell it still hurt and it would for a long time to come. I cuddled her close and kissed her forehead.

"I have to hope he'll come around, baby."

"Carter can be stubborn," she murmured. I smiled to myself in spite of the situation.

"You guys are a lot alike that way," I murmured and she laughed and lightly slapped my chest.

"I wish I could argue the point, but I really can't," she said softly.

I heaved a big sigh. I couldn't imagine what it would be like being so at odds with my flesh and blood like she was with her older brother right now.

"I'll be glad for this weekend," she murmured. "I've done what I can with getting things moved, but getting the rest of the heavy stuff out of there and the walls started, the silks hung… it'll feel like a real start, you know?"

"I agree," I murmured.

"A real start to our future," she said.

"I'm proud of you, baby."

"Yeah?" she asked.

"Yeah. You were handed a fuck-ton of lemons and made some fabulous lemonade."

"Well, I don't know about that," she said, laughing. "I can't say so unless I start turning a profit and the gym picks up business."

"I think everything is going to turn out great," I said.

"Yeah?"

"Yeah. I think you're due some good things for a while."

"Hmm," she hummed, a happy sound and cuddled close to me and I laughed into the dark.

"You're something else, you know that?" I asked.

"So are you," she whispered. "So are you."

28

*C*laire...

"Today is the first day of the rest of your life," I told my reflection.

"What?" Angel called from the kitchen. I smiled, it was like he didn't want to miss a thing.

"Nothing," I called back a little louder. I didn't want him to think I was silly or stupid for the daily affirmations I had begun to tell myself. I was trying to think positive, which was a lot harder to do than it sounded, especially with a thoroughly-poisoned mindset.

"You about ready?" he called.

"As I'll ever be," I said, coming away from the bathroom sink and stepping back out into the main floorplan of the houseboat.

"You're going to do great. Hell, I was amazed at what you got accomplished already."

"I said I would do most of it myself," I said with a raised eyebrow. Really, I'd only broken down all the cardboard and packing materials that'd been piled up near the defunct weight equipment. I'd also gotten started on some of the painting, going as high as I could on the walls with the primer until the lift could be brought in to get all the way up. We had the lift for a couple of weeks; renting that thing had been one of the bigger expenditures by far, right along with the sprayer rentals for the painting.

There would be at least two, maybe three work parties needed to get everything accomplished. Today was just the first.

We took a car to the gym, mostly because I had two big boxes of silks that I'd had delivered to the house so I could be sure to get them. I took one while Angel took the other and we threaded our way through the gym to the back section I would be in. Already there were people assembled and introducing themselves to each other.

"Hi, Thierry! Hey, Anya! Glad you could make it," I greeted two of my Circus peeps as Angel and I set down our burdens of boxed silks.

"Aleksi and Giada are on their way," Thierry said as we kissed each other's cheeks. I went to Anya and gave her the traditional European greeting as well, then went and hugged all of Angel's club family who had arrived. Golden and Lys weren't there yet, but Aly was, and Yale. Also, Poe, Driller, and Oz were there.

"Whoa, can't get this party started without us!" Skids cried from the doorway, and he and Reflash came through, with Backdraft, Lil, Youngblood, and Chrissy right behind them. The men each carried a ladder. Two short A-frames and two collapsible rigs; I couldn't begin to guess at how high they went, but it looked like they went pretty high, which would be useful for getting primer on the walls while the lift was in use getting things up on the ceiling.

"So, what's the plan?" Youngblood asked.

"The plan is to wait for us!" Aleksi called from the door as he and Giada came through.

We greeted each other and I made introductions, and just as I was about to dole out orders, a larger-than-life voice boomed out, "The Queen has arrived! You all can bow down. Yes, yes, I accept your adulation!"

I laughed and so did everyone else as Pasquale sauntered in, like he was walking the runway during fashion week, looking like Effie Trinket in the last *Hunger Games* movies in a drab grey, skin-tight jumpsuit, his bald head covered in a red bandana 'Rosie the Riveter' style. He had the cuffs of his coveralls rolled up above his work boots, which were paint-splattered and had seen better days. But as fabulous as he walked and looked, he also looked like he was ready to work, and that he was no stranger to it.

It was wonderful. He was a contradiction all over the place and I loved it. Despite his work-ready attire, he still rocked a face plied with makeup – done to ostentatious perfection as always. He came and gave me the traditional European greeting my circus people had.

We went through more introductions, just in time to do it all over again when Golden, Lys, Manolo, Blaze, and finally Narcos, with his shy, quiet woman, Everleigh, always clinging to his arm, arrived.

"Okay, I really think that's everyone," I declared, only to be stopped by a hearty, "Nope!"

McGowan, Ringold, Reynolds, Jefferson, and Colt came through dressed in old sweats and apparently ready to help as well. I frowned slightly, "Not that I'm going to turn down the extra help, but I thought I was on my own for this."

McGowan chuckled. "Had to show you up somehow, didn't I?"

"More like our mammas raised us to clean up after our own damn selves," Reynolds declared. "Have to say, you did pretty good knocking this pile down all by yourself."

"It was just a day or two of flattening cardboard and taking it out to the recycling dumpster."

"Well, I brought my truck to haul this shit down to the scrap yard," Ringold declared.

"I got my pickup out there too." Youngblood jerked a thumb toward the three big roll-up bay doors on the other side of the space.

"Good deal. Less trips, and you can keep the cash the scrap place gives you for the use of your truck and the trouble," Ringold told him

"Sounds good." Youngblood gave a nod.

"Right. With the doors up, it's going to get pretty cold back here, so everyone might want to keep their jackets on. Circus people, watch yourselves. I don't want you getting hurt with performances coming up."

Several of them exchanged sidelong glances, and I cocked my head, raising an eyebrow.

"Guys?" I asked, leaving it open for someone to explain what those looks were for.

Thierry spoke up, "We all quit."

"What?" I demanded sharply.

"Right, you guys talk this out, we're going to get started," Skids declared. McGowan was already hitting the button to roll up the outside doors, cold air blasting through the space.

"Make sure that door to the main space is shut, would yah?" he called out. Everleigh detached herself from Narcos' arm and went to make sure the doors were closed. My circus people closed in around me.

"You guys, you *can't* quit. You're here on work visas!"

"It's already done," Giada said, waving a hand dismissively.

"Most of us leave the end of the week," Anya said.

"Fourteen of us quit all together, the day we got the email from corporate stating Milo would remain director and you were no longer employed with the company. Most of us emailed notice back right then and there," Thierry said.

"But *why?*"

"My darling girl, enough was enough," Giada declared.

"Milo is a tyrant," Anya said. "If not you, then he would have moved on to any one of us. We couldn't let that happen. It wasn't right."

"More of us are coming, just some wanted to go to rehearsal today to say they quit as well." Aleksi shrugged.

I teared up and reached out and pulled all of them into a group hug. I didn't know what to say. I was so absorbed; I didn't even notice that Angel stood nearby in case I should need him. I was more than a little overwhelmed by the love and support.

"Come, we have work to do, no?" Thierry asked with a grin, but his eyes were watering too.

"Yeah, let's see how far we can get."

The answer was, *really far.*

We got the walls completely primed, the hardware bolted into the ceiling beams, and the silks hung by days' end. The silks from the circus weren't among them; those were going to be returned to the prop room as surreptitiously as they been removed in the first place, by one of Aleksi's friends who hadn't quit – yet. It would hardly be fair to my new employers to have stolen goods openly on display in their gym. The eight practice silks were all solid colors, mine were black shot through with traceries of silver, not as beautiful, but better for teaching; as long as I didn't wear black clothes, what my arms and legs were actually *doing* as I moved would show well against the silk for my students.

The walls were still to be painted in a mural of the night sky, some chandeliers hung between the silks, mirrors put on the walls – jeez, there was still so much left to do! A lot of us were sitting on the cement floor, taking a break before we wrapped the silks in plastic to protect them from the paint that had to still go up, when McGowan and the other gym co-owners came through the doors carrying mats between them. They laid them out them under the silks.

"What's this?" I asked, smiling. "It's still too early for mats, yet."

"We figured it was time for a little performance. We still have yet to see what you can do," Colt said.

"Oh, I don't know…" I shook my head and Aleksi called me a liar in Russian. I scowled at him and shot back something about his mother.

"Your accent is terrible and my mother is a good woman," he said, laughing.

"Fine," I said. "Get over here and help me stretch."

The bay doors were closed but the high windows were open to vent the paint fumes from the primer. It was cold in here, and I was a little worried about not being able to warm up properly. We'd had cold nights at the circus, though, so I knew what to do to prevent injury.

"Somebody needs to find music," Giada said, and she was already scrolling through her phone.

"Find something contemporary," I said, my feet planted against Aleksi's, hands in his as he pulled me over myself towards him gently. "Easy," I told him and he eased off just a bit.

"Contemporary…" Giada said, voice pondering.

"As in 'none of the performance music from the Night Circus'. I'll be glad if I never have to listen to any of that again."

"How about Christina Perri's 'A Thousand Years'?" Aly asked, looking at her own phone's screen.

"I don't think I know it," I said, and she played a little bit of it.

"Oh! I do know it, that's a good one. Yes. That, please."

"Okay, how do I connect to your speaker thingie?" she asked Backdraft. He chuckled and went over to her.

"It's a Job Rocker, and open up your Bluetooth and find the list of devices to pair to."

"You know, that song goes well with the fourth act routine and we're all here," Thierry said and I thought about it.

"The setup is close enough, we could do it if the 'audience' was over there."

"Grabbing more mats," Aleksi said and got up, jogging out to the main gym, Thierry following him, and in no time we were as set up as we were going to be, everyone gathered on the mats to watch. A bunch of the guys were standing at the back, several cradling their women, and I fought not to giggle at how it reminded me of a bunch of first graders waiting for storytime, the way they sat. I think it was the blue mats.

Angel came over to me and helped me to my feet with a hand down.

"Be careful," he murmured and I smiled up at him.

"Always," I promised.

Excitement fizzed through me, the low-grade buzz of adrenaline taking hold, knowing I was about to perform. Really perform, not practice, not a one-off thing, but a real, choreographed set. And not just for a group of people paying to see me, but for people who, for all intents and purposes, had thrown all-in with me, declaring themselves family, treating me better than my own family had.

I stood on my toes and planted a quick kiss against his lips as everyone took their positions. I was glad I'd worn a matching set of underwear today, because we were all pretty much going to need to strip down to them for this. I unzipped my jacket and handed it to Angel. He understood, we'd talked about my performing and the best ways to do it. If I kept my pants on, it would hinder the glide of the silks. You really needed just skin or a slicker nylon or pantyhose kind of material only.

Athletic leggings worked, too, to keep the fabric from binding up. Skintight was best, or nothing at all. Since I didn't have skintight, the black boy shorts and black sports bra I had on under my boat-neck tee would have to do.

I kicked out of my shoes as I lifted my shirt over my head, and uncomfortable laughter broke out among the spectators.

"Didn't realize it was that kind of a show," Driller joked, and I caught Thierry likewise stripping down to his black skintight boxer-briefs behind me. Everyone was stripping down to their most appropriate degree of dress for the parts they had to play. Thierry and Anya immediately started to climb their white silks while Giada and Aleksi stretched and practiced a few lifts off to the side, getting a feel for one another like they usually did.

"I love you," I told Angel and stepped back, grabbing a silk in either hand behind me. He blew me a kiss and stepped away, and I hoisted myself up off my feet, keeping my arms straight, pushing off with one foot, raising the other knee artfully. The silk's light material fluttered behind me and I 'flew' in a light arc, away from the spectators, sailing cleanly over the mats.

"Oh, wow!" one of the girls blurted and I touched back down. It had been nothing, really. It looked far more impressive than the tough stuff which I would be getting into soon. I raised my arms, striking a pose, gripped high on the silks and drew myself up, my arms coming down until I had risen off my feet again, only this time, I kicked the silk in a wrap around my foot and stood, climbing the silk as if it were rope, to take position. Thierry and Anya flanked me on silks behind and to either side of me.

I looked down and checked with Giada, who nodded, and got myself wrapped and cradled like I was supposed to be. I checked on Thierry and Anya, who were on their marks, and gave a nod down to Giada. She turned to Aly and said lightly, "Music, if you please."

Aly hit play and the opening notes came through the speakers. Giada let down her hair and ran lightly across the mat below me, Aleksi following, reaching out artfully. Giada dipped and swayed, twirled as if caught in an eddy of wind, and touched fingertips with Aleksi.

He drew her in flawlessly, Giada spinning lightly on her feet until her back went to Aleksi's chest and they swayed back and forth together. The vocals hit and she went into the first lift, bowing back, tumbling into Aleksi's arms, the two of them making it look effortless. They danced beautifully, a combination of acrobatics and dance with a level of skill that was unparalleled.

The music went on into the second verse and still they danced together, a marriage of skill and ability and then the chorus – and I tumbled and dropped. My arms went out as I took wing, I was vaguely aware of Thierry and Anya echoing my grace a step behind me as we perfectly danced and twirled in unison above Giada and Aleksi, mirroring each other in perfect synchronicity, until it was my solo moment.

My counterpoints stopped and I rose, arching, legs split, silk wrapped just so, as I danced nearly twenty feet up, imagining I was one with the sky itself as I twirled and bent, reached and arched, sinuous and grace-ful, my movements controlled, making everything look as smooth as the silk I hung from.

I curled in on myself, supported, and reached down to twirl the tail of the silks to get a good spin going, elongating my body, hanging upside down by my feet, drawing my arms in, going faster and faster until I flung out my arms and arched forward, stopping my spin as the last note died. Everyone came to rest and applause erupted, cheering and whistles. I gasped for breath and held my position for the proper count before letting myself down. I gripped the silks in front of me with my hands and kicked out of the bindings, controlling my body and lowering my feet below my head with carefully-crafted precision before letting myself down the rest of the way smoothly, hand-under-hand.

My feet touched the floor and I turned to the applause and raised my arms. My castmates joining me. We grasped hands together, Thierry on one side, Anya on the other, Giada beside Thierry, Aleksi on the other side of Anya, me in the center. We took our deep bow and rose, all smiling, and broke apart, all going to each other and hugging tightly.

"Well done," I breathed, and even more important, "Thank you."

"That is what this should be, always," Aleksi said, his blue eyes sparkling.

"That is what could never be with the Night Circus, not anymore; that is why we go," Anya echoed.

"I love you guys," I said, tearing up again. "I'm going to miss you so much." We huddled in a knot, a big group hug, and we cried. We couldn't help it. This was a perfect ending, but still, it wasn't how this was supposed to end.

ngel…

"Aww!"

"Oh, no!"

Everyone looked stricken at the sudden but inevitable tears. I looked over the faces of my brothers and my sisters and smiled. They all genuinely felt for Claire and I could see she'd been accepted. She was one of us. One of their own, and that did my heart good. I knew when she got past this, it would do her heart good, too.

She'd been even more amazing than the first time she'd performed and pretty soon the little knot of performers broke apart and our people surged off the mats to go talk to them.

Aly gave a joyous shriek, and put out her arms and hugged Claire, crying, "Oh, my God, you can teach me that right? I so want you to teach me that!" She turned to Yale and said, "I can learn how to do that, right?"

Yale laughed, his hands buried in his pockets and said, "We'll see."

"Pleeease!" Aly begged.

Lil went to Claire and said, "You've inspired me for days! That was phenomenal. I can't wait to get back to the writing cave. Seriously, you have to let me write you into a book as a character."

Claire laughed, kind of incredulous. "*Me?*"

"Yes, you!"

"Um, okay…"

I smiled and let the love and enthusiasm sweep through me and surround her. Golden stepped up next to me and raised an eyebrow, smirking. He nodded a few times and stuck out his hand and I grinned and took it with my own. He shook it and I laughed.

"Congratulations, bro. If she's that passionate, that good at what she does and she feels that way about you, I don't think I could ask for anything else."

"Thanks, man."

Claire made it back to me and I hugged her tight. She swayed in my arms and laughed, and looked up at me, asking, "You going to tell them?"

I nodded and called out, "Hey, yo, yo! I got something to tell you guys, so listen up!"

Everyone settled down and looked our way.

"I asked Claire to marry me and she said yes. We'll let you know wedding plans as soon as we make them."

"Shut the fuck up!" Blaze called, excited.

"Holy shit, bro, congratulations!" Backdraft grinned.

"Reception on *The 10-13*," Reflash declared and I laughed.

"Wouldn't have it any other way," I told him.

Hugs, handshakes, laughter and even some tears. It was a good way to start a life. The best way.

Claire looked up at me and I smiled and murmured, "Welcome home."

She grinned up at me and reached for me, whispering against my mouth before she kissed me, "There's no place like it."

30

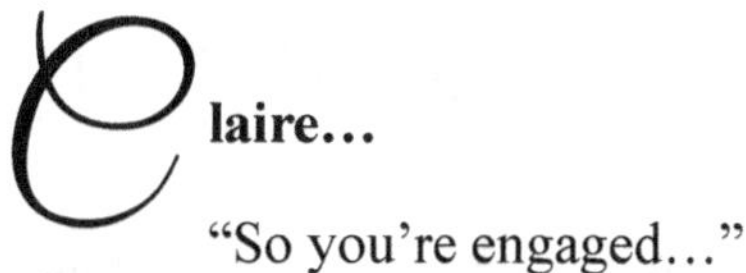

laire…

"So you're engaged…"

I froze up and turned slowly. I'd just finished my evening class. My studio space had been open for weeks now and I was happy. It was nice, having the ability to tailor my schedule around Angel's.

This was unexpected, though. I swallowed hard and turned around to face Carter. He stood in the doorway, his hands buried in the pockets of his khakis. He shrugged his shoulders, his white tee-shirt and light blue, short-sleeved button-up shirt standing out starkly against the glittering night sky painted on the wall behind him.

He looked at his brown loafers, and said, "Would have been nice to know when it happened, but I, I, uh, get why you didn't tell me."

I sniffed, my eyes brimming already, and asked, "How did you find me?"

He pulled a postcard out of his pocket and held it out. It was one of the advertising mailing promotions the gym and I had sent out to let Indigo City know I was here and what we now offered. There had been a crazy amount of sign-ups. We didn't anticipate a lot would stick around, but business was promising enough that we were looking for a belly dance instructor and a couple of yoga instructors to teach classes out of my space when I wasn't using it.

"And how do you know I got engaged?" I asked.

He huffed a bit of a laugh and scratched the back of his neck, "I just watched you take that ring off your necklace and put it on your ring finger. Doesn't take a rocket scientist, Sis."

I rubbed my lips together and said, "It's been a long time since you called me that."

"Really?" he asked, surprised. Then he thought about it and nodded slowly. "Yeah, I guess it has."

"What do you want, Carter? Because I'm not too keen on letting you hurt me again."

"I want to fix it," he said, and the look on his face said he was genuine.

"Mallory followed through?" I asked. It was just a hunch, but pretty spot-on.

"That obvious?"

"Never figured you would come here on your own, otherwise."

"That's where you're wrong. I *am* here on my own."

"Let me guess. You want me to talk to your wife?"

"No. Wow, I really was that big of an ass…"

"Yeah, Carter. That's putting it mildly." I shook my head.

"Look, I've got to go." I hefted my gym bag up onto my shoulder and he reached for it.

"Let me carry that for you."

I jerked my shoulder back out of his reach, twisting my body.

"It's okay, I've got it. I'm a big girl, now. You aren't responsible for me anymore."

"Shit," he muttered. "At least let me walk you out while you wait for your driver," he said.

"I drove myself, and you're a big boy. You can do what you want, too. Hell, you already did."

"Wow," he said. "I mean it, Claire. I'm really sorry. I want to fix this."

"I don't think you can," I told him, and went around him.

He fell into step beside me and said, "Please, let me try."

"Oh, now you want to try? Figured out there were some consequences? Feeling pretty lonely?" I asked.

"Yeah, to both, and I know I deserve it but – "

"No 'but's'. Just to let you know, how you're feeling right now? Been there, done that. More than three years' worth of it."

"Look, I saw the video," he blurted, and he was getting worked up.

"Which one?" I asked flatly. "There are several."

"The one of you and that director guy. I had no idea."

"I only tried to tell you, like a thousand times," I said. I would so not cry. I wanted the carrot Carter was dangling in front of my nose, but I was super cautious, which hurt in and of itself, to be honest.

"I know, and I didn't listen. All I heard was the same old complaints about this dance instructor or that coach. I just – I couldn't seem to see you as anything other than the bratty little kid sister dogging my steps."

"I know, I get it, I was a burden mom saddled you with because she didn't have anyone else to rely on. I totally get it. I ruined your life. Well, congratulations, you sort of ruined mine right back. And to answer your question, yes, Angel asked me to marry him the night you decided to go thermonuclear on our relationship. I lucked into finding a man who actually gives a shit about me and wanted to do anything he could to just make it better, and I recognize that, and I want that, and I'm finally figuring out that I deserve that. So seriously, just –" I let out a frustrated breath. "Just *fuck off*, big brother. I can't and won't do this again with you."

"Claire! Claire, stop! Wait!" He caught me by the upper arm and I stopped and waited for all of two seconds before I raised my eyebrows at him.

Someone cleared their throat, and my and Carter's heads turned on a swivel, in unison. McGowan came around the front desk wrap, his arms crossing over his big chest as he asked, "Everything okay here, Claire?"

"Yeah, Mike. It's just my asshole brother."

McGowan hitched up with a laugh and grinned, shaking his head. "Nice to meet you, Asshole. Mind taking your hand off your sister?"

Carter dropped his hand and said, "Actually, it's Carter. I *am* an asshole, but our mom gave me a proper name."

Okay, I was impressed. The Carter of a few weeks ago would have tried to break it off in McGowan's ass for that shot. Actually, McGowan would have never made it far enough to take it. I would have had my ass chewed up one side and down the other for calling Carter a name. For a half a second it felt like there was hope that I could and would get my brother back, before I slammed the lid back down on the box.

"I've got to go," I said. "I'll see you tomorrow."

McGowan gave a nod and said, "Night, Claire. Don't be an asshole, Carter. Your sister has an entire department of angels looking after her now."

"I'm trying not to," Carter said. "Believe me."

I'd already started walking away by then, though. He caught up to me in three lanky strides. There was a reason my older brother had played basketball. He had the height and the long legs for it. Ate up court like nobody's business.

"What can I do?" he asked when we hit the sidewalk. The freezing air was a shock to the system.

I picked my way over the salted sidewalk to the lot next door and said, "Nothing. I just want to go home."

"I mean it, Claire. I'm sorry, and I'd do anything to fix this, just, please…"

There was a note of desperate pleading to his 'please' that stopped me by the gate. I sighed, my breath pluming the air around my face.

"I'm glad you're working your issues," I said. "I'm sorry if I don't know if it's enough. You really fucked me up, Carter, and I'm leery."

"I mean, what if I told you I want you to be a part of Gracie's life?"

I shook my head. "I already am, and are you seriously trying to use my niece as a bargaining chip?"

"What!? No! I didn't mean it that way, I… *Shit!* I really can't win with you *or* Mal."

"There's a reason for that," I reminded him coldly. "Or did you forget you put your ego above my nearly dying."

His face pinched and he looked away from me, his eyes misting. He sniffed and turned back to me and said, "You scared the shit out of me with that."

"Could have fooled me…"

Tears leaked out of his eyes and I came up short. I couldn't remember the last time I saw my brother cry.

"I'm being real," he said. "You scared me so bad and all I could do was get angry and I held onto it and the next thing I knew it got so big and so out of control and I couldn't put the fire out. I let it eat me alive and it burned everybody, everything I cared about, and I'm so sorry. Please just let me make this right."

"How'd you get here?" I asked.

"I took a car. Mallory took ours when she moved out with Gracie last week."

I felt my shoulders drop.

"I just saw them earlier this week; she didn't say anything about moving out."

He gave me a sad, crooked smile, like he couldn't make his mouth work enough to give me a whole one. A tear dripped off the end of his nose and he sniffed, swiping an arm across his face.

"Did you ask?"

I shook my head. "We don't talk about you. My choice. Last thing she mentioned was that you guys were in therapy trying to work things out. She told me not to give up yet. When she stopped bringing you up altogether, I pretty much gave up on the idea you ever cared at all."

"Man." He shivered and I frowned.

"Where's your coat?"

"Ah... I left it in the car. Driver had it like a million degrees. I didn't even think about it when I got out. Son of a bitch."

"You're having a red-letter day," I said dryly. "Come on, get in." I hit the button on my key fob and my car unlocked, the back hatch opening up. I stowed my bag back there and he looked over the car, nodding.

"It's nice," he said finally. "Angel help you buy it?"

I fought not to roll my eyes. "Nope. Did it all by myself... used all my own money -everything."

"I'm getting used to the taste of shoe leather, believe it or not," he said, opening up the passenger door.

I shot him a look over the roof of the car and said, "Oh, I believe it."

He laughed a little and got in the car.

"Taking me home?" he asked.

"Actually, it's my night to cook. Thought we'd stop by the store, pick up a few things and that you could maybe try a take two on that dinner."

"Think Angel will mind?" he asked.

"Guess we're gonna find out," I said, and started the car.

"Great," he muttered and sounded nervous.

I felt my lips twitch as I tried not to smirk.

"Be grateful Angel's nothing like his identical twin," I said.

"There's two of him?"

I rolled my eyes. "I just said he was nothing like Golden, didn't I?"

"Okay, fine. Also, I'll bite. Why should I be glad that Angel isn't like his twin?"

"Because, one, Golden's a cop, and two, one of his favorite life mottoes is 'God forgives so I don't have to.'"

"Okay." He clapped his hands down on the top of his thighs and rubbed them back and forth as if to dry his sweating palms. "And you're sure you want to marry into this family?"

"Hey," I said tartly, "this family wanted me when my own didn't."

A sober silence ensued and he raked his bottom lip between his teeth.

"Touché," he said, quietly.

I didn't say anything else. Just let him marinate in that truth all the way to the grocery store. The next thing that was uttered was a somber, "What are we getting?"

I let him carry the basket as we wound our way through the produce section and down aisles. I settled on making a pesto chicken I'd learned from Giada, who I missed terribly. She was back in Italy. Aleksi had managed to get a visa from the Italian consulate and had gone with her. I was glad for that. I'd been afraid of what might happen to him if he went back to Russia.

He was trying to figure out how to come to America, but with the way things were right now, I felt he was better off in Italy.

The drive home held a little inane chatter, but not much. Once we got through the door back at the houseboat I asked him, "You know how to start a fire?"

"Not something I've ever really had to do, but I could take a crack at it."

"No time like the present to learn." I had him help me bring in some wood from the port side of the wrap-around lower deck and opened up the wood stove. I showed him the basics and let him get it going while I washed my hands at the kitchen sink.

"Kind of a unique bathroom," he remarked.

"Yeah, we had the blinds closed the last time you were here."

"Mind if I close them again? It's a little creepy staring at your bathtub from the kitchen and living room."

"Go ahead," I said. "Angel is probably going to want to get a shower when he gets home, speaking of. I should text him and give him the heads up that you're here." I dusted off my hands from the basil I'd just torn up and put into the food processor to grab my phone and swore when I saw the time.

"What?"

"He's already on the bike by now and on his way home."

"Oh. Well, with any luck, he won't punch me in the face or anything on sight."

"Wrong twin," I reminded him, and he kind of blinked at me, startled, and said, "You're really not joking about that, are you?"

"Mm, nope. Although I'm pretty sure Golden wouldn't actually hit you. He *is* a cop, after all."

"Right, wouldn't want to lose his job, I guess."

"Pretty much the only thing that would make him think twice about it. Angel will be nice because he's Angel and lives up to the name. I wouldn't expect the same out of Golden, though."

"Where do these guys get their names?" he asked.

It was a safe topic, so I told him the stories behind Golden and Angel's names.

"And how did you meet these guys, again?"

I stirred the pasta in its water and sighed, leaning against the kitchen counter. I told my brother the truth. The full truth this time. Not the watered-down version that Angel had given him. Carter sat at the dining room table, speechless.

"Oh, my God… Claire," he said finally.

"I know, I know! I shouldn't have left him like that."

"Okay, setting aside for now that my sister is even capable of a one-night stand – which I thought mom and I raised you better than that –" I cut him off by barking, "Hey!" at him but he ignored it and just pushed on, "Yeah. Wow. Whoa. Not sure how to process this one. Just give me a minute."

"Well," I said after a moment of silence. "I guess one thing is apparent from this little nugget of wisdom."

"What's that?" he asked.

"I'm definitely your sister, because before this little repentance-thing you have going on right now, it's pretty much exactly the kind of thing you would have done, leaving like that."

He winced and didn't say anything at first, then finally said, "You're right."

"Guess we can both be assholes," I said softly, a tentative peace offering.

"Yeah," he said, just as softly. "I guess we can."

31

*A*ngel…

I don't know exactly what I had expected when I got home, but what I hadn't was finding Carter sitting at our dining room table. I slowly shut the door and eyed him as I walked past to get to my fiancé. I leaned down and kissed her and she sighed in contentment against my lips. I set my lid aside on the counter, out of her way, and turned to face Carter.

"Carter," I intoned, shrugging out of my jacket and cut, taking it over to the coat-tree by the wood stove and front door.

"Ah, hi, Angel."

"What are you doing here?" I asked.

"Um, Claire invited me to dinner."

"Did she, now?" I glanced at Claire to make sure he wasn't feeding me a line of bullshit and she gave a barely-perceptible nod.

"He showed up at the gym," she said.

"Ah-huh. Why?"

"I wanted to apologize to my sister," he said sincerely.

I went over and dropped into a seat near his and eyed him. "I see." I was being carefully neutral. My curiosity burning, I gave in and asked, "How's your wife?"

"Packed up and left me last week, took our daughter with her."

"I see. I'm sorry to hear that," I said.

He blinked and his brow furrowed slightly; he opened his mouth to say something, closed it, and finally settled on a really confused-sounding, "You really mean that."

"I do."

"Told you he was the good twin," Claire said with a wry smile. I had to smile, too. We'd had dinner with my brother and Lys just the other night and had gotten into the whole 'Who was the evil twin' debate. Once again, Golden had won the title of evil twin, even though both of us were as far from the true meaning of the moniker as we could get.

Carter cleared his throat, and said, "Yeah, well, I guess I should be glad you got this one."

"I know I am," she said, and I didn't need to turn around to confirm that she was smiling. I could hear it in her voice. I felt my own lips twitch.

"You guys good, then?" I asked.

"No," Claire answered readily and Carter's face fell. "But we'll get there eventually," she said grudgingly and I watched hope spring in the other man's eyes.

"Good deal," I said and got up to help set the table, kissing her one more time on the way by and murmuring, "It smells good."

"Thank you," she said softly.

"You want a beer, Carter?"

"Uh, yeah. Yeah, that would be great," he said.

The tension in the house dissipated some and I nodded and got two beers out of the fridge.

I kept an eye on Claire the entire meal, the conversation turning mostly to a walk down memory lane. By the end of the meal, there was more laughter than sadness and I figured I could feel a little more confident that this was on the up-and-up, that there was some real hope of them working their shit out. Well, really, that Carter was working his shit out.

"I'll clean up," Claire murmured finally, at a natural lull in the conversation.

"I should get going," Carter said before looking at his sister and saying, "Thank you."

"For what?" she asked and the tension and nervousness was back as we all felt close to sideswiping topics we didn't want to get into.

"For this. For, um, giving me another chance."

"I haven't fully committed that far yet," she said.

"Okay, then for giving me half a chance, tonight." He nodded.

Claire nodded too, and said, "Sure, but you go back to being that asshole, we are so done. I meant it, Carter. I won't even let you close enough to hurt me like that again."

"I understand," he said, standing up. "I don't want to. I mean it. I'm sorry, and being sorry, really sorry –"

"Means never doing what you're sorry for ever again, otherwise it's an empty apology," they said in unison.

Both of them cracked a smile, and I think their mom was in the room. She had to be.

"Right, well."

"I'll walk you out," I said.

"Can I have a hug?" he asked Claire, and she set down the plate she had in her hands on the edge of the sink and came around. They hugged, bodies tight and tense and I think her brother choked up a little. Looked like he'd gotten the wake-up call he'd needed. Good, that was good.

"Good night," Claire said. Her voice was strained with her own threatening tears.

I swung my jacket and cut on and asked, "Where's your coat?"

"Ah-ha," he let out an embarrassed laugh. "Accidentally left it in the back of the rideshare I took to the gym."

"That sucks, hang on. Let me grab you one of mine. You can give it back the next time you see us."

He nodded and I ran upstairs, grabbing down my thick, warm, canvas construction jacket out of the armoire. I jogged back down the steps and held it out.

"You still got your phone, wallet, and keys, right?" I asked.

He nodded, "Yeah, we live in the city. I don't keep that stuff in my jacket. Pants, always."

"Fair enough," I said. "Be right back, babe."

"Okay," Claire said, and she was a little subdued. I couldn't tell if it was that she was sad her brother was leaving or not. I had even money that she was all over the place emotionally at the moment. I would pick up any pieces when I got back to the house.

Carter had his phone in his hand, using the app to call up his ride. I opened the door and he stepped out ahead of me. We walked down the dock in silence and I opened up the gate at the end. He stepped through and I followed him out to the parking lot.

"Hey, listen, thanks for not being a jerk. I know, I totally deserve it and," he gave a nervous laugh, "to be honest, I'm kind of afraid of what you're going to say right now. I'd almost rather you just punched me in the face and got it over with."

I gave a shrug, hauled off and belted him right in the jaw. I hit him and he hit the ground. I bent down, grabbed him by my jacket and hauled him to his feet as he sputtered and spit out crimson. I dusted him off while he moved his jaw back and forth with his hand.

"Better?" I asked.

"Hell, no!" he cried.

I shrugged, "Need me to do it again?"

"No! No, I'm good."

"Good, now that I have your attention, I'd like to make it clear that you've abdicated making any decisions for your sister. No telling her what to do, none of that shit. You talk shit, you make her feel anything less-than, I'm going to do a whole lot worse, you feel me?"

"I thought you were supposed to be the good twin," he said, and I loomed, on purpose.

"I *am*."

"Point taken," he said quickly.

"Good."

"You really love my sister," he said, and it wasn't a question, but I answered it anyway.

"With everything that I am and then some."

He nodded and said, "Good. I feel like we kind of got this backwards. Like I should be the one threatening you with bodily harm should you screw things up?"

"That's traditionally how this goes, but you kind of fucked up first, so here we are."

"That's fair enough," he said, and sucked in a breath muttering, "you hit like a truck."

"Want me to check you out?" I asked.

"What?"

"I'm a medic. I broke you, now I feel like I should put you back together."

He kind of laughed and shook his head. I switched on my penlight and checked him out.

"Eh, you'll be fine. Just put some ice on it when you get home. Fifteen on, fifteen off."

"You're confusing."

"Not the first time I've heard it, probably won't be the last. Your ride's coming."

He nodded, "Well, thanks for dinner – not so much for punching me in the face though. That I could have gone without."

I shook my head, mouth tight. He laughed and nodded.

"Once again, fair point, well made, sir. Fair point, well made."

"Right. If she's receptive, see you in a few weeks. Go fix the rest of your family, if you can," I said.

He nodded.

"I'm trying to. Really, I am."

"I believe you. Otherwise I would have pitched your ass off my boat."

He laughed, "I like you, Angel. God knows why, but I do."

"Exactly. God knows why. Take care of yourself," I said. "I mean it. I hope you come to the best resolution with your wife and that you find peace with each other."

"Yeah," he said, opening up the door to the Prius that rolled to a stop. "Me, too."

"Night, Carter."

"Night, Angel." He got in and shut the door and I watched him pull away, my hands buried in my pockets.

I heaved a sigh and went to see how much damage had been caused to my woman who was waiting inside. I figured it would be pretty bad. There were points she'd looked fragile. She'd come so far the last few weeks and I was worried about a setback, that she would get discouraged.

I expected tears, and I found them when I got back inside. She was sitting in one of the living room wingback chairs, the dishwasher running, humming along in its wash cycle. I went to her and picked up her hands in mine.

"You didn't get into a fight, did you?" she demanded, looking at my red and swollen knuckles. I shook my head.

"No. Let's just say your brother and I came to a man-on-man sort of understanding. It's done and over with. No hard feelings, no grudge."

"Seriously?" she asked, and I could tell she didn't believe me.

I laughed a little and murmured, "Let's just say I gave him the talk every brother is supposed to give the boyfriend."

She sniffed and sighed, "You didn't hurt him too bad, did you?"

"Not even close, babe."

She looked like she was at war with herself and finally let out a pent-up breath and said, "I really don't know whether to be mad at you or disappointed that you let him off so easy."

"I wouldn't say he got off easy," I said. "But I didn't fuck him up as hard as I wanted to either."

"Oh God," she groaned and covered her face with her hands. She tipped forward slightly and I put my arms around her and cuddled her.

"It's okay, *mi alma*," I whispered. "Over and done with. Just like that."

"I don't understand how guys can do that," she said. "Just punch each other out and be fine after that. Go out for beers and be best friends."

"Technically, the beer came first, and I don't know about best friends," I said laughing.

She put her arms around me and laid her head on my shoulder.

"Can we just take a bath, have a drink, and forget about it for now? Talk about something happy?"

"That sounds perfect." I smiled and she leaned back.

"Good."

"Go on up and get naked," I told her. "I'll draw the bath and get the beer."

"Two beer night for you?"

"Yeah."

She laughed, "At least things are better."

"Yeah?" I asked, checking in with her, making sure.

She nodded gently, "By no means healed, that's going to take a lot more time, but I think they could be on the mend."

I smiled. "I'll take it."

"I thought that was supposed to be me," she said with a wink, standing. I swear this woman could turn anything into a sexual innuendo and I loved her sass.

"Oh, you will be," I told her, giving her a slap on the ass as she headed for the stairs.

"In that case, sparkly bath-bombs ahoy."

I mock-groaned.

"You're going to make me look and smell like I got dipped in unicorn jizz?"

"Shut up!" she cried, but she was laughing.

I chuckled and got the bath going. I opened up the fresh bottle of champagne I had in the fridge. Not because of any special occasion, but because I knew it would make her happier than a beer. She called from over the railing, "What are you doing?" after the cork popped.

"You'll see," I called back.

I filled the tub and dropped in two of the bath bombs she kept in a basket on the corner of the tile surround and she came back down in her robe. I opened up the blinds, went up and got out of my clothes, dropping them in the hamper and shrugged into my own robe.

Claire was already in the tub by the time I got back downstairs. The blinds up, our view unimpeded, she huddled at the foot of the tub waiting for me to get in behind her. I did and she slid back into my arms, leaning against me. I handed her one of the champagne flutes and she smiled.

"We haven't done this in a while," she murmured.

"That's why I did it." We clicked glasses and sipped.

"I love you."

"I love you, too, baby." I kissed her shoulder and she sighed out, her body relaxing. I worked my mouth from the outside swell of her shoulder, along the leading curve to the side of her neck. She hummed out in pleasure and I slid my hands over her body.

"Keep that up, you're going to get laid," she said.

"That *is* the whole point," I whispered in her ear, my fingertips finding her clit beneath the water. She jerked slightly in my grasp and I teased her body. She shivered against me and put a hand over each of mine, encouraging the one at the apex of her thighs to touch her just like *so,* dragging the other to her breast and encouraging me to give it a squeeze.

I grew hard behind her, my cock stirring against her back.

"You are so getting whatever you want," she said.

"I already have what I want," I told her. "Right here, in my arms."

EPILOGUE

*C*laire…

    I laughed hysterically as Angel kicked open the hotel room door and carried me across the threshold. I loved how he carried me as if I weighed nothing, and to him, I probably did. He was used to lifting people of all shapes and sizes onto stretchers, after all. He set me down and I wound my arms around his neck. He bowed his head and kissed me and I melted, molding myself to the front of his body.

We'd been together a year and a half and still, kissing him was like brand new, every time, and we tended to kiss a lot. We'd just been married, today was the first day of the rest of our lives and it felt amazing, exhilarating, and I suddenly couldn't get me out of this dress, him out of that tux, and into bed with him fast enough.

"God, I love you, *mi alma*," he murmured against my mouth.

"Not as much as I love you," I whispered back, my lips curving into a smile.

The wedding had been perfect, held at Angel's church. My brother had walked me down the aisle. Mallory and Carter were moved back in together and working things out. Gracie had been our flower girl, Manolo bearing the rings. Every single club brother had been a groomsman, their women bridesmaids. Giada and Aleksi had even come, as well as several others in my circus family from far and wide overseas.

The gym was successful, and I had been repaid and then some. They had made me a full partner, and I was even performing again. Life was good. Better than good, and I was sharing it with a man so good, so pure, I couldn't have even dreamed him. It was still so surreal.

"I need you," he gasped.

"Oh, my God, get me out of this dress," I demanded.

His fingers worked frantically at the line of buttons down my back while my fingers fumbled at the fastenings holding him in his tux. If it were a race, I won by a wide margin. He was three-quarters undressed while I was only halfway there.

He grunted and shoved the material off my hips and the beautiful dress puddled at my feet. He hauled me up against his body and I wrapped my legs around his hips, climbing him like my silks until I was a head and shoulders taller than him.

"Fuck that's hot," he muttered and took me to the bed, throwing me down. I bounced twice and he dove over the top of me, his hands bunching in my hair, holding my head back so he could feed at my mouth with his own.

"Fuck condoms, I'm on birth control and if we get pregnant, we get pregnant. I don't care!" I gasped and he chuckled low and dark.

"Glad we're on the same page." He pulled my pantyhose off and took my panties with them, gazing on my naked pussy with heated desire. His look was hungry, but not for anything involving food – unless I was the main course.

I really wanted to be the main course. I wanted him inside me so badly.

In my mouth, in my pussy, hell in my ass, I didn't care, as long as he fucked me. Forget about making it good, he didn't even have to try to make it good. He always knew just how to do me to make me come screaming and God, I wanted that, I needed that. I needed him so badly.

"Hurry up! Oh, my God, you're killing me!"

He laughed and shoved his boxer-briefs down in front, his cock sprang free, throbbing and I bet it ached as fiercely as I did. I wrapped my fingers around it, firm but gentle, and his hips jerked. He made a strangled noise somewhere between a cry and a moan and let me stroke him a few times as he pulled me into a better position to get inside me.

"Sit up," he demanded, and knelt on the bed. I sat up and he bodily picked me up. I reached between us and guided him into my entrance, sinking down onto him as he thrust up. We met somewhere in the middle in a passionate explosion.

My body wasn't ready, but the pain was sweet, the pleasure that chased it intoxicating. His big arms wound around my body and crushed me to him as I buried my hands in his short hair and kissed him fiercely. He let me stop for a while, cock twitching inside me as my pussy grew accustomed to his wide girth. When I was ready, I began to move, rolling my hips, and I swear his eyes rolled back into his head.

"Oh, God, Claire... Fuck yes, like that. Just like that, baby. Fuck me, yes."

"Mm," I sucked in a heated breath and it hissed between my teeth as I rode him. He felt impossibly long inside me at this angle, teasing a deep spot that touched off a spark, lighting my fuse, which did a slow burn, the pleasure building, euphoria filling my veins, driving me absolutely insane as I silently begged for it to reach critical mass and send me exploding, launching me up among the stars.

I arched back, bending fluidly over his arms, leaning to where he somehow felt like he went even deeper and I ground against him. Oh, the way he looked down at me. So hot, so possessive in all the right ways. Encouraging, filled with love and light, his eyes smoldered with desire, painting me in exquisite ecstasy wherever his gaze swept over my skin. He took one arm away, holding me effortlessly with just the one, his other he used to trail his fingertips along my collarbone, between the valley of my breasts, over the slightly raised ridges of my abdomen, to the top of my sex.

He dipped his fingers into the wetness where our bodies met, where I rode him, before swirling that moisture around my clit. He teased me, he tantalized me, until I begged him to stop playing and to touch me. He gave me what I asked for and I closed my eyes and fell. I fell through the mattress, through the floor, through the nine floors of hotel below us and the through the underground. I fell and fell and fell and was burned up at the molten core of our love for one another, the fire sweeping through my body, out from my center, along every vein, sparks flitting along every nerve.

I opened my eyes and it was just me and Angel, flying among the stars.

Wait, no, that wasn't right. While the fairy lights, the stars and sparkles, were real and white-hot at the edges of my vision, I was safe. The ceiling of the honeymoon suite resolving into focus behind Angel's head, but still, he had a halo of those white-hot lights.

"You all right?" he asked between panting breaths, as the lights that's seeped across my vison, began to recede back to the edges from where they'd come.

I swallowed hard, barely able to croak. I tried again, flicking my tongue against my lips.

"Again," I whispered.

"My pleasure," he said, laying me down.

He drove into me powerfully and I gasped, the gasp cutting off the surprised cry he wrung from me. I gripped his shoulders and raised my knees, letting my legs fall open to give him better access and he took it, grasping my thigh with one hand, the other curving up under me, his hand gently cradling my neck as he half-pulled me down to meet his upward thrust.

"Oh, God!" I screamed, and he took it for the invitation it was, ramping up the intensity until I went supernova in his grasp. I came back to myself slowly, my body dewed with sweat, pussy drenched, from me, from him, I didn't care. I just wanted, needed more.

"Kiss me," I begged and he kissed me. "Fuck me," I pleaded and he laughed, panting, and said, "Just gimme a few minutes, baby."

I whined, and he laughed again and cuddled me to him. A few moments went by and he slowly started to move inside me again. I moaned, and lay, boneless and languid beneath him as he moved inside me. Slowly now, more intimate, more loving and careful than what we'd done before.

"Do you know just how much I love you?" he whispered and I bit my bottom lip and shook my head. It felt lazy, like I was adrift and the world had gone soft around us. He smiled and said, "Oh, I was hoping you could tell me."

I smiled and arched like a cat beneath him and he slid his arms around me, holding me close as he continued to languidly fuck me. My pussy was so wet, his cock glided in and out of me with barely any effort. It was the sloppy, lazy lovemaking that came after good sex and led into a total, satiated exhaustion, and I wanted that. I wanted him to love my body into a fucking coma. I wanted him to hold me like this and for us both to sleep for what felt like a thousand days after this.

I was drunk off his love and I didn't ever want to sober up, not if it felt like this.

We loved each other late into the night. So. Much. Sex. It was amazing. I couldn't get enough of him. I didn't want to, I hoped this would never end. I made him promise it would always be like this.

"Forever and ever?" I breathed.

"Forever and ever, Amen," he whispered against my mouth.

Amen.

I liked the finality of that.

Amen.

The End

ALSO BY A.J. DOWNEY

The Sacred Hearts MC

1. Shattered & Scarred

2. Broken & Burned

3. Cracked & Crushed

3.5 Masked & Miserable (a novella)

4. Tattered & Torn

5. Fractured & Formidable

6. Damaged & Dangerous

The Virtues

1. Cutter's Hope

2. Marlin's Faith

3. Charity for Nothing

The Sacred Brotherhood

1. Brother to Brother

2. Her Brother's Keeper

3. Brother In Arms

4. Between Brothers

5. A Brother's Secret

6. A Brother At My Back

7. A Brother's Salvation

Indigo Knights

1. Her Thin Blue Lifeline

2. His Cold Blue Command

3. A Low Blue Flame

4. His Wild Blue Rose

5. Her Pained Blue Silence

Paranormal Romance (with Ryan Kells)

1. I Am The Alpha

2. Omega's Run

3. Hunter's End

ABOUT THE AUTHOR

A.J. Downey is the internationally bestselling author of The Sacred Hearts Motorcycle Club romance series. She is a born and raised Seattle, WA Native. She finds inspiration from her surroundings, through the people she meets, and likely as a byproduct of way too much caffeine.

She has lived many places and done many things, though mostly through her own imagination…An avid reader all of her life, it's now her turn to try and give back a little, entertaining as she has been entertained.

Stalker Information:
www.ajdowney.com